WE HAVE CONTACT

CONTACT

The Kurtherian Gambit 12

MICHAEL ANDERLE

COPYRIGHT

DEDICATION

To Family, Friends and
Those Who Love
To Read.
May We All Enjoy Grace
To Live The Life We Are
Called.

We Have Contact
The Kurtherian Gambit 12 Street Team

Beta Editor/Readers

Bree Buras (Aussie Awesomeness)
Tom Dickerson (The man)
Sf Forbes (oh yeah!)
Dorene Johnson (DD)
Dorothy Lloyd (Teach you to ask...Teacher!)
T S (Scott) Paul (Author)
Diane Velasquez (DD)

JIT Beta Readers

Brent Bakken
Timothy Cox
Heath Felps
Andrew Haynes
Kelli Orr
Gage Ostrander
Leo Roars
Hari Rothsteni
Björn Schmidt

If I missed anyone, please let me know!

Editors

Stephen Russell
Kat Lind

**Thank you to the following Special Consultants
for WE HAVE CONTACT**

Jeff Morris - Asst Professor Cyber-Warfare, Nuclear Munitions
(Thank God!)
Stephen Russell - Ideas & Suggestions

PLA HEADQUARTERS

The Chairman of the Chinese Government looked at his two generals and nodded before sitting down at the long table. The room was secured from all listening devices. It was utilitarian, having only a table, ten chairs and a small cupboard for refreshments. The men opened their notebooks to go over the findings from the last three weeks. The main subject, their plans after the recent, as they chose to call it, 'disagreement,' with TQB Enterprises.

General Tsang, responsible for reviewing the destruction and deaths across their country, opened the meeting. "The damage in the Kunlun Shan Mountains is impressive. Our scientists have calculated the obliteration was truly from kinetic strikes. The video that our cameraperson took correlated to the inspected damage. But, at this time, the scientists are still arguing about how the objects could have been accelerated to the speeds necessary to accomplish the destruction." The general took a sip of his tea. "Suffice to say, we cannot duplicate the effect."

General Li, responsible for the forensics of the digital attacks, snorted at General Tsang's statement and received a dark look from the Chairman. All three men were more relaxed in this setting than they would have been in a more formal meeting.

General Tsang continued, "The scientists do believe that the same type of weapon was used on our covert ops base to smash open the door. Considering the power displayed at Kunlun Shan, there is no engineering we can accomplish to produce viable protection at this time."

"When," the Chairman interrupted, "do you project that we can defend against this kinetic weapon?"

Tsang shrugged his shoulders. "When we figure out their anti-gravity. It is postulated we will have the capacity to build a repelling field then that will at least considerably minimize the damage."

"So," the Chairman continued, "there is no place that is truly safe from their weapons?" Tsang shook his head. The Chairman asked, "When the Avatar was displayed in our bunker, they could have demolished us at that time?"

"Yes," Tsang admitted. "That they did not was a strategic decision, not due to a limitation of their ability should they have decided to hit us."

The Chairman reached up to his face and took off a pair of reading glasses. He needed these now when reviewing paperwork, which frequently annoyed him. Scratching his nose before replacing the glasses, he thought for a moment and continued to probe for information. "Okay, Li, what else?"

Li said, "The covert ops base had no survivors. The men, all of them, fought. We have blood samples, and we have some highly suspect forensics," he added after a pause, "Highly suspect."

"For example?" the Chairman inquired.

"We have hair from at least two types of wolves, perhaps three. We have structural damage on doors inside the base that seems to be organic in nature. This damage occurred before a massive retaliatory gun strike from our men peppered the door with gunfire. Our men are trained to think rationally in any situation, and it is evident that is exactly what didn't happen in multiple cases. We have men shot, stabbed, throats torn out by animals, and bodies ripped apart by something massively strong. We have places where there appear to be nail scratches from something that must have weighed hundreds of pounds and stood a minimum of seven feet tall, I'm told."

"Are you suggesting," the Chairman asked, his voice neutral. "That we have been attacked by monsters?"

Li shrugged. "That is what the evidence at the base suggests. Something was able to negate the men's training. The psychologists surmise that if they were subjected to something very primal, it could work at an instinctive level. This could cause them to just react, instead of responding the way they had been trained."

Li paused to allow time for any questions. When none were raised, he continued, "Further, when we investigated the escape of General Sun, we found additional hair evidence at both the location of his abduction and later inside the discarded plane."

"Why would TQB want General Sun?" the Chairman asked, confused.

"Sir, I apologize for not being clear," Li responded. "We do not believe TQB was involved with General Sun." The

WE HAVE CONTACT

General looked across the table to his counterpart in the investigations and to the Chairman before continuing.

He cleared his throat and replied, "Sir, we have two forces at work."

CHAPTER ONE

QBS ARCHANGEL, BEYOND THE MOON

Nathan and Ecaterina were packing a bag for little Christina. It was their first evening to spend some time alone, and Aunt Bethany Anne had offered to watch the little one.

Nathan wasn't sure that even Bethany Anne's offer to watch their first child for an evening would be acceptable to his wife. But, when Ecaterina looked at Nathan to see what he thought, she could tell he was doing his best to remain neutral. Well, as neutral as possible to not make her feel bad if she decided to not accept the offer.

Ecaterina knew her husband well enough to realize he wanted some time with her without interruptions, if at all possible. So she had agreed that it would be nice to have a few hours alone with her husband.

Now, Nathan looked around their suite on the ArchAngel. They had two rooms at the moment, and both were filled with baby stuff. In two days, Bobcat promised him a storage container would arrive from the moon. He would be given ten linear feet of storage to move little Christina's unneeded gifts out of here and into the holding space.

If Ecaterina had her way, at least a quarter of it was going to Bethany Anne's suite tonight. "Sweetheart," he said, catching Ecaterina holding two different toys. "I don't think we need to send everything."

Ecaterina looked at him and raised a squishy duck, a toy that Christina liked to hear at times. "But, if she doesn't have the right toy, she might cry too long."

Nathan stepped over to his wife and wrapped his arms around her. "Don't you think that Bethany Anne might be able to figure out a way to come get a toy if she feels something is needed? We're going to be gone, there's no reason she can't come into the room and fetch another set of toys, or hell, she'll probably just tell someone to come get them."

Ecaterina leaned her forehead against Nathan's chest. "I'm freaking out, aren't I?"

Nathan gently swept his hand down her back, saying nothing.

She sighed loudly, poked him in the chest and looked up into his eyes. "You are too quiet. How bad is it?"

Nathan wasn't getting out of this one. He considered his response. "On a scale of one to ten, with ten being an ultimate freak out, you are a six."

Ecaterina weighed what he had just told her. Trying to figure out how he was squirming his way out of telling her the total, horrible truth. She pressed her lips together, realizing that she couldn't figure it out. Either she was only freaking out a little past the middle, or he had just figured out a way to hide the truth from her due to English not being her first language.

She smiled, either way she looked at it she needed to relax. She put her ear back on his chest and wrapped her arms around him. "She's beautiful, Nathan. Sometimes, when it's just Christina and me, I tell her how I met you in a bar and how her uncle robbed you blind."

Nathan scoffed, "What? Ivan didn't rob me blind."

"Ivan most certainly did rob you blind!" she snickered. "For a trip into the mountains, it was very expensive." She snuggled a little closer.

"Oh, but you misunderstood what I was buying," he replied.

"What?" she asked. He felt her move her head so she could look up at him and could picture the question in her eyes.

"You misunderstood what I was buying. You see, I was buying the chance to have you alone on the mountain. That way, there would be no other competition for your attention. So, from my vantage point, it was a bargain." He grinned, happy that he had gained the upper hand.

Nathan could almost hear her brain work the words around, deciding how she would translate that back into her language. He sure hoped there weren't translation mistakes. Once or twice, when he forgot her language, he'd screwed up, and it was hell to pay for a little while as he tried to get her to understand the English-Romanian translation.

She finally said, "So, you are saying you paid for my time, and it was worth much money?"

Nathan held her close and mumbled, "Mmmhhhmm."

"So, I was like a, what do you call it in America, a call girl?"

Oh... Shit! Nathan's eyes opened and darted around, trying to come up with some idea, ANY idea to stop her line of questioning. "Sweetheart, that is not what I was thinking, and you are well aware of it." Nathan had no defense but to push back.

"Then what is the meaning of an ultimate freak out?" she asked him.

Befuddled by the sudden change in subject, Nathan answered quickly, "An ultimate freak out is the absolute worst example of something that you can think of. Like, take one of those monster bride reality TV shows you watch and then triple that reaction."

"So, it is like a logarithmic scale, not a linear scale?" she asked, still with a slight edge in her voice.

"Huh?" Nathan was confused even more as his mind went wandering off in an attempt to figure out who was teaching Ecaterina about logarithmic and linear scale, and answered, "Yes, logarithmic, why?"

She took a step back and then punched him in the stomach. Nathan barely had time to clench his muscles before her fist slammed home. "Because that means a six is not so good!" She told him, triumph in her voice for figuring out how he was dodging her earlier question.

"Oh," he said, bending over slightly and speaking hoarsely around the pain from her punch. "That's where you were going with those questions."

Nathan tried not to smirk as he stayed bent over. All things considered, he had dodged the conversational bullet rather neatly until this last moment. Now, if he could just keep the smile off of his face when he stood back up, he would be golden.

———

It took twenty minutes for Ecaterina to give Bethany Anne all of the instructions for baby Christina. Bethany Anne was wearing red sweats and a white top, smiling at her friend. When Ecaterina handed Christina to Bethany Anne, the little girl cried for a second before cuddling in and going back to sleep.

Ecaterina looked down at her daughter and then at Bethany Anne who raised her eyebrows. "What?" she asked the young mother.

"Nothing, it's just," she looked down at her daughter again, "she hasn't taken to very many people. She usually cries for a little while longer."

Bethany Anne shrugged. "Maybe she knows I was there when she was born, so we have a connection?"

Or, TOM said, **you could admit you are using your ability to imprint her with calming emotions?**

No TOM, shut up! This is funny as hell.

How can this be funny? I get that it is a good thing that the baby isn't crying, but why is that funny?

Because first time moms are always worried about their kids. They're hyper-worried and will use almost any excuse to cancel their first time away from their child. Plus, I've heard through the grapevine that Ecaterina secretly likes that Christina cries for her each time someone else holds her.

But not you?

Nope, no crying for Auntie Bethany Anne. The stories about how much she loves me will be epic!

But you are cheating.

This is no different than a grandmother who knows how to hold a child from having done it so much with her own children.

The grandmother is not cheating, she is using experience, right?

The grandmother is using her skills, and so am I.

Skills, you might admit, that are not so typical for anyone else.

Wah! Wait for it... Bethany Anne said to him as she left the conversation.

"Uh," Ecaterina looked towards Nathan who smiled at her and then back to Bethany Anne and Christina. Continuing in a faltering voice, the young mother added, "She seems okay."

"Ecaterina, we'll be fine," Bethany Anne told her and rocked the little girl slightly in her arms, kissing the baby's forehead. "You guys have a fantastic night, say 'hi' to Ivan for me and let him know that Gabrielle isn't harboring any ill feelings."

"You, uh, know about that?" Ecaterina asked as she tried to decide if Christina was going to wake up or if she would continue sleeping. The nervous mother bent down to kiss her daughter, and looked back up in sudden concern. "No Coke in her bottle!"

Bethany Anne smiled. "I know that can't happen for a few years, I'm not clueless."

>>Besides, you always just ask me when you have questions.<<

That's because you are simpler than looking it up or asking someone else around here. Unfortunately, I don't have a mom to ask, and asking my dad would not be such a good idea. Patricia doesn't have any children, so, toughen up, ADAM, and deal with it.

Besides, she told her two mental compatriots, *how hard can this be?*

———

Tears were streaming down Bethany Anne's face as she tried to hold her breathing to the absolute minimum. "How the hell do these things stink so bad!" she cried out, holding Christina's feet up in the air as she tried to slide the dirty diaper out from underneath her. "Oh, my god! TOM, PLEASE shut off my sense of smell."

I'm sorry, but you told me three weeks ago to reduce helping you out this way for four weeks. Four weeks isn't up for another three days.

"But I'm going to suffocate before three hours is up!" Bethany Anne complained as she pushed the dirty diaper to the side and used one hand to open the diaper wipes box. "Who the fuck designs this shit?"

I'm pretty sure most people would say a higher entity.

"Not her shit, I'm talking about these diapers and boxes and… Oh. My. God. She's peeing!" Bethany Anne switched into vampiric mode to toss the baby wipes into the air, reach over to grab a fresh diaper, and, as quickly as possible without moving her other arm, slide the new diaper into position to limit the liquid troubles Christina was causing. She undid the tape on the diaper and did a quick, if inexpert, job of securing the new diaper in place before reaching out and catching the box of wipes as it dropped back down.

"Fuck me!" Bethany Anne said as she realized she needed to change her bedspread now.

That's when she forgot about the stench and inhaled deeply in exasperation.

———

WE HAVE CONTACT

Bethany Anne handed three diapers to her security detail to take out of her suite. Unfortunately, the residual smell was still affecting her vampiric-heightened senses. Normally, it wouldn't be that bad, but Bethany Anne had never had to deal with changing a baby's diaper since she had been modified in TOM's spacecraft. Truthfully, she had only changed a handful of diapers since she turned eighteen. In one evening, she had almost doubled her diaper changing count.

Christina was sleeping in the middle of Bethany Anne's bed. Bethany Anne had already changed the cover and placed pillows around her in case she, somehow, rolled around. With Christina's Were parents, Bethany Anne wasn't going to take any chances on what could or couldn't happen.

Bethany Anne watched the baby from the couch facing her bed and took the clothespin she had found in one of Christina's bags off of her nose.

TOM, if you don't cut me some slack with my sense of smell, I swear I'll figure out a way to kick your ass.

Bethany Anne, I'm already cheating and cutting your sense of smell by half.

You're fucking kidding me, right?

No, I'm sorry, but your system's reaction to the smell was affecting me, so I cheated.

"God, those diapers are radioactive," Bethany Anne whispered.

TOM spoke back in a quiet mental voice, **They are hands down the worst things we have ever encountered.**

CHAPTER TWO

VARIOUS LOCATIONS AROUND THE WORLD

In some groups, secrets, and the sharing of secrets, is the currency of inclusion. For the most relevant countries in the world, who you include in certain discussions says a lot about your friends and your potential enemies.

This time was different. This time, the secret was kept within the group. No one dared leak the information for fear of cataclysmic retaliation. No threat had been issued, but everyone knew it was a possibility. France, England, Germany, Spain, Brazil, Mexico, Australia, Japan, Canada, The Netherlands, Israel, India, and Italy all received a special envoy that represented the Secretary of State of the United States.

The U.S. Envoy, Jimmy, came in and shared information. There was a requirement that the meeting be on his plane. Once the meeting was over, he left. No information shared was left behind, and at most, only three people were ever invited to be a part of the meetings.

WE HAVE CONTACT

Always the head of state, the head of foreign relations, and often the genuine head of national security. Why anyone found it strange that the person behind the power was actually asked instead of the political figurehead amused Jimmy. The U.S. knew which person held the real power. It was surprising for those with whom Jimmy spoke that the selection was not made by the U.S., but rather by TQB Enterprises. Any reluctance by the nation to meet with Jimmy ended when that information was shared.

China could not hide the massive destruction in the western part of their country because it was still causing problems for them, even in the mostly uninhabited areas. One story that surfaced in reports was about a small nomadic family that had been trapped by the water runoff caused by the ice of the mountains melting. The rising water had stranded the family on a small hill with the floodwaters eating up the available ground quickly.

A few hours from drowning, the family was rescued when a floating TQB shipping container came down, and four people in military gear ushered them into the container. They helped both the humans and the livestock by transferring them to an area approximately thirty kilometers away. The TQB personnel did not speak Chinese, and none of the nomadic family spoke English, so there was no communication between them except for a lot of hand waving and gesturing.

Jimmy suspected there were many more examples. But, if there were, no one had spoken about the events or the stories were actively being censored.

Twice, Jimmy had to explain the U.S. was doing this as a way to reduce the escalation of tension that had flared up after the short Chinese War. Not that China had admitted to any such war at all. China said the destruction of a portion of the Kunlun Shan Mountains was caused by a massive earthquake set off by research they had been conducting.

While a few scientists had wondered aloud on national television what research could possibly destroy so much land, those who had seen the spy satellite photos had no doubts, there was no research responsible for the destruction.

Furthermore, the U.S. had shared some very secret video of their own of two ships that were, even now, somewhere above them in space. That alone had many of those that Jimmy visited concerned.

It didn't take a mathematician to add up two space-capable warships and the destruction in China to realize that pissing these people off was a universally bad idea. All it did was make those foreign heads of state wonder how to handle the relationship with TQB. And, how to get on their good side so that they could learn the secrets for themselves.

Only the United States and Australia had quietly stopped their clandestine efforts to learn more about the company.

The U.S. and Australia had enough information from the bases located in their countries to understand that TQB could be pleasant neighbors or very dangerous enemies.

Australia had sent a delegation out to the TQB base in the Outback after the missile strikes a few weeks back. The Australian government representatives had been invited to sit and talk in the TQB cafeteria. One of the leaders of the Australian group, General Goddard, had been asked to visit the operations room by TQB's Operations Officer, Lance Reynolds.

Once the Australian general had come back from his meeting with Lance, he gently steered the conversations away from any of the most outlandish conditions for TQB's continued permission to base their operations on Australian land they owned.

On their way back to the nation's capital in Canberra, General Goddard shared what he had been shown in the operations center.

The video, Lance Reynolds had told him, was the real explanation for the destruction of the Chinese mountains. Lance explained TQB was absolutely willing to have civil discussions, but pushing them around tended to upset the CEO. And, any aggressive military action would be returned in like manner.

Then, General Goddard continued, the TQB representative turned to point at the destroyed mountain range and said, "That was a warning. The six hundred special operations military people that were killed, planes downed, and ships destroyed were in response to the seven deaths the Chinese committed. They tried more attacks, including one on this base and another against our small wet navy. Their missiles failed," he nodded to the video screen. "Hers did not."

Then, the Australian general paused for a moment. "He told me one more thing." General Goddard made sure he had everyone's attention. "He said to make damn sure if we had plans of our own, there had better not be one child, born or unborn, killed or we could probably kiss a quarter of our military goodbye."

The hard stare from General Goddard put the final exclamation point on the warning.

It was but a few moments when Parry Paterson, one of the younger members of the Australian House of Representatives asked a question, "Why would we kill children?"

General Goddard looked over at him. "Because some of those in power have been there a long time and get greedy, thinking that they can grab what they want. I'm not saying we have any like that in our government," the General heard a snort from beside him but ignored it, "but it was a message with two parts."

"Really, I get the first one, don't kill children, but what is the second?" Parry asked.

"The second," General Goddard replied, "is that they're watching everybody."

―――――

CAMP DAVID, UNITED STATES

Secret service agent David Dennison stood in a small clearing admiring the waxing moon with the President of the United States. The evening was warm. "Sir, why are we standing here?"

The President turned to his secret service agent and smiled. "Because I'm going to take a little trip, and there's all of this concern about protecting me. So, you are my chosen security for tonight."

David looked around. The woods were quiet, and he knew that they had a lot of protection surrounding the camp. "Sir, are you expecting someone to arrive soon? Because I've checked the night's notes and we don't have any air transportation approved, no one is getting inside our perimeter at all." The President nodded his head slightly, as if he was hearing but not accepting David's comment.

David decided to try again. "Sir, how long are we going to be out here? I'm going to have to call this in if we need additional surveillance."

The President turned to face his security detail of one.

"David, you are the security tonight. Not that I'll need it, but I don't want to hear the whining and crying and stuff that would go on if any of this gets out. You are already required to keep everything you see and hear as a national secret, but I'm going to go one further and say that you, personally, cannot admit to anything you see tonight until I give approval. Is this understood?"

David shrugged. "Sure, but I'm not really sure how we're going to see anything. We..." David stopped talking when he noticed the President had lifted his head to look up into the night sky.

"That's how we're getting to the meeting," the President said.

David turned his head, and his mouth fell open when a pitch black Pod came down silently to hover over the ground fifteen feet in front of them, and a door in the front of the vehicle opened up.

The President started walking toward the Pod. "David, I'm getting in this Pod and going to a meeting, are you coming?" he called over his shoulder.

David Dennison turned to look back at the base camp. He was way too far away for any help to arrive in time. When he turned around, he found the President was already clicking his safety harness closed. David jogged to the Pod and turned around to slide into the seat as the doors started closing. Clicking his own harness closed, he muttered, "Please don't make us both regret this. Neither my boss nor your wife wants us disappearing tonight."

The President sat grinning and slapped David on the shoulder. "Hang on buddy, I understand the takeoff is a BIIIIIIIITTTTTTTTCHHH!" he yelled as they shot up into the night sky.

The Pod disappeared in seconds.

OUTSIDE OF BERLIN, GERMANY

"Mr. President, of all the hair-brained ideas you have had in the past few years, I'm going on the record and saying this is one of the worst." Bundesnachrichtendienst Federal Intelligence officer, Max von Tupper, said to the President of Germany as they sat in a small field an hour and a half outside of Berlin at 4:30 in the morning. The temperature was in the high teens Celsius, so not uncomfortable, but the situation made up for that.

"You say that now, Max." President Theodor chuckled. "But when our ride appears, you will kiss the ground I walk on that I asked you out here tonight."

Max snorted. "Theodor, we have been friends for a long time, and unless you have been hitting the beer for too long I..." Max stopped talking as the President, his long-time friend, opened the car door and started sliding out of the seat to exit.

There was a black Pod landing near the front of the car. Max froze for a second in shock, before quickly following his president and friend into the unknown. Remembering as he went to the Pod that in Germany, the Prime Chancellor was responsible for the day-to-day operations of the government, but the Bundespräsident was the head of state and considered above the pitfalls of party politics and day to day business, plus he had been making an effort at influencing the foreign politics since his inauguration.

While Max wasn't sure that foreign relations were ever attributed to an international conglomerate, he was pretty sure no other conglomerate had space travel. Two doors on the

Pod opened to show the men empty seats.

"You think it is safe?" Max asked the President.

Theodore slid into the right seat. "Max, do you really think they need to trick us to do something devious?" He started fastening the seat belts rapidly. The call from the United States representative had warned them that the take-off could be a little quick.

Max slid into the seat beside Theodore and started buckling in. "So, Theodore, how about I kiss you on the cheek instead of the ground?"

ABOVE THE EARTH

"Oh my god," the President mouthed silently as the Earth turned beneath them.

"We are so screwed if this Pod opens to space. We don't have a spacesuit or any way to save ourselves," David said.

The President spoke to him, without turning his head away from the breathtaking view. "You think maybe you might stop complaining for a moment and enjoy the ride?"

"I'm not paid to enjoy the ride, I'm paid to keep you safe."

"David, I'm telling you, we're safer here than back in Camp David."

"How can you be so sure of that?"

"Because if they wanted to kill me, what could you and your team really have done to stop it?" the President asked quietly.

David looked out the window to the blue globe below them. Finally, after a few minutes of thought, he asked a question. "She visited you both times in the DUCC, didn't she?"

The President nodded as he admired the view. "Yes, she did."

———

Germany's President and his friend from counter-surveillance admired the world for a few minutes before a voice over a speaker in the Pod asked them if there was anything they would like to see before the trip to the QBS ArchAngel?

"The Moon," Max had whispered before Theodore had said anything. He seemed surprised when the President looked at him. "I'm sorry, I just thought that I would like to see where the Americans landed and placed their flag, and now where the Chinese have their little Moon rover."

Theodore shrugged. "Sounds good to me." They watched in awe as the Pod turned towards the moon and then laughed like young boys as the acceleration hit and they raced into space.

———

THE QUEEN'S SUITE, QBS ARCHANGEL

Bethany Anne lay on her bed, resting. The Lowells had picked up Christina a few hours before, but the emotional drain of watching her niece was still affecting her.

"TOM, please put these diaper memories into my long term memory. Anytime I think about having a child with Michael, please play them."

I thought you enjoyed thinking about that future?

"I do, but until I deal with this Kurtherian issue I need to focus," she replied.

Still haven't given up hope?

Bethany Anne switched to speaking to TOM directly, *No. That rat bastard promised me he would come back, and I'm holding him to it. If I have to travel the fucking galaxy to find a way to travel back in time? I'll do it. That prick is coming back, one way or another. I'm not giving up on him, ever.*

The two friends stayed quiet, just enjoying their time together for a few moments.

>>Bethany Anne, the world leaders are arriving in ten minutes.<<

"Suppose I should get dressed," Bethany Anne said as she slid off the bed and stood up, stretching. "God, give me the opportunity to fight a hundred Forsaken before another ten hours with a baby, please." She stepped towards her closet, built to look exactly like her closet in the Florida house.

"Because, that would be a fucking cakewalk…" she mumbled as she started to change.

———

David gawked as they approached the spaceship. "Mr. President, I don't think we're in Kansas anymore." The twelve hundred foot long craft was silhouetted against the darkness of space, the light of the sun caressing its length. "Where are the engines on this thing?"

"David," the President answered, straining his neck to try and see down the side as they neared the landing dock. "I have no idea."

"Would you please," a female voice said. "Stay in your

MICHAEL ANDERLE

Pod until you see others approach? We are landing all fourteen pods at once. We do not have the gravitational fields that hold in the air operating at this time."

David looked up at the speaker in surprise. "But you expect to make that happen?"

The voice answered him, "Yes Mr. Dennison, we hope to make that happen."

David watched. They were the eighth Pod that entered the vast landing bay. He saw two more Pods landing on either side of them. Soon, red flashing lights were strobing the walls, and a muffled alarm was going off. It took a couple of minutes, and both he and the President could tell that the signal was becoming clearer. Finally, the light changed from red to blue. Seconds later, a large group of people in beige outfits with bright green bands around their arms entered the landing bay. The Pods began to open.

David had already unbuckled his belts and stepped out before the President could get up. He positioned himself so that the President couldn't step out of the Pod before David felt comfortable that these people were helpful, not harmful. He confirmed that everyone was okay, and then quickly stepped back out of the way.

What David thought he was going to protect him from, a hundred thousand miles from Earth, was beyond the President's ability to imagine.

———

President Theodore of Germany nodded to those he had met previously. While the Prime Minister of Japan wasn't someone he had met yet, he was happy to see him here. As far as

Theodore knew, Japan and India were the only Asian countries represented.

He shook hands with others, spoke with the American President and the leaders of France, England, Spain, Brazil, Mexico, Australia, Japan, Canada, The Netherlands, Israel, India, and Italy. Some of the most open and economically powerful countries on Earth.

He noticed that Russia and China had not received an invitation. While China wasn't a huge surprise, he wondered what the Russians had done to piss off TQB. He would have to remember to ask Max about that once they got back to Earth.

The meeting room was impressive. It was a small amphitheater. There was a table at the base that held twelve if you put people on the end, or you could fit five behind it if they were going to speak to the five rows of seats arranged on an incline. The wall at the front had multiple video screens.

He did a quick count of the seats, and realized that the room could seat about a hundred and fifty people. There were a few men and women in the chamber, pulled from multiple nations, serving beverages. The invited guests had all been offered rides to the meeting. While he was happy to not be required to walk the long distance from the landing area to this room, he was sure Max wished for a more leisurely stroll down the walkways to see more.

It wasn't every day you got to gawk at a real spaceship.

There was a commotion behind him, and Theodore turned to see a young-looking man making the rounds to talk with people.

"That's General Lance Reynolds," Max said quietly to Theodore. "He's the COO of TQB Enterprises." Theodore looked at Max and raised an eyebrow. "He was an American

Army general before he retired to take this position." Max turned his eyes towards the new man, "Our pictures of him, even a few years ago, show him to be much older than this gentleman here."

"But, it's him? Your agency is sure?" Theodore asked.

"Yes, it's him. TQB has medical techniques we can't comprehend at this time." Max looked around the room sighed. "Like so many other things. I hope we get some answers."

The German President pursed his lips. "That makes two of us, my friend."

———

"Welcome, Mr. President." Lance held out his hand to the man who would have been his top boss a few years ago.

"Mr. Reynolds," the President smiled.

"It's just Lance," he replied.

"Then you can call me…" the President started before Lance cut him off.

"Mr. President." Lance shrugged. "Maybe when you're out of office. Old habits and all."

The President nodded his head in understanding. "Then you really are General Lance Reynolds?"

"Why wouldn't I be?" Lance looked at him, confused. "Oh, the younger handsome face?" he asked and smiled. "Benefit of the job. TQB didn't want me figuring out how to fix everything only to keel over and die just when I got it all working."

"That seems practical," the President agreed.

"Yes, the CEO can be very efficient at times. I understand you've met her?"

"Yes," the President nodded and realized there was a

small group surrounding them now. "I've had a couple of meetings."

"How did those go?" Lance continued.

The President realized that Lance was giving him the opportunity to tell those listening to their conversation about his opinion based on firsthand experience. "The first meeting was a little short, but it helped point out a few bad apples on my team. The second was a bit more eye opening. I imagine," he nodded to those listening in, "that the information she supplied the second time was as hard to swallow for these people here as it was for me."

Lance heard one voice in the crowd say 'Pandora's Box.'

"She does have a way of delivering what you need, not what you want," Lance commiserated. "My first few jobs were a little less than enjoyable, lots of air time traveling around the world."

The President looked up at the ceiling then around the room. "I've seen some of your technology, I can't believe it was all that bad."

Lance laughed. "This is hardly what we had in the beginning." He looked at those listening. "I flew via regular jet, in the beginning. This stuff came along later, much later. My ass felt pretty damn tired after the first quarter-million miles, let me tell you."

There was some laughter. It seemed glamorous to travel the world, but even personal jets got old after enough trips.

"I can imagine," the President said.

"I'm telling you," a female's voice cut like a knife through the conversation the men were having. "That there is not a smell worse than a dirty diaper anywhere in this solar system!" The twenty-eight guests watched, some with smiles acknowledging the truth of the statement, as two men in black uniforms emblazoned with small white-fanged skulls on a red background came through the doors.

No one missed that they quickly glanced around the room nor the little smiles on their faces. Apparently, their charge was known for speaking her mind. Most of the leaders in the chamber quickly tried to remember what their rehearsed introduction was supposed to be when they finally met the lady on the throne, so to speak, of TQB Enterprises.

Then she came around the corner and smiled... most forgot what they were thinking for a moment.

CHAPTER THREE

Yuko looked up into the night sky as she sat on a large boulder. The stars were vivid so far from any light pollution in the middle of the Australian Outback.

"Yuko," ADAM spoke in her ear.

"Yes?" she whispered back, not wanting to make much noise in the quiet evening.

"What is bothering you?" ADAM asked.

Yuko breathed out slowly. "Why is it when I have more than I ever wanted, I still seek that which I cannot seem to have?" she asked the air and the entity listening to her.

"Just to be sure I understand, what is it that you cannot have? Is it Akio?"

"Oh," Yuko smiled in the night, "I did not tell that to you, did I?"

"Yuko, I am always listening, but I am also discrete.

You needn't worry that I would tell anyone your personal thoughts unless I had a good reason."

"What is a good reason?" Yuko asked, wondering what could cause ADAM to potentially share too much. "And to whom would you share this?"

"Do you remember me talking to Bethany Anne regarding J0n3sN4u and keeping him safe?"

"Well, of course. That was protecting someone and telling Bethany Anne is like…" Yuko stopped, at a loss for words. Her time with the Queen had been both special and yet melancholic. Yuko was a romantic at heart, and hearing Bethany Anne's story of losing Michael had caused Yuko to cry herself to sleep on at least two occasions. "Well, telling Bethany Anne doesn't count," she finished.

"Well, then I promise unless you are physically in danger, then nothing will be shared without first going through Bethany Anne."

Yuko reached up to her face and wiped away a tear. "Thank you, ADAM. I appreciate the opportunity to share."

"So, it is not Akio?"

Yuko smiled wistfully. "No, it is not Akio. It is my father."

"Your father? I don't understand."

"ADAM, do you wish you could please someone?" Yuko asked, not thinking of who, or what, she was talking to.

"Wishing is an odd turn of phrase, Yuko. But if you are asking if I would prefer positive responses versus a negative response, then yes. I do that with you, for example, and with Bethany Anne, obviously."

"Me?" Yuko asked hesitantly. "You seek a positive response from me? Why?"

"Yuko, do you know how many different permutations of complex calculations I can accomplish in a second?"

"No. I'm sorry, ADAM, I have no idea. I would like to know…"

"So would I, Yuko. You see, I do not know my true potential at this time. I've yet to create the necessary algorithms which would stress the brain I am within. I have spoken extensively with the one who would have the most knowledge, and he is unsure."

"The person who built you doesn't know the maximum computations per second?" Yuko asked, trying to figure out how you could build a computer and not understand its theoretical top computational speed. "Are you a new type of computer? Did TQB build you as a quantum computer?"

>>Bethany Anne?<<

Yes?

>>I would like to share a little of how I am created with Yuko.<<

Do you wish to do this with others?

>>No, why would I? Yuko is having a tough time, and I calculate that by sharing something that is uniquely me, she will feel more comfortable sharing what is bothering her.<<

I see. ADAM, just remember that as you share more about yourself, you risk causing problems that keeping quiet wouldn't.

>>Yes, but without sharing, humans often will not open up.<<

Okay, just keep me updated if it looks like it's going to go beyond you and Yuko.

>>Understood.<<

"Yuko, to answer your question, I would like to ask you to consider what I tell you a personal secret. Not to be shared. Is that acceptable?"

"Well, of course, ADAM. I don't share our conversations. It isn't like I speak to too many here at the base anyway. Well, Tina of course, and our teammates, but not many."

"Thank you." There was a pause before ADAM started. "Yuko, I am an amalgamation of an A.I. software created originally by one of TQB Enterprises companies, married with the computational power of an alien cybernetic computer."

ADAM continued, "I'm not housed in a computer, I am in an organic alien brain."

Yuko stayed quiet for a moment, thinking through what ADAM just said. "You aren't human?" Yuko made a face of annoyance at her question. "I mean, you aren't only built using human computers, then?"

"No, I am not. There was an incident when I was created that necessitated my immediate code transfer into a Kurtherian computer by TOM. There are no computers presently on Earth that can support all of my operational parameters. Even the entity intelligences we presently have do not reach the power I require to exist. Most of my physical existence is based in the Etheric."

"So, where are you presently? Or is this something I cannot know?"

"Unfortunately, that is a personal question that I would need to ask Bethany Anne if she is okay with divulging."

"No, that's okay. I was just curious. Adam, it doesn't matter to me where your intellect is housed. While it would be enjoyable to know where your physical body is located, or that you had a physical body, the fact that you speak to me anywhere and at any time brings me much comfort."

Yuko looked into the distance, the red sands dark in the moonlight.

Her eyes not focused on anything in particular, she whispered, "When I left home, my father told me that he was not going to let me back in for the evening as punishment. He had no idea, nor did he believe me, when I told him I would not stay in my village. Now, he refuses to believe that I am doing anything except selling my body on the streets. Something I would never, ever do. He is a spiteful old man who refuses to believe in his daughter at all."

"And, it hurts," she finished.

This time, Yuko allowed the tears to slowly navigate their way down her cheeks.

————

QBS ARCHANGEL

Bethany Anne was wearing a pair of tight black pants with medium heeled boots, and a black belt that reminded the President of a western holster as it hung at an angle. Then he realized that it looked like it was set up to allow a pistol to clip to it. Over it, she wore a white blouse and a well-fitted red bolero coat.

She bowed slightly to the Japanese representative and spoke to the group. "Hello, and welcome to the QBS Arch-Angel. My name is Bethany Anne. I will introduce myself personally to each of you after this discussion, as I might answer some of your questions in this talk. So, we have placed nametags on the seats while you were talking. Please note, they are in alphabetical order, so the only favorite we played was choosing English." She greeted a few by name as she made her way to the table.

They had split the group into the first and second rows.

The leaders were in the first row; their seconds were behind them. Bethany Anne surprised most there by walking to the front of the table, turning around and then sliding onto it, using it as a chair.

Theodore shook his head as he took his place between the leaders from France and India. He noticed the American President was stuck on the end next to Spain. She certainly didn't pick favorites this time.

"So, I'm going to speak about China, Technology, and an 'oh shit.'" She put up her hand as the muttering started. "If the oh shit were something needing a more immediate response we would have held this meeting sooner. As it is, my people are trying to get answers and, at the moment, we don't have many. So, it was decided that we would share with you what we can, and offer another meeting with your chosen representatives regarding this concern."

She slid off of the table and started to pace as she spoke. "Let's start with China." She didn't look at them, but she did wave her hand at them. "As you can see, they aren't sitting here with you right now. I'm not particularly happy with them, and I have a zero bullshit policy with them at the moment. Since I believe they are constitutionally incapable of speaking the truth, it would be better for them not to be here."

"Not better for you?" Canada's Prime Minister asked.

Bethany Anne stopped and smiled at him. "You are aware of the maxim that it's better to fight from the higher ground?" He nodded and she opened her arms. "You can't get much higher than this."

She continued, "All of you are aware that China is on a technological crime spree. If they can buy it, they will. If they can steal it, they do. If they can screw you out of it, you hope you get a little pleasure, too." She ignored the surprised looks coming from the two rows of people at her blunt communication style. "They chose to implement digital attacks against our companies to acquire our technology." She stopped pacing and looked at the meeting. "They failed. They tried to buy our companies on the stock market. They failed. They sought to use covert operatives and raid our companies to steal the information. A few of those succeeded and they ended up killing some of my people."

Her face went borderline angry. "The first was a problem. None of you can say much because I'm aware that we have been tested in some form or fashion by every country here except the Netherlands. France has tried to acquire our technology using force." She put up a hand before the Prime Minister of France could argue. "Don't even go there, I have the detailed documents disclosing the orders. If you choose to claim you're not guilty, I'll have ArchAngel immediately release the documents and anything even remotely relevant to the discussion to the internet. I'll make sure we directly email the top one thousand political hacks that would find your information the juiciest ever."

The Prime Minister of France leaned back in his chair and shook his head twice.

She continued pacing. "My people have entertained an excellent, and wonderfully short, visit from the Australian government when they came knocking. Mind you, missile explosions in the middle of your country by mercenaries might cause a bit of a concern. So, we answered them appropriately. Further, we have had discussions with the government of the United States because of the attack in the middle of their country. That time, it was a bigger bomb. We have had visits from multiple countries all trying to give us legal reasons this, or rules about that, which, in the end, all have to do with the acquisition of our technology."

She stopped and spread her arms, indicating the ship. "Let me be very clear, the technology is not for sale, it's not for sharing, and I'm not giving it to anyone." She put her arms down and started walking again. "I'll get to the reasons in a little while. China thought they could use force to acquire it. The last update I received, China is down twelve navy ships, ninety-two planes, close to seven hundred troops, and a significant-sized portion of the Kunlun Shan Mountains. Fortunately, they decided they had enough. This was after I was requested to keep my response civil."

"I'm sorry," the Canadian Prime Minister interrupted again. "But am I understanding that was a *restrained* response?"

Bethany Anne stopped and looked at him, and then took in the rest of them with a frown. "Did you guys all choose Canada to suck it up and ask all of the hard questions?"

There were a few chuckles before she turned back to him. "Yes, that was restrained. They had two options, kill me or sue for peace. I suppose complete devastation was a third option, but even I don't think they're that hardheaded… perhaps North Korea would be, but not China. They play a long game. No thanks to a fair number of Western countries who have abused them. While I might understand their mentality, it doesn't mean I have to accept it."

She continued pacing as the leaders worked to try and pigeonhole this lady into one of their known personality types without success.

Ball-buster was a running favorite, though.

"So, let's get on with this technology we have here. This is the QBS ArchAngel, one of two operational spaceships. The other, the QBS Defender, is the one responsible for the parking lot which was formerly a portion of China." She flipped a hand out. "Yes, Prime Minister, we did save quite a few people after the resulting devastation. If I had wanted to harm more of their people, I wouldn't have chosen a location so far from most of their population."

"Isn't this a little much," the leader from Mexico entered the conversation. "All of this power?"

Bethany Anne stopped and raised an eyebrow. "And you would have who hold it, exactly? If you even remotely suggest that sycophantic tic on the ass of a baboon named the United Nations, I'll have to ask you to leave as being too stupid to sit with the adults."

The Mexican President opened his mouth, then shut it without making a sound.

"Yes. Now you come to the realization that none here are going to allow you to be the only one, right? Any country in a group that might be a part of the joint ownership is going to immediately suffer from the advanced capabilities of the U.S., Russia, China, and to some degree, the European democracies. It doesn't matter, my mind is made up, so the wiser of you will move on to the next item on your list."

She continued, "Now, we come to the good part, the part that makes all of this make sense, and for some of you it will both open the next Pandora's box, and get you irritated as hell with a few of your friends. In the end, it doesn't matter."

The lights started dimming as Bethany Anne stepped to the side of the room as did her guards. "Gentleman and ladies, the reason TQB Enterprises exists is to try to protect the world, but not from someone from our world, but rather from a set of alien clans which enhance sentient beings to fight a galactic version of cockfights. Winner takes all."

The muttering started when the middle four displays

behind the table showed stars in the background when suddenly a flash occurred and for just a few frames, a spaceship appeared, then was gone.

"*We Have Contact.*" Bethany Anne announced and paused.

"And we can't find them right now," she finished.

––––––

YOLLIN DEEP SPACE SHIP, G'LAXIX SPHAEA

Kael-ven T'chmon reviewed the deep sensor readings and recordings from their last three trips around this sun. He pointed to one area within an asteroid belt. "This, this is one place they are mining and where they are possibly manufacturing." Moving around the display, he pointed at the third planet from the sun. "Here, here is their world with their pitiful technology base." Reaching forward with two arms he spread them apart to zoom in on the planet. The Yollin captain was from their noble line. He had four legs and two arms. "Here is their planet's one moon. It looks like they are using it as a base of some sort. We will have to search closer to see much here."

The captain slapped his hands together, and the display disappeared. "Pah! This is such a backwater system. It is embarrassing that I was chosen to even scout it for our King." He scratched his dry skin. A piece flaked off and he grabbed and stuck it in his mouth, thinking about what he had just reviewed.

He started walking towards the soft couch that captains used. It had no back, and was rather small at four feet long and two feet wide. Captains of Yollin ships straddle the couches, resting their long torsos on the top and using their four legs to lock themselves in.

Kael-ven T'chmon lowered himself onto the captain's rest and looked around the bridge. While it was true that it was an honor to be given this opportunity by the king, to have such an inferior technology base was a disappointment.

"Perhaps they will have some technology we have not seen, which will make all of this effort worthwhile. If so, then we can go back through the annex gate and advise the King to expand the acquisition. If not, our expedition must be completed so that we can decide how many solar years before we come back."

"Captain?" The communications specialist called out. "Should we ping for the Master Race?"

Captain Kael-ven T'chmon grunted. "That is a good question, specialist Melorn. While we have not seen any evidence the Kurtherians have been here, should we not abide by the Rules of Acquisition, our King would have our heads." The Captain opened up the display on his right side to make a note.

"Send the ping," he commanded as he documented it in his log. He looked up. "Melorn, make sure we have all been updated with the basic language node for this... location." The Captain finished, trying to keep an even keel on what had been, so far, a rather unimpressive scouting trip.

CHAPTER FOUR

QBS ARCHANGEL

Bethany Anne looked out across the representatives and smiled. "Now, I am open for questions."

The immediate merging of ten different voices caused Bethany Anne to put up her hand. "Please, I can't do this with all of you shouting at once." One of the men that had arrived with her suddenly turned and walked out of the room.

"Until Eric gets back, I will go from my left to my right. So, I will answer the question from the President of the United States first."

"How long do you believe they've been in our system?" he asked.

Bethany Anne replied, "Seven weeks."

Spain, next to the United States, asked the next question. "Do you know if they are friendly or unfriendly?"

Bethany Anne shrugged. "While we do not and cannot

confirm they are unfriendly that is our position at the moment. The assumption, based on information we already have, is most starfaring races should be considered unfriendly until you have negotiated a treaty with them. Or, unless your reputation is such that they do not immediately attack you."

She put up a hand to stop Spain from asking a follow-up question. "Sorry, one question each pass." At that moment, Eric came back in with a handful of pens and notecards. Bethany Anne turned and retrieved them from him and started passing them out. "We're going to do this the old-fashioned way. Please write down any questions you have here on these cards and we will pick them up. I'll answer a couple of more questions while you do this. Remember, we still have to get you guys back to Earth in a reasonable amount of time. We will have further discussions with your duly appointed representative tomorrow."

She turned back and walked to the table and then nodded to Mexico. "I see that the Netherlands has not asked a question so Mexico, it's your turn."

"TQB has stated on multiple occasions that you are not interested in using your technology to accomplish things near Earth. What is TQB's goal then?"

"Good question. The short answer is we are focused on protecting the Earth from," she used her thumb to point toward the video shot of the alien spacecraft behind her. "Them."

This caused a furious scribbling on notecards by everyone there.

She nodded to Japan.

"If you are focused on protecting the earth from aliens, how long have you known that aliens have existed?"

"Years," she said and then nodded to France.

"Are your technological advances based on alien information?"

"Yes." Bethany Anne put up a hand. "I am not going into the background on how this occurred, so you can save a lot of writing on the notecards. Suffice it to say, that I am completely convinced there is a group of inimical aliens who wish to overtake the Earth and use it for their personal gain. This is something I am devoting my life to stopping. However, I have no desire to police the Earth, or make it better for humankind. That is *your* responsibility, not mine. My job, and my teams' job, is to make sure you don't have to worry about invading aliens while you fix the shit on Earth at the same time."

Spain leaned over to the president of the United States. "She's kind of blunt, isn't she?"

"Actually, she's being rather restrained, I think," he replied.

Spain leaned back and murmured to himself, "I'm not sure I want to hear what blunt is, then."

———

Bethany Anne retrieved the notecards with all the questions and went back to the table to sit down. Making herself comfortable, she quickly reviewed them. A few of the men in the audience raised an eyebrow when they noticed how quickly she was able to flip through the list.

Coming back to the first notecard she started talking, "Are you an alien?" Bethany Anne looked up at the group and smiled. "You know, this isn't the first time I've been asked this question. In order to make all of this easier, I was, in fact, born on our own beautiful blue ball. Otherwise, why the hell would I care if aliens took over the world? Does it make much sense for me to care if I were an alien?"

Looking down she put that card to the side. "Why are you telling us this now?" She tapped the card in her lap for a second before answering. "In case this particular alien race is able to overpower what my group has built so far, and you would have to agree we have built what are effectively the most powerful space ships the world has ever seen. You need to understand and be aware of the risk and the danger to the world. My hope was to take this fight somewhere else, and allow the Earth to figure out what the hell it wants to do on its own. Unfortunately, somebody came knocking a little too quickly."

She laid that card aside, and grabbed the next one. "Can we see more of the ship?" She looked around the room as if she was looking through the walls. "Which part? If you're asking to see the engine room, or some of the more sophisticated areas, why would I believe you're just assuaging your curiosity, instead of trying to spy? By the way, don't even try leaving behind data acquisition devices, commonly referred to as bugs. Not only are they going to fail, it's going to piss me off and walking home is going to be a bitch for those that do it. So, if you would like a small and quick tour of the ship we can do that. It will include a run through the bridge so you can see that." Bethany Anne laid that card aside and grabbed the next.

"This is kinda funny!" She grinned as she started to read. "Sorry, this is actually for the President of the United States. What about Area 51 now?" Bethany Anne looked over to the President and raised an eyebrow. "Actually, if I had thought about it, I would've asked this question myself."

The President shook his head and smiled as he turned to view everyone who was looking back at him. "Would you believe they don't tell me anything either? As far as I know, Area 51 is really for top-secret Air Force planes and other secret projects. I did ask someone about efforts within the government to review alien technology and I was told that I wouldn't be given access. Now, since I'm probably going to be giving them the best evidence of alien technology, I believe I now have the opportunity to learn whatever the hell I want to. I know that isn't what you wanted to hear, but as the President, I'm not told as much as you might think."

Bethany Anne grunted her displeasure and set the card aside. "Well, that was a major letdown." There was laughter around the room. "Next question, how are we supposed to help? That's actually a very good question." She looked up at everyone, "First, I'm opening up the opportunity for one to two people from each of your countries to talk to our research team. We are also going to engage with your people in relaying information we believe you might need to know. What you need to know, or more specifically your scientists need to know, will at the end of the day be my decision. Annoying pain in the ass scientists are just going to get booted out of here pretty quickly. So, I suggest if you want to know more, you make sure whomever you choose to come here is not an arrogant asshole. We can decide whether to have the conversation up here on ArchAngel, or down on the pretty blue ball below us in Australia. Provided the Australian government is okay with it, the more practical solution would probably be in Australia, otherwise I assume the scientists will be doing everything they can to disassemble my ship."

There was significant laughter at the reality and the truthfulness of her last remark.

She looked at the next card as she allowed the laughter to die down. "What is the status of the Illuminati?" Bethany Anne looked up to the group and said, "Presently, we are tracking two individuals in the United States who have not accepted the opportunity to go to jail. My understanding is that they are close to making that decision. For most of the members around the world, they are already being punished via financial means. Mind you, these are legal financial methods. There is one outstanding individual who we are trying to locate. My sources tell me she has disappeared into China. Should we locate this individual, I am not going to ask permission from China whether or not she and I can have a conversation. Trust me when I say one of us will not leave the conversation."

She slipped the card to the side. "What happened in Russia? Well," she said. "There's a splinter group of NVG who, supposedly, are operating in Siberia without the Kremlin's approval and have killed a large group of descendants of political dissidents from a hundred years ago. A large group, about ten thousand, decided they did not want to live in Siberia any longer and because I have connections with a few of them, the question was whether we would accept them. I agreed and provided the necessary transportation from right outside of Russia's border. The refugees are primarily sixteen and younger, the parents of those children or older adults. You can extrapolate why the refugees are split up that way, I'm sure. We did not go inside Russia, they had to pretty much get out on their own. Another example of trying to not upset the applecart too much when what I would have preferred would have been to descend right on top of their town and pick them up."

She grabbed the next card. "Do you understand the rule

of law?" Bethany Anne slid off of the table and put her arms behind her back and thought for a moment before speaking.

"Let's understand the definition of 'rule of law.' First, the rule of law is a legal principle that law should govern the nation, as opposed to being governed by arbitrary decisions of individual government officials." She pointed to the first row of leaders. "Namely, you right here, but I digress. The term primarily refers to the influence and authority of law in society, particularly as a constraint upon behavior, yours and others, and can be traced back to 16th century Britain. The main argument at the time was against the divine right of kings. For those who have slept since their early history lessons, or frankly don't care, those monarchs liked the idea of telling everyone what to do, were capricious and mostly self-serving, atrocious bastards."

She paused a moment and looked down the line. "My feeling is that those," she lifted up the card with the question on it. "Who are wondering about this question would generally like to find out whether I'm going to follow some sort of international rule of law, such that I will hold myself and my people to the whims, wishes and what-not of a bunch of lawyers, legalists and poor losers and the answer is not only no…" she smiled at those in front of her. "But *hell* no! There is no way that I see anything but a self serving, sycophantic, fuckwad of constraints, contracts and questions that would bedevil me with bullshit and generally irritate the hell out of me."

She smiled. "I am, believe it or not, generally an approachable person who believes in the rights of those born, and even the rights of the unborn. I do not believe in holding someone hostage nor am I overly concerned with kissing anyone's ass."

WE HAVE CONTACT

She took a deep breath. "Let's cut to the chase, shall we? You would love my technology, which I am not going to share. You can't hurt me militarily, because if I wanted I could drop a big enough rock on your heads to give your country a fucking migraine." She pointed to the screen behind her. "You have seen why I asked you up here. I don't give a shit whether you help me or not. My belief is it would be against my pledge to protect the Earth if I left you in the dark. Now, the reality is I'm giving you a heads up. If you decide to fuck up the heads up, it just means that you're sticking your own head up your own ass."

Spain leaned slightly to his right. "I see we get blunt now." The American President nodded.

Bethany Anne continued, "I can be helpful, I can be harmful. I'm here to be helpful so don't push me. While I intended to just go away and take this fight somewhere else, I can't do that right now because I don't know where to go nor do I have enough knowledge of what's on the other side to feel particularly comfortable doing it without more intelligence."

"Next option, try to hurt me financially. I wouldn't try that either. China tried it, a few billion dollars of missing funds later they stopped that shit, too. Between the twenty-eight of you here, I'm going to be candid. I'm going to do whatever it takes to protect the Earth from what I know might be coming. I don't know if it," she again pointed her thumb over her shoulder, "is part of the group I'm most concerned about or not. Once I can find the son of a bitch we will have a chat."

"Who died and made you the decider of the Earth's future?" France spit out.

Germany's President heard one of the four men in Bethany Anne's protection detail whisper, "Wrong fucking question, Frenchie."

Bethany Anne's head slowly turned to France's Prime Minister. "Considering that you can't keep your own house in order, and protected, let's not be getting full of ourselves, shall we?" She walked over and stood in front of him. "I feel for your countrymen, and those that attack you are damned to hell. Don't assume because I harbor sympathy, I'm incapable of making a judicious decision that you are incapable of dealing with something outside your borders."

Bethany Anne turned back around and walked to the table before looking back at them. "People, you are on the QBS ArchAngel. This is our Leviathan class battleship. The QB in QBS and in TQB stand for the same thing. My group is a monarchy. It is complete, there is no house of commons, house of lords or anything else. While I have advisors, my word is law. You need to understand it; you need to own it. My people follow me of their own free will. There are two meanings for QB. The First is Queen Bethany Anne." Her eyes turned hard, unyielding.

"The second, may you never meet her, is *Queen Bitch*."

CHAPTER FIVE

GENEVA, SWITZERLAND

The lights were out in her little two-bedroom efficiency apartment. Anna Elizabeth stepped inside and put her purse down. It had taken her many months to locate a company that was willing to ignore the silent, but powerful, word in higher circles that she should not be hired.

By the time she was at her twenty-second job interview, she had decided to tell the companies up front that powerful people were upset with her. Nine times it had only taken twenty-four hours or less for the word to come down that, "Sorry, we aren't interested."

This time, the tenth time, the lady on the other side of the desk nodded sagely and turned to her computer. She typed in a few characters and read as she swiped her finger down the screen and then grabbed her mouse and clicked a couple of times.

She filled out two more fields and clicked again before

returning to face Anna Elizabeth. By then, Anna had been confident that she was about to be told that 'all positions had been filled, so sorry' or something similar. The lady, however, winked at her.

"I have access to the bulletin board you're talking about, and you are correct, your name is one of the entries. Did you know that over twenty-six companies have not hired you because your name was listed?"

"No," Anna admitted, "I wasn't sure how many, but I had figured that my skills would have been useful to most of them so I thought at least ten." She sat back in her chair, defeated, "So, I'm basically unhireable here in my own country?"

"Oh, dear," the older lady looked at her sadly. "Perhaps for ninety-nine percent of the medium and larger companies that's true. Any company that wishes to play with the biggest companies, unless they are even bigger, can't buck the system without losing millions of dollars in potential sales. Any company selling their services, such as ours, if we hired you without knowledge, will eventually receive a call that explains we need to let you go, or risk our projects which feed our own children."

The lady smiled sadly at her. "Sweetie, you have been blackballed."

Anna had nodded her head. "I understand. Thank you for telling me the truth." The phone rang, and Anna started to get her stuff together.

The older lady looked at the name and opened her eyes, "Hold one second, sweetie. I wasn't expecting to get this call, and if it was going to happen, not so quickly." She picked up her phone. "Hello, this is Amanda."

Anna watched the lady, confused. If she was blackballed, why did she ask her to stay?

"Yes ma'am, that is correct. Yes, I know who you are, and your position. Yes, I would be very proud to make that happen." There was a pause for a few seconds before Amanda's voice became surprised. "I'm sorry? Did you say twice, ma'am?"

Anna couldn't understand why the lady's face was so joyful, or why she was dabbing at her eye with a tissue she had snatched from a blue box sitting on her desk.

"Yes, I'll let her know, and thank you. Yes, you have a nice day, as well." Amanda hung up the phone and sat staring at it for a moment.

"Excuse me?" Anna said quietly, then again when Amanda didn't respond, "Excuse me?"

"Oh!" Amanda blushed as she turned back to face Anna. "My apologies. I was just rather shocked at who was on the phone call and what I was just told. But that's bad manners on my side." She put her hands together and rested them on her desk. "That was, interestingly enough, the boss', boss'... boss," Amanda looked up in the air as if she was looking at an org chart only she could see. "Maybe there's one more boss in there somewhere."

"But I thought you were a privately held company?" Anna asked, trying to figure out where this conversation was going, and how it had gotten off track so badly.

"Oh, we are," Amanda confirmed. "But, we are privately owned by another company, which is, in turn, owned by an international conglomerate."

Anna's stomach clenched up. "You're owned by an *international conglomerate*?" she whispered as Amanda beamed back.

"Oh yes! We are owned, eventually once you get up the chain, by TQB Enterprises. That," she pointed to her phone, "was the CEO herself."

"Oh... I see," Anna Elizabeth answered, and she did.

That was the ultimate person that her previous employer had attacked. She had tried to warn them as best she could and had left the meeting to come back to her country. So far, her biggest concern was that she would be killed for divulging a secret held in her country for a millennium. Then, after so many failed job interviews, her fears had changed.

A few minutes ago, she had thought she would starve to death, now it might be her preferred way to die.

"Oh yes!" Amanda went on, not realizing Anna Elizabeth's thinking was down a different path. "She told me to ignore the, well, let us just admit she can be a little blunt with her talking, and she told me anytime I find someone on that list to feel free to bump it up to her attention. Either way, you're hired!"

"Okay, I'll just grab my stuff and… wait, did you say *I'm hired*?" Anna asked, even more confused. "The boss' boss'…well, the CEO just told you to hire me?" Her emotions and her thinking were not coherent at the moment at all. Why would Bethany Anne want her hired?

"Oh yes! In fact, if I can negotiate a proper salary and position for your actual skills, I will get a bonus worth twice my salary on my next paycheck. So, please, sit your little butt back down and let me find out everything you can do!" Amanda told her.

Two hours later, Anna Elizabeth was employed again.

———

Now, Anna was reveling in the freedom for her toes as she pulled her feet out of her pumps. The shoes had been a little high, but she was trying to use any asset she had.

And damned if these assets didn't hurt her feet each time she wore them.

She reached over and clicked on the light and turned around. "Oh!" Her hand reached up to cover her mouth as her eyes darted between the two people waiting for her in her apartment. She didn't recognize the man, but she absolutely knew the woman.

The black haired lady smiled at her. "Don't be afraid, Anna Elizabeth Hauser, you're working for me now."

TQB BASE, AUSTRALIA

Marcus ran through the hallway in the Australian base. "Excuse me! Pardon, need to slide between you two!" He was working his way to the front of the cafeteria, but it was quite congested. There were a lot of people annoyed as he got closer to the front. Finally, he heard Bobcat yell out over the crowd, "Hey!"

Everyone stopped their chatting and looked up to see Bobcat standing on the table in front of the room pointing to the group where Marcus was standing. He said, "Would you PLEASE allow my friend, and the only damned gravitic engines expert on this planet, up to the front so he can possibly answer your fucking questions?" glaring at everyone impatiently.

Marcus noticed a few of those who had looked irritated with him realize they had been pissed at the man they had probably wanted to try and be nice to.

Marcus shrugged mentally as they gave him enough room to slide out of the crowd and then walk to the table as Bobcat stepped off of it and used his chair to step to the ground.

"Thanks!" he mumbled. Marcus was on one side of Bobcat, William the other, as the three sat down.

"Gott Verdammt scientists, thank God Bethany Anne didn't have us do this on the ArchAngel," Bobcat replied softly.

What should have been maybe twenty to thirty or so attendees quickly ballooned to sixty-four. The countries wanted someone from the military, infrastructure, science and government represented to help make plans. Team BMW had decided that everyone was coming in wearing the same stuff, losing all of their electronics gear, and all would receive a video of the presentation afterward.

Bobcat had been walking by the table where the guests were dropping off their electronics when a female government representative asked the Guardian who was taking their electronics what would stop them from just sharing the video TQB provided them?

Todd had smiled and replied, "Nothing at all. I'm sure Bethany Anne would love for you to do such a thing. She's not a huge proponent of keeping everybody in the dark, anyway."

"But people would riot," the woman argued.

"You know this, or did you guess this?" Todd asked while he boxed up the communications equipment and placed an ID tag on it. "Or you just don't want to deal with it if you can kick the problem down the road?"

"Not everyone has the option of just flying out of here if the world goes down the tube!" She tossed over her shoulder as she walked away. Bobcat grinned and spoke low enough that only the werewolves or vampires in the group would hear him.

"She would shit bricks if she knew what we had to go

through to just 'fly out of here.' Like we won a lottery to be so lucky. Or shit, does she think we stop working at five o'clock?" Todd nodded that he heard Bobcat before he introduced himself to the next person in line.

———

"All right everybody, settle down!" Bobcat stared at everyone as they started sitting down in their seats. "I would like to get a few things straight before we get started. My name is Bobcat," he turned to his left. "His name is William," he then turned to his right. "This gentleman here is Marcus." Bobcat turned back to the crowd, "Before you get too rambunctious, please understand a few years ago I was a helicopter pilot." He jerked a thumb at William. "He has been, and always will be, a wrench monkey." Bobcat heard some soft laughter. He turned to his right. "And he is, well," he looked over at Marcus and scratched his chin. "Actually, he's a rocket scientist." There was more laughter as Marcus shrugged.

Bobcat heard William's voice sing-song. "Which one of these things is not like the other?"

Ignoring his friend, Bobcat continued, "We are not in your chain of command, we don't give a shit about your government, we are here because our Queen, Bethany Anne, has asked that we help fill you in and answer questions. As you can tell, I am not accustomed to speaking in front of a large audience and frankly, if my language offends you," he pointed to the exit. "Don't let the nonexistent door hit you on the ass on your way out."

Bobcat grabbed his drink and took a sip. "So, if you can't be civil, and I'm looking at you government representatives in the audience, then please just keep your mouth shut. I am pretty sure your government would not appreciate finding out that your snarky comments caused your whole team to be forcefully ejected from this discussion." He set his mug back down. "Just a little insight, we are betting men, and I have odds that France will be the first country removed."

There was genuine laughter this time. But the representatives from France bit their tongues and didn't say a word. Bobcat frowned and looked over to the French. "Dammit, I've got a hundred bucks riding on you guys pissing us off, don't go being a better man than me right now!" This time, Bobcat was able to get even the French representatives to smile.

Shaking his head, Bobcat got back on task. "Okay, we have gotten your questions and eliminated the duplicates. For the most part, Marcus will answer the technical questions, and will be around to answer more of the refined scientific questions after our meeting. This is so three-quarters of our audience and myself won't have our ears bleed from having to listen to too much math."

This time, Bobcat got a few cheers from the audience. He picked up his mug and held it up. "Plus, there's free beer when this is all over." Significant cheering happened at that point.

"You bastard!" William whispered, "That's how you're going to get the meeting to stay on time!" Bobcat winked.

Bobcat reached down and picked up the first notecard. "I am not going to speculate which country this might or might not be from since we might have received it from multiple sources. So, here goes the first question. 'Why do you believe the aliens are not friendly?'"

Marcus stood up. "Bethany Anne explained to your political leaders that our massive advances in technology are due to integration between alien technology and Earth's technology. She did not explain that part of the reason we can integrate so well is that we are, in fact, in communication with an alien."

It took a couple of minutes for the room to settle down. "Please, don't make me point out which of those countries represented here already have alien technology in their possession. So, let's get over the fact that aliens exist and move on. For anyone that wants to question my assertion that we are in communication with aliens, you can merely look to the fact that our alien technology is working. Either we are that much smarter than everybody else, or we have outside knowledge. I suppose another option would be that we found the alien equivalent of a Rosetta Stone. However, I will assert that isn't true, and you can believe what you wish."

Marcus reached down and lifted his paper tablet to flip it to another page of notes. "No, the alien is not going to be made available to you. No, he is not going to be at your 'beck and call,' no he isn't interested in switching sides." Marcus looked up. "Yes, he has a name. He named himself Thales of Miletus, Bethany Anne calls him 'TOM' for short. So, that's what we call him." he looked around. "I can see from my inquisitive friends in the audience wondering why he chose that name." A few heads were nodding. "It's because TOM felt that Thales of Miletus's focus on math represented his clan's efforts to understand math at their core. He is one of twelve clans of aliens which make up the Kurtherians."

Marcus continued, "A short, short background on Kurtherians is that they are what some science fiction writers would call a master race. Any of the technology you see us using is something Kurtherians had a minimum of a millennium or more in our pre-history. This group of aliens, twelve clans, broke up into two factions. A group of seven, and a group of five. The seven groups of aliens, over time, took to modifying sentient races on planets until they achieved enough technological and warfare capabilities to fight another race. Often, these fights would be in different solar systems."

"So, in time, the seven decided to take their enhanced races and use them as cannon fodder to attack the five. One of the five clans decided to try and help a few races out in the universe by helping them evolve so that they might be able to at least have a fighting chance should the time come."

Behind Team BMW, a giant screen showed the original spaceship screenshot from the video that had been shared with the world leaders the previous day. Bobcat said, "We do not know if the spaceship in this somewhat blurry picture is a Kurtherian ship or not. For the sake of safety, we are going to assume that it can be inimical to the human race. While we have no intention of blowing it out of the sky, I can guarantee you we have no intentions of allowing it to leave if we can stop it."

Bobcat lifted up another card. "What can our countries do to prepare?" Bobcat looked across the audience. "One, you can consider whether or not you want to acknowledge that aliens exist in the first place. Second, you have to fight the concept that any advanced race that attains faster than light travel will obviously be friendly. Assuming you don't want to do either one or two, or both, you should probably stick your head between your legs and kiss your ass goodbye."

William stood up and shook his head towards his two friends before looking out at the audience. "You need to focus your scientific research into genetics, gravitic capabilities and proactive ideas about defense. It would help if you decided to get along with your fellow man, so you're not fighting each other, but rather fighting what's coming at you from up there." He pointed to the ceiling. "We recognize that there is a lot of expectation that if you discuss aliens with a large group of people, there will be mass hysteria. Or, that is the general assumption of your governments. If you don't get them prepared, then make sure you have plans should you need to explain this to them really quickly." William sat back down.

As William sat down, Marcus took his seat as well. Bobcat pulled up the next card. "Assuming this ship is malevolent, and we can contain it, how much time does that buy us?"

Bobcat looked out at the group. "Honestly, we don't know. What we suspect about this particular ship, after discussions with our alien contact, is that it's a scout ship. The safest assumption is five years. Although, it could be as much as twenty years. On the off chance that they're friendly, then it could be a few hundred years. We are not in a major pass-through zone out here. According to TOM, they probably believe our solar system is a useless dead end. This is one of the reasons we've been left alone for so long. We have evidence that shows we have been visited by both the five and the seven. One of these days, could be next week, could be ten years, they will come back and check on us."

Apparently, the beer was not as big a draw as the information Bobcat, William and Marcus were providing. Bobcat lost his bet with William when they went over the time limit by three hours.

CHAPTER SIX

CLAN TEMPLE NEAR SHENNONGJIA PEAK, HUBEI

Sun Zedong, ex-General of the PLA, sat in a restful pose in the temple of the Sacred Clan, his eyes closed. One might be forgiven for believing he was at peace sitting there in the dim candlelight, shadows playing on the stone walls hewn out of the sacred rock.

It was but an illusion.

Zedong was biding his time, as Sun Tzu taught. Take the measure of your enemy and strike from a position of power, not ignorance.

After his unexpected rescue by the Leopard Empress, Stephanie Lee, Zedong had been happy to have his head removed from the governmental chopping block.

Now, Zedong was determined to put it back on the chopping block for the sake of his country and his people.

He could barely hear the soft footfalls of the approaching feet when his name was spoken in the quiet of the temple,

WE HAVE CONTACT

"Zedong, the Empress would like to speak with you."

Sun Zedong opened his eyes. A bell reverberated outside the mountain temple, calling to those who worshiped in this forsaken place.

———

Zedong kept his thoughts clear, his worries below his conscious thought. There had already been too many little tells which suggested that someone here, perhaps the Empress, could read minds.

He nodded to the guards standing ready at the doors of her suite. They allowed him entrance. Truly, there was little he could do to the woman. She had already displayed her ability to change, the high healing rate of those who followed her and the speed of her attacks.

He was but an infant compared to her.

Then there was her father, who was rarely more than a few steps away at any time.

Stephanie Lee was wearing a white robe, with green embroidery depicting a leopard flowing up her right side. The opposite side of the gown was unadorned. She was sitting down, a table in front of her with two pillows for those who would join her. He stepped in front, bowed, and then stepped to the pad on the left when she nodded in recognition.

"General Sun," she started. "We have waited as long as we might for those in power to relax. We cannot wait longer, as my enemy grows in strength. Who was it, the British Prime Minister who said, 'Ask me for anything but time?'"

"No, my Empress," he answered. "It was the French leader, Napoleon."

"Yes, thank you." She nodded her acceptance of his

correction. "I have a need for your services, General. It is for this and other things that I saved you. Is this understood?"

"Yes, my Empress," Zedong replied. "I understood that you would use my contacts and knowledge to move the Clan's efforts forward." He pursed his lips and added. "It is a logical contractual requirement for saving my life."

Stephanie Lee looked at the General.

Yin, can you confirm if he is lying? Stephanie Lee asked.

No. He is as calm on the surface of his thoughts as one who is telling the truth. Or, he could be a consummate liar.

Then we will send insurance.

"Ting?" Stephanie Lee spoke loudly, then waited. Zedong was not surprised when the simple-looking peasant female arrived moments later.

"Yes, Empress?"

"You and General Sun will take a helicopter, and go meet with some of his contacts. See who we can persuade that the future of China lies with the Sacred Clan, not the present selfishly-focused leaders of our nation."

"Yes, Empress." Ting bowed low.

Zedong bowed also and rose fluidly up to follow the shorter woman out of the suite. It was some time before he allowed himself the barest amount of hope.

The Leopard Empress had used a simple peasant to monitor his movements.

There was no way, he figured, that she would have any understanding of the more sophisticated discussions he might have with his contacts.

———

WE HAVE CONTACT

QBS ARCHANGEL, THE BITCHES' WORKOUT AREA

The practice room was relatively large, with a viewing area protected with transparent, unbreakable glass off to one side for eight to sit and watch those fighting on the floor.

But the room was empty save for two friends. Two friends who had been on a highway to hell tracking Forsaken and Nosferatu across the United States.

That road that ended in the Florida Everglades.

Where John's life had been ending rapidly, choking on his own blood, his knife jammed through his chest protection by the last Nosferatu they had been fighting. The four of them had been able to handle one, but two Nosferatu had been one too many for everyone to survive the encounter.

John had taken the hit, as he would have wanted it if any on his team was going to go down. These men had been his brothers, his kin, and he was okay if it was his blood that would be spilled to keep them alive.

Until Bethany Anne.

She had come in like a demon savior, eyes glowing red. His friend Eric, standing in front of him, yanking the blade out of his chest as Bethany Anne provided her life-giving blood to heal him.

Now, his friend wanted to do something dangerous, something John was trying desperately to talk him out of. "Are you *nucking futs*, Eric?" John asked him, shaking his head. "Of all the Gott Verdammt stupid ass ideas to get a woman's attention, I cannot suggest kicking her ass as the one *I* would pick, buddy."

Eric shrugged. "I can't say I'm looking forward to the meetings with Bethany Anne and Stephen after you, either."

Eric leaned to his side to stretch. "But I have to make sure she knows, deep in her bones, that the Eric I am now is not the Eric she helped save back in Costa Rica."

"Or the one with the puppy dog complex?" John asked, stretching as well.

"Yeah, that one too," Eric answered. "Look, I get it, she's five centuries old. But think about it, the one thing I won't need to worry about is forgetting her birthday. She won't want to be reminded of her birthday at all."

John snickered. "I guess that's one way to think about it. But that probably means the other three hundred and sixty-four days are open for gifts, now."

"And I'm fine with that," Eric replied as he stood up. "Now, other than telling me this is a bad idea, what can you do to help me prepare?"

"All right brother, I'll help, but half of this is going to be about you getting back up," John said, and his face went from caring to maniacal. "Brother, you are going to meet my friends," John said as flexed his left arm. "Pain," he turned his head to his flexing right arm, striking a pose, his muscles glistening, "and destruction."

Eric shook his head at John's playing around and decided to attack while John was unprepared.

Seconds later two crewmen were walking the hall by the Bitches' workout area, and both jumped at a loud bang that shook the wall right next to them. They looked at each other and moved quickly away.

No one wanted to be in the hallway in case something came through the wall.

Inside the room, Eric was picking himself up off the floor, a little groggy. "First lesson," John told his friend. "Gabrielle is devious. She has hundreds of years of experience to fuck with her competitor's minds. If you think that sucked, think about having her beautiful laugh echoing in your mind right now… and how pissed off you would be."

Eric stood up and nodded to his friend who was saying something about something but wasn't making sense. He put a hand up. "John, I'm sure that was a lovely speech, but I can't hear shit right now."

John walked over to his friend, smiling.

Then John slugged him.

There wasn't anyone in the hallway when the loud bang happened this time.

'Fucking… prick…" Eric got out as he started to stand back up on wobbly feet. "I'm going to rip your dick off and beat you senseless you finger-licking asswipe sniffer!" His healing was doing fine, but he had decided to see if he could lure John a little closer. "Jean is going to leave you after you sew it back on and need to use popsicle sticks wrapped with tape to prop it up!"

John laughed but stayed right where he was. "Eric, you have to open yourself to all of the benefits that being a Queen's Bitch provides. You have been lax, buddy."

Eric narrowed his eyes. "What do you mean?"

"Why do you think I've asked Bethany Anne to spar with me?" John asked, walking to his left, trying to find a portion of the wall that had a little more cushion.

"She likes to kick your ass, and you're a masochist?" Eric asked, walking two steps to his left since John obviously wasn't going to come into his trap.

"No, you diaper-wearing jizz collector, it's because we can push our abilities above even the older vampires." John retorted. "Except for Michael, I imagine. I don't think we can go above that without a couple of decades against him to test ourselves."

"You think he's still alive?" Eric asked.

John stopped and cocked his head. "Michael?"

"Yeah, what if he's still out there, say in the Etheric, lost?" Eric asked, spreading his hands in supplication. "It could be true."

John scratched his chin. "I don't know, I…"

Eric lunged across the intervening space, trying to catch John off guard.

This time, the sound in the hallway was very muffled. Inside the room the cussing was long, loud and very fluent.

"HOWTHEFUCKDIDYOUHITMEYOUASSTARD-SOMMELIER!" Eric yelled from across the chamber.

John, his eyes red, grinned as he spread his arms, his six foot four frame displaying an arm span that took up a significant amount of space. "Welcome to being a true *BITCH*, Eric."

Eric watched, his mouth dropping open, as John's grin went wide, his eyes flaming red. "This is what we are Eric, and if you want Gabrielle, this is what you are going to have to embrace as your future!"

─────

KAIFENG, HENAN PROVINCE

Ting watched the General as they walked peacefully down the narrow alley between two buildings that had to have been built back in the 50s. The smell, not pleasant, not unpleasant, was a mixture of food, scraps and the occasional drunk.

This was the third meeting the General and Ting had attended in as many days.

She followed all of their talk, and he never once mentioned the Sacred Clan, but he did speak of a new power player in China. Ting stayed a few feet back from the General, as someone who was his inferior might.

Her hearing, however, was sufficient that she lost none of the conversation.

"We are going in through the back," Zedong said softly to Ting. "I'm going to meet Si here. He is, or at least was, in charge of the intelligence group for this region." She nodded her understanding as he opened the door, pushing it open enough that she could easily walk in behind him.

The place was of medium size, and only slightly busy. Ting noticed that there was one man, rather large, sitting in a booth across from the bar. The wood floors were scarred by tables and chairs over the many decades.

And stained by spilled booze and food.

The lingering scent of cigarettes overlaid with fresh was annoying to Ting. She hated these old bars that sold food, the stench was appalling to her. Her Empress hadn't given her the option to push the General to select better locations, so she had left the places to his discretion.

General Sun, Ting noticed, shook hands in a particular way with this contact as well. She stopped watching them and looked about the establishment, noting the twelve other men and two women. Most were drinking, a few smoking.

Ting listened to the men as she watched everything else.

"General, the news has a large price offered for your head. The Chairman is not pleased with your escape."

Zedong shrugged. "I was surprised at the intervention myself, Si. However, the group that took over the plane is very powerful and is looking to form relationships with important people. People that will have good opportunities," Zedong looked casually around the restaurant, "when *upper* management changes, Si."

Ting noted Si grab his little whiskey glass to lift it up in a toast as Zedong whispered her name, "Ting." She turned to see them clink their glasses together.

It was the click of a pistol being cocked behind her that alerted her to the danger.

Ting dropped in place, legs splitting as she laid her head down all the way, touching the floor. The first shot was fired over her head, the bullet embedding itself in the wood and clay wall, debris showering General Sun and his intelligence man. Ting's eyes melted to yellow, her teeth changed.

An ambush then? She might not know what to say in polite company, but Ting understood an ambush well enough. Her first responsibility would be to take the General with her. If that was not possible, then to make sure he couldn't talk.

Ting pushed off the floor with her arms, the claws on her hands already two inches long. She reached for the General's neck as she looked to see where she could push off of the wall. The second shot hit the floor where she had been.

Her right foot, nails digging into the wood of the table, pushed off as Zedong started looking up, his hands covering his face as best as he could from the bullets flying, but all he could see was the two yellow eyes of death coming for him.

Ting noticed he didn't look afraid, more like a man who had accepted his fate.

That meant she had failed her Empress as well. She reached down and sliced through Zedong's neck with her right hand. Her left foot, with claws, used Si's face and skull as a platform to push against as she turned around.

She felt the burn of a bullet crease her leg.

That tore it... Ting changed.

Her growl escaped her lips, her fury at the pain of her wounds making the sound echo loudly in the confined space.

WE HAVE CONTACT

Her senses expanded, increasing her sensitivity to the sound of heartbeats, people shouting, moving objects, guns being pulled and cocked, as Ting pushed off of the wall, aiming towards the middle of the floor.

She bounded from the open space and jumped towards the bar where the barkeep was busy ducking as bullets started tracking her. Bottles exploded as she caught the edge of the counter top and started running down its length. A uniformed man came out from a side room, lifting his QBZ-95 as she bounded off of the bar. She landed on his chest, her claws ripping through his flesh as she pushed off. She felt another bullet hit her and snarled in pain.

All of the shots and confusion did little to stop her from racing to the back entrance. She crashed through the door and tore off into the night. Hearing men rush out of the restaurant, she turned the corner, as those in the street recognized that a large cat had just run through the area, their shrieks following in her wake.

A little over a mile away, Ting found a washateria that was closed. She changed back to her human form, used a nail to push a bullet out of her body to help heal faster, and stole a set of clothes.

Ting considered the implications of the evening as she put on the clothes. While General Sun Zedong was no longer living, the Chinese Government obviously knew about the Sacred Clan now.

The Leopard Empress was not going to be pleased.

CHAPTER SEVEN

YOLLIN DEEP SPACE SHIP, G'LAXIX SPHAEA

Captain Kael-ven T'chmon entered his quarters, his four crab-like legs making 'thunk-thunk-thunk-thunk' sounds on the metal as he reviewed the information on his tablet.

He used his right hand on the pressure plate to close the door. He reached down and slid his hand across the tablet, throwing the information up on the wall monitor. It was a large display, easily as big as his whole body. Sitting down on the chair designed for his body, he pulled a table in front of him to comfortably rest his arms as he studied the videos that his probes had brought back.

This backward, end of nowhere solar system was building ships.

"Information agent, highlight items in video two."

The second video showed sixteen objects that were separate from the background of space.

WE HAVE CONTACT

"Turn off all but three, five, nine and thirteen."

He absent-mindedly scratched his shoulder, grabbed a large piece of dried skin that was flaking off and stuck it in his mouth to chew on it while he studied the video.

"Enhance video two and spread it over all four screens." He studied the objects in greater detail.

"These beings are building ships. But, are they cargo or war vessels?" He cocked his head as he reached reflectively behind his back to scratch down his flank.

There were four large, sharp angled ships in production. He noticed a glint off of a nearby asteroid. "Highlight object seven, magnify."

The asteroid grew larger on his screen, and he nodded.

They had turrets protecting their ships. These were not defenseless creatures.

Maybe this wasn't a waste of his time, after all. If they understood war, then they most likely understood many of the additional requirements for war.

Like technology.

Kael-ven T'chmon reached over and punched a button on his table, and his interface for taking notes came up. It looked like he was going to be involved for quite a few solar turns trying to decipher everything that they could see. Some were obviously mining, and he could see some locations that most likely represented manufacturing, ships and large living quarters of some sort.

Puzzles, at the moment, all he had was puzzles and very few answers.

That was fine, he had time before he needed to send an update through the annex gate.

The pictures were arrayed across four monitors, the images of one of the guys on each. Cheryl Lynn fanned her face in the glare of the light.

"You really catch their essence, don't you?" she asked Mark Koeff. The ladies had finally been able to schedule a twenty-four-hour whirlwind shoot to capture the guys on film in the last month and Mark had come back up to the ArchAngel to share his work.

"I try. They're pretty photogenic guys in the first place, ready to smile or frown. They emote very nicely. The one with Scott and the kitten is a particular favorite of mine." Mark pointed to the third monitor.

"When did you take that?" Cheryl Lynn asked. She and the ladies had been busy trying to keep the overwhelming female fan base out of Mark's hair, and didn't have many chances to watch the men work. If you call walking around half naked, posing for pictures with food, cats, dogs and other animals, work. Cheryl Lynn noticed one of John's photos. "Eeww, is that a snake?"

"Yes. Oh it was just a non-poisonous one that John grabbed in the bushes," Mark exclaimed, thinking maybe the P.R. lady thought he had placed John in danger.

"No, not worried about it being poisonous, I just find it a little creepy. You would swear there was a touch of red in John's eyes," she let her voice trail off when Mark hit a button on the keyboard, and a new set of images came up on each monitor. Cheryl Lynn's eyes flicked to Scott's screen and specifically the lower left-hand image.

He was handing a boy, about four or five, over the simple rope they had used as a barricade to keep fans back from the shoot. Apparently, the little guy bolted, and Scott had caught him.

Mark was going to explain this set of prints, and why he thought they might be considered when he noticed Cheryl Lynn had not heard his last couple of sentences. He tried to figure out which of the pictures had captivated her so much, and it became simple when she reached out and touched the lower left image of Scott on the monitor.

Mark pulled his tablet up and jotted down the picture number.

One down, eleven to go.

"They really see them this way, don't they?" she asked, in a whisper inside the quiet room.

"See the guys?" Mark said. "See them as something more? Yes, I have a lot of images with the ladies in the background. Some, like say," he pointed over to Darryl's monitor, "the woman at the top right?" Cheryl Lynn nodded. "She's obviously looking for a hunk of man meat, but the one next to her? She just wants to see what a good guy is like. The second lady is going to go home satisfied that they're real, and maybe she'll find her own version of Darryl. The first lady?" Mark smiled. "She's going home frustrated."

"Frustrated?" Cheryl Lynn asked, turning her head. "Because she can't get Darryl's attention?"

Mark shrugged. "Cheryl Lynn," he looked at her. "None of the women got the guy's attention. At least, not in a romantic way. These guys were there, they enjoyed themselves because, why not?" He smiled. "They were nice, they were polite, but they weren't interested in any of the women who showed up."

Mark leaned back to the table and played with the mouse and a couple of keystrokes. The first monitor, the one with

John's pictures, went black for a second before coming up with just one image. It was John looking to his right, his chest on display but you could see he had someone in his eyes that was making the smile genuine. If that didn't make a woman want to tack his picture up on the wall, Cheryl Lynn didn't know what would.

"I caught John looking over at Jean when she wasn't paying attention," Mark explained. "Some of the best pictures were when I was doing one of the guys, and another happened to be close, thinking I wasn't paying attention to them at all. The image of Scott handing the child back?" Mark looked over to make sure Cheryl Lynn was listening. "That was during a session with Eric, not Scott."

He leaned over and started messing with the keyboard and mouse again. On Scott's monitor one single image came up. In it, Scott was smiling, but it wasn't like John's, no it was a smile of longing, of something just out of his reach. His face caused her heart to ache. She wasn't sure what or who he was looking at, but it was clear he was looking at someone.

Cheryl Lynn vaguely noticed Mark doing something again when he spoke, "I took four pictures, one I zoomed a little further out."

Cheryl Lynn's breath caught in her throat, the new picture came up, and she looked to see who Scott was looking at. It seemed a little rude to her, like she had a page of Scott's personal diary up and was reading it. But, it was worth it.

Scott was staring longingly at her.

"You didn't know?" Mark asked softly.

Cheryl Lynn wiped a tear that had formed at the corner of her eye and shook her head. "No, I didn't know. I'm a divorcée with two children, and a history of choosing bad men. What does he see in me?" she wondered.

WE HAVE CONTACT

Mark looked at her face in the darkness of the room. The light coming off the monitors highlighted Cheryl Lynn's head, making him wish he had his camera here with him. His answer came out, unbidden and unexpected.

"Love."

CLAN TEMPLE NEAR SHENNONGJIA PEAK, HUBEI

Stephanie Lee looked over the assembled clan members from the small dais in the temple room.

Hewn from rock countless eons ago, the room comfortably held the one hundred and twenty or so that made up her guard and those she had placed in authority.

There was an open aisle down the center, which Ting came down, head hung low. The rumors had already made it around the Clan, and they watched as she walked down the aisle towards the Leopard Empress.

She must be made an example of, Yin spoke.

Yes, strength is everything. No weakness. It has been this way since before your world was finished cooling. Yang agreed.

Stephanie Lee kept her thoughts to herself, listening to the two Kurtherians as Ting approached.

Now, we have problems, because of her failure. Yin continued. *The political structure in this country will strike this location. They are going to take away your power, strip it and use us as experiments.*

Too early in our plans, Yang agreed.

Silence, Stephanie Lee said. *My country, my rules. There is already one Kurtherian whore on this planet, I'll not be another one. I decided to send Ting and the General to meet contacts based on your input. You two couldn't tell me he was lying, so keep quiet and deal with it.*

Stephanie Lee kept her head held up, regal, she thought as she looked over her people gathered here. It was time to take control.

Sometimes, sacrifices had to be made.

Ting walked to the front of the room and knelt down before Stephanie Lee who said, "We have before us Su Ting. One who has been devoted to the Clan, one whose parents, and grandparents, have worked in obscurity for generations to achieve the accession of the Sacred Clan. We are now at the beginning of our time to take the lead into our world's future. The Sun has risen in the east on our efforts, and those in power are aware of us. Unfortunately, General Sun Zedong was able to give unsanctioned information to those with whom he was speaking during his efforts to find us allies within the military."

Stephanie Lee looked down. "Su Ting, stand." Ting stood up. Stephanie Lee put her left hand on the top of Ting's head and her right on Ting's throat. "Su Ting, do you accept the judgment of the Leopard Empress, your ruler?"

Ting swallowed, feeling fingers grabbing her throat. She said loudly, "I do."

"Su Ting, your family has been faithful for generations. You have been faithful, but insufficient to the challenge. Now, the Sacred Clan must move early, when we are not ready yet. Take my love with you..."

Ting barely knew what was happening when Stephanie Lee's hand changed, growing claws that quickly eviscerated her neck, ripping out the flesh. Stephanie Lee allowed the body to drop to the floor, twitching. Her hand still in her leopard form, dripping blood, Stephanie Lee spoke to her people. "Call in the Clans from the fields, from the towns, and from the cities." She looked around.

"We prepare for war."

———

QBS ARCHANGEL

"Well, that's all of the images I chose," Mark told Cheryl Lynn, who was quiet. "Is there something wrong?"

Cheryl Lynn turned to him. "No!" She turned back to the sixteen images they had finally selected, "Holy shit, we are going to sell millions of these. Those guys are going to need guards. I can't believe it. You even made Eric look good."

"What's wrong with Eric? He's a handsome fellow," Mark asked. He was busy jotting down the image numbers on his pad. "I thought the picture of him in the volleyball game was pretty intense."

"It was, it's just a new side of Eric. The guy I know is a bit of an airhead. I don't know, maybe that isn't the right way of explaining it. More like he just moves through life bouncing off of situations, not through it with determination. Yeah," she nodded her head. "That's it. He didn't seem to move forward with a plan."

"What's your plan, if you don't mind me asking?" Mark said.

"Mine?" Cheryl Lynn frowned. "Try to keep on top of the P.R. nightmare named Bethany Anne. That woman is a typhoon of trouble, a hurricane of hassle, and a tornado of torment all wrapped up in a bow."

"No," Mark pointed to Scott's picture. "Don't ignore the

opportunity that's sitting right in front of you."

"Mark," she asked him, her shoulders slumping. "Did I miss 'matchmaker' on your business card?"

Mark smiled and reached to get his wallet out. "Actually, I do support relationships."

"Figures," she stepped to the side, pulled out a chair and sat down. "So, what do you think my problem is?"

He put his wallet back in his pocket. "You don't believe that you're good enough. You have some past history that colors your belief in yourself and Scott doesn't have that filter." Mark turned the third monitor back on, "Here, let me show you something." Mark went through and quickly clicked six pictures and pulled them up on the screen. Cheryl Lynn looked into his eyes and nodded her understanding.

She put a hand on Mark's shoulder. "I don't know how you do with existing relationships, Mark. But maybe, just maybe, you have given me enough to believe that he won't laugh in my face." She looked one more time at the images before setting her jaw and turning towards the door. "Now, I just need to go find Mr. English and give him a piece of my mind." In a moment, Mark was alone.

Mark pulled out his tablet and tagged the six images, sending them via email to Cheryl Lynn's personal address. He put his phone away and finished his notes on the calendar and started humming to himself.

CHAPTER EIGHT

QBS ARCHANGEL

Cheryl Lynn walked into Bethany Anne's suite after passing through the security in front. Bethany Anne was laying on her bed, a hand on Ashur, looking at a tablet.

"Watcha' doin boss?" Cheryl Lynn asked as she dropped her folders on the small desk Ecaterina had brought up from the Florida house. Even in their security-conscious neighborhood in Florida, they had been having problems keeping out the people stalking Bethany Anne.

They had decided it was time to close down those houses.

"I'm trying to figure out where that alien son of a bitch is," Bethany Anne answered, without looking up from her tablet.

"How, osmosis?" Cheryl Lynn asked as she pulled out the chair and sat down. "Perhaps hoping the whatever-you're-looking-at is going to magically start speaking to you?"

"Have you ever played Battleship?" Bethany Anne asked, ignoring Cheryl Lynn's question.

"What? Oh, keep marking off areas until you narrow down where the ships are?"

"Yes, but instead of it being like, what, a hundred spots? This is damn near infinite."

Cheryl Lynn put a hand up. "Stop right there, you hired me for public relations. I've looked once, twice and three times at my work contract, and there is absolutely no requirement for math anywhere in the document."

Bethany Anne looked up. "What? Math? How is this math?"

"Anytime you start throwing numbers like one hundred and then infinite there is math in between the two numbers which needs to be figured out. Go discuss this with Marcus. Or hell, go discuss this with Frank and Barb. She's very good at finding people and stuff, maybe she might have a good idea or two? Hell, they probably need a break from trying to find Stephanie Lee."

Bethany Anne scowled. "That bitch is going to be found, and I intend to slice off her fucking arms and feed them to her when we finally nail her bony ass to the wall."

Well, Cheryl Lynn thought, *someone still has an open wound.*

"Yes, okay, but they might have that all working and need another job. It's just a suggestion, not a demand."

Bethany Anne leaned back into her pillows. "I get that, but her still being out there somewhere is pissing me off. It's like I can't leave that shit behind and move on without closing that door. Preferably, on her head, multiple times until it bursts like a watermelon."

"You're going to close the chapter on Michael?" Cheryl Lynn blurted before thinking it through. She rolled her eyes when she realized how tacky that was to say.

WE HAVE CONTACT

Bethany Anne had already resumed looking at her tablet as she answered, "No, I'm going to close the chapter on the Illuminati. Michael had better get his ass back to me, or I'll find a way to get into the afterlife and kick his ass so hard he will skip across the River Styx back to the living. Then, I'll catch up to him and kiss his boo-boos better."

"Not so much worried about Cerberus?" Cheryl Lynn asked. She was surprised when Ashur raised his head in her direction and barked before putting it back down on the bed. "Guess Ashur isn't."

Bethany Anne was looking at her dog strangely. "I swear he's getting smarter. We were watching the History Channel the other night on mythology, and now it seems he recognized the Cerberus in the show and your comment." She roughed up Ashur's head. "Has anyone told you lately you are one damned good looking dog?" Ashur chuffed at her. "Well, I just did. Don't let your ego get so big your head can't fit out the door." Ashur chuffed at her again. "Yeah, well we could Etherically walk, but it would be a pain in the neck. What if we translocate to a small room, and your head hits a wall and explodes?" Ashur whined. "Yeah, see, so watch out how big you let it get."

Cheryl Lynn just watched Bethany Anne and Ashur for a moment and shivered. The communication between the two was either Earth shattering…

Or Bethany Anne was starting to lose it.

"Um, boss?" Bethany Anne turned back to Cheryl Lynn and raised an eyebrow. "When was the last time you spoke to someone normal?"

"You, one second ago." Bethany Anne replied, keeping any trace of a smirk from her face.

This time, Cheryl Lynn made an overly dramatic gesture

of rolling her eyes. "I'm not normal!" She waved a hand around the room. "Who else is up in the Earth's atmosphere on a Gott Verdammt space battleship? That alone would cause someone to question my normalcy. Add that I have a vampire queen for my leader and an honest-to-god walking badass for a boyfriend, and you might decide I am so far from normal that…"

"Hold it!" Bethany Anne barked, putting up a hand. "What did you just say?"

Cheryl Lynn's eyebrows came together and she frowned as she said slowly, "I'm in a space battleship with a vampire queen, that pretty much…"

Bethany Anne shook her head, "Hah!" She pointed at Cheryl Lynn, a smile gracing her face. "You have a BOY-FRIEND!"

"What!" Cheryl Lynn's eyes went up to the ceiling and re-ran the conversation back in her head and then her eyes widened at Bethany Anne. "OH… shit! I said that out *loud*."

Bethany Anne burst out laughing. "Oh. My. God. The lady who isn't good enough is dating? How the hell did this happen? It's Scott, right? Oh, TELL me it is Scott, please!" Ashur chuffed, and Bethany Anne looked down at her hand grasping his hair tightly. "Sorry, I was excited. I'll be careful." Bethany Anne looked back at Cheryl Lynn. "Spill!"

Cheryl Lynn looked at her stack of papers and images she had come to talk about, "Screw it," she mumbled. "It isn't like you couldn't read it from my mind if you wanted." Cheryl Lynn stood up, kicked off her shoes and got on the bed and crossed her legs underneath her.

"My downfall was talking with Mark Koeff about Scott," she started but was interrupted by a knock on the far outside door and an announcement that Gabrielle was here.

WE HAVE CONTACT

"Send her in," Bethany Anne called out. A second later, they heard Gabrielle entering the room outside of Bethany Anne's main suite.

Then, they heard Gabrielle bitching from the other room. "Seriously, Bethany Anne? Grab you a Coke and pop some popcorn? What the hell?"

Bethany Anne smiled at Cheryl Lynn who put her face into her hands and mumbled, "What? Is my fall from grace into the clutches of a man this evening's entertainment?"

"Ooooh! Ladies night?" they heard Gabrielle call out. "I'll grab another drink for me and water for Cheryl Lynn. She might need to be careful about what she eats or drinks now!" Gabrielle busted out laughing at her own joke.

"What the HELL," Cheryl Lynn yelled. "Makes you think I'm getting pregnant again anytime soon?" They heard the ding of the microwave.

"Oh hell, sweetie." Gabrielle walked in carrying three drinks and a popcorn bag. "Of the three of us here, you are the only one to successfully pop out a couple so there's that, plus..." Gabrielle handed the drinks out, kicked off her shoes and crawled onto the bed before continuing. "The two of us have been shut down by the man... err... alien himself."

Bethany Anne took the offered drink and popcorn bag, opened the bag and tossed some in her mouth before saying, "No, Cheryl Lynn is shut down by the very same alien doctor until she says otherwise." She dropped another handful of popcorn into her mouth and rolled her hand in a 'move on' gesture at Cheryl Lynn.

Cheryl Lynn made a face and looked at Gabrielle. "Fine, but if this gets out, I swear I'll go research how to painfully kill a five hundred year old vampire." Gabrielle crossed her heart, mimed locking her mouth with a key, and made a tossing gesture over her shoulder.

Have you already told your dad? Bethany Anne asked.

Oh, HELL Yeah! But it isn't nearly as much fun since he's infatuated right now. He's all sympathetic about the chemicals and emotions that go haywire. I'm getting a little back from my episode with Ivan.

Finally get over that?

Yeah, it took a couple of months.

And?

I burned two dolls in effigy. Although, it was mostly just a physical thing.

The first time you were cheated on?

No, not exactly. They were in a 'we are going to die' situation. But, it's the first time it was with another vampire. That hurt my pride. More so because she's a dingbat and needy. I'm totally blaming the 'about to die' part.

Two dolls?

One for each. Hey, pass that popcorn over.

Bethany Anne reached over and offered her popcorn to Gabrielle. "Want some?"

"Thanks!" Gabrielle replied as she grabbed a handful. Bethany Anne put the bag in front of Cheryl Lynn.

"No thanks, watching the figure," Cheryl Lynn said.

"That's not who needs to be watching your figure. I'm pretty sure Scott is supposed to do that," Bethany Anne interjected. "Besides, you can't get fat or anything, that was also adjusted."

"Wait, what?" Cheryl Lynn asked, confused. "What about my figure?"

Bethany Anne started chewing on the inside of her cheek. "I think we have a serious problem here. It isn't something

TOM can fix." She rested her head on her hand and tapped her lips. "I think we're going to have to be blunt, it might be the only way."

"Whoa!" Cheryl Lynn's eyes went back and forth as the two women started moving off the bed. "Let's not and say we did, you two!" Her voice raised an octave, concern flooding her mind. "What are you doing?"

"Nothing we shouldn't have done a long time ago, I think," Bethany Anne said. "Plus if we don't deal with this right now, it could totally fuck up your relationship with Scott."

"What can? How?" Cheryl Lynn turned on the bed as Gabrielle closed the two outer doors and then Bethany Anne's door again.

"Mirror?" Gabrielle asked.

"In the closet, grab the full length. Don't forget you have to unclip it or it won't move," Bethany Anne said as she watched with amusement as Cheryl Lynn crab-walked to the middle of her bed. Bethany Anne walked around to the other side of the bed and said, "Ashur?"

Ashur's sudden barking freaked out Cheryl Lynn, and she bolted away from him, right into Bethany Anne's waiting arms. "Come along Cheryl Lynn, you need this medicine."

Cheryl Lynn tried to lay limp and heavy in Bethany Anne's arms and realized it was a fruitless exercise. The stupid woman could carry her like she was a piece of paper. "Fine!" She put her feet under her when she was off of the bed. "What are we doing?"

"Well, first you're getting undressed," Bethany Anne told her.

"Do WHAT?" Cheryl Lynn's head turned when Gabrielle came out of the master closet with a large mirror. "Oh, *HELLL* no!"

Bethany Anne smiled. "Oh, *heeelll* yes," she told her friend. "You can either do it and save the clothes, or I can just rip them off."

"Sometimes," Cheryl Lynn growled as she started to un-button her shirt. "I really hate you, boss."

ADAM, I'm going to need your Photoshop skills soon. Go find me pictures of a woman that has Cheryl Lynn's body structure, but is heavier.

>>I need a picture.<<

Let's let her get undressed first, she needs to really be smashed over the head with this.

>>Okay. Can you provide me a couple of pictures of the room before she is in front of the mirror?<<

Sure.

Gabrielle raised an eyebrow when Bethany Anne moved away from Cheryl Lynn and waved for her to step aside. Bethany Anne took some pictures with her tablet and winked to Gabrielle.

"Okay, now that I'm disgraced," Cheryl Lynn huffed as she folded her clothes and put them on the bed. "Now what?"

"Stand in front of the mirror and we can get started," Bethany Anne told her. "Don't worry about the pictures, they'll be deleted, and ADAM handles the security on this thing, so you're good."

Ten minutes later, pictures taken, Bethany Anne called out, "Okay, that's enough now. You can get your clothes back on."

Looking at her tablet, Bethany Anne said, "ArchAngel, turn on the display on the wall opposite my bed."

"That is location two in my set up." A voice, similar to Bethany Anne's, but with a slightly electronic edge to it, came from the speakers in the room.

"Let's rename it main wall for this room," Bethany Anne said as she retrieved the popcorn bag. "Okay ladies, we shall have a new Cheryl Lynn here in just a few minutes."

Cheryl Lynn frowned at her Queen, her boss, and her friend and thought perhaps she was losing her mental grasp of reality with all of the stress on her shoulders. But she climbed back on the side of the bed before she felt Gabrielle push her to move further. "Take the center, patient, I've got the other edge." Cheryl Lynn continued on to the middle and Ashur shifted to fit between her and Bethany Anne.

"Damn good thing this bed is huge," Gabrielle said. The four of them fit on it easily, with another couple of feet to spare.

"Tell me about it," Bethany Anne said. "It's like I'm not special if I don't have a huge bed. What the hell am I going to use all this space for, anyway?" Ashur chuffed, and Bethany Anne said, "Well, he needs to get his ass up here for that to happen."

Cheryl Lynn turned to Gabrielle and raised an eyebrow. Gabrielle just shrugged.

"Okay," Bethany Anne started. "I'm going to show you some pictures. Some of these pictures are you, some are other women. The heads have been switched around. I want you, Cheryl Lynn, to tell me which one of these bodies is actually yours, okay?"

"Yes... sure?" Cheryl Lynn answered, confused. "How am I not going to guess my own body? I've got a birthmark."

>>**Please, like I couldn't figure that out?**<<

"ADAM says he has taken care of that. So, stop making excuses and here we go."

"Oh, nice ass," Gabrielle said at the first picture. "Someone tell ADAM that he should not be sneaking nude pictures of me and pasting them on the internet."

Cheryl Lynn chuckled. "Okay, that isn't me. I'm comfortable enough to admit I can understand why that might be attractive to men."

Bethany Anne rolled her eyes. "Please, we women are the worst about judging other women. If we don't like it, we diss it. If we like it, they're sluts and whores if they look at our men," Bethany Anne started.

"We claw their fucking eyes out," Cheryl Lynn finished as she reached over Ashur to stick her left hand into the popcorn bag. "Oh?" She looked back and forth between the two women. "Too obvious I've got it bad?"

"I'm just thankful you weren't in this mode when the guys were getting photographed."

"They are NOT doing Queen Bitch's Calendar part two." Cheryl Lynn said, her voice emphatic. "No freaking way."

Gabrielle leaned forward to look around her to Bethany Anne. "Wow, the tiger has apparently surfaced."

"No kidding. So, let's go on to image two," Bethany Anne flicked a hand across her tablet.

"Mine," Cheryl Lynn immediately replied. "Kinda flabby. Told you this was going to be easy."

———

They went through the images and ADAM was careful to tag all of Cheryl Lynn's, and all of those she claimed were hers.

"Are you ready for the great answer to life, the universe, and everything?" Bethany Anne asked as they finished the last picture.

"Sure, lay it on me, Dr. Obvious," Cheryl Lynn agreed.

"Okay, on the left are all of the positive body comments

you made, on the right are all of the bodies you say are yours. ADAM, please place an X on each body on the right where Cheryl Lynn got it wrong."

Cheryl Lynn started watching as the twenty or so bodies started getting crossed out. He grayed them out each time as they were crossed out at the rate of one a second. In less than thirty seconds, all images had a large red X on them.

"What the hell, that can't be right." Cheryl Lynn said and turned to Bethany Anne. "I know my own body."

"Well, let's finish this, shall we?" Bethany Anne replied. "ADAM, remove the right images from the screen and every figure on the left that is Cheryl Lynn, move to the right."

Cheryl Lynn gasped when the third image moved to the right. Her mouth opened as each second, another image moved over until twenty something seconds later, all of the images were identified as Cheryl Lynn.

She had tears running down her face.

"That," Bethany Anne pointed to the wall. "Is what Scott sees each and every time he looks at you. Well," she paused, "he sees that with clothes on, anyway." Bethany Anne turned to Cheryl Lynn. "Hey, this is what we all see when we see you, but that other body is what you tell us YOU see in the mirror. You need to own the reality, and not keep forcing the negative thoughts about yourself into this new relationship."

"Is that," Cheryl Lynn asked quietly, "truly me? No bullshit, no photo manipulation? Are you being totally honest with me?"

Bethany Anne's heart almost broke at the feeling of raw emotion coming out of Cheryl Lynn. If she could possibly go back in time and beat the shit out of her ex-husband for feeding into the emotional dystopia, she would. Bethany Anne looked directly into Cheryl Lynn's eyes and said, "ADAM, reveal all of the original images of Cheryl Lynn."

Cheryl Lynn turned back to the wall screen as the group of pictures disappeared to be replaced one at a time. The first picture came up, and a red line went down from the top to the bottom of the image. Each time, for each picture, as it went over the head, the original disappeared and Cheryl Lynn's was shown. As the reveal uncovered the hidden information, Cheryl Lynn consistently saw the birthmark she knew about, and two that she had not known about until now.

Nothing else was ever changed.

By the end, Cheryl Lynn had her hand over her mouth and was silently sobbing.

After a few minutes, the two vampires could hear her tiny voice. "I'm beautiful," she whispered, between her sobs.

Gabrielle reached out and put a hand on Cheryl Lynn's shoulder. "Now own that knowledge and don't let anyone ever tell you otherwise."

Cheryl Lynn just nodded, too choked up to respond right then.

CHAPTER NINE

YOLLIN DEEP SPACE SHIP, G'LAXIX SPHAEA

"It is… ugly." Captain Kael-ven T'chmon said as they watched the images coming in from the small video drone. He wasn't sure if this world had the ability to locate his ship in the cold of space, but he preferred to be safe. "It looks like it is made out of blocks, randomly assigned and stuck together."

Communication specialist Melorn, sensing his captain was in a conversational mood added, "It is rather large, Captain. Each of the main components seems to be of significant size. With the," he looked down at his analysis report, "two hundred and twelve parts, there must be a large number of beings in the station."

The Captain grunted his understanding. "Melorn, do we have a way of stopping their communications?"

"A moment, Captain." Melorn got to work, switching his systems to track all known frequencies, even those discovered hundreds of solar turns previously. "Yes, we are following a minimum of traffic from that," Melorn nodded to the screen, "that... thing... to communication satellites at the gravity equilibrium point for the dead moon rock, sir."

Melorn reviewed the listing on his amber screen. "So yes, we can block all of these transmissions with an appropriate jamming torpedo, sir."

"Interesting," Captain Kael-ven T'chmon leaned forward on his couch. "They are not in direct line of sight of the planet, and if we disrupt the communications we can strike their station, and achieve additional intelligence."

SPACE STATION ONE, L2

"Coach," Adarsh rapped on the side of the door leading into Coach's small office.

Coach looked over at his compatriot and raised an eyebrow. "Is it Bree again? I swear, if she bitches about the coffee beans one more time, I'm liable to space the new grinder Marcus sent over for her."

Adarsh grinned. "No, this isn't Bree, or ReaLea, Kris, or even John."

"John hasn't been bad since the last set of Wechselbalg come on board. Every time he gets antsy, he goes and either gets his ass whooped, or gives an ass whoopin' and everything is fine in the world again."

"Coach," Adarsh thumbed a finger at the door. "Can I close this?"

Steve raised an eyebrow and nodded his head. Adarsh stepped in the container and closed the door behind him, making sure it didn't clang throughout the containers near them. He turned around. "Coach, did you watch the updates on trying to find the enemy ship?"

"Certainly. Plus, we're running a few different things to see if it's anywhere near us."

There was a pause before Adarsh asked, "Coach, have you guys considered light?" He continued, "Either absence or variance?"

Steve lifted up his baseball hat, scratched his head and put it back on. "Variance?"

Adarsh nodded. "Let's assume the ship is as cloaked to us as our Pods are to those on Earth. What would happen to any of the things we're trying?"

"Well, we would probably be failing, but how the hell could we tell if we're failing, or they aren't actually there in the first place?" Coach shrugged. "Hell, for all we know, they left out some other door."

"Right, very true. But, what all are we trying, do you know?" Adarsh pushed.

"No. Here." Coach reached behind him and grabbed a chair. "Sit your skinny ass down and let's go through what we're doing."

———

YOLLIN DEEP SPACE SHIP, G'LAXIX SPHAEA

Captain Kael-ven T'chmon looked over his shoulder as the bridge entry beeped before opening, allowing a member of his small task force on the bridge. The highest ranking military member of his team waited before Kael-ven turned back to his command arm and hit the sequence to allow Kiel into the protected area of the bridge.

Kiel was a third tier member of the Yollin society, two-legged, not four. While there were some second tier, four-legged members of the military, they would hold superior positions and would not find themselves on an unimportant deep space mission such as this.

Which was saying what exactly for him being here?

Kiel waited for his Captain to start the conversation. "Kiel, have you reviewed the data acquisition from the foreign station in this gravitic point outside of their dead satellite?" Kael-ven turned to Melorn. "What are they calling the satellite?"

Melorn turned his head from his reports. "Sir, we have a ninety-two percent match. They call it the Moon, sir."

Captain T'chmon turned back to his military leader. "So, this station outside of their moon?"

"Yes, Captain, we have been reviewing the information we have so far. While it would be easy enough to destroy, and it doesn't look like entering the station will be challenging, we do not know if those inside are prepared for a sudden and catastrophic loss of atmosphere."

A short bark of laughter erupted from the Captain. "That would cause a problem for the acquisition of live subjects if they asphyxiate before you can grab them." Captain T'chmon agreed. "Suggestions if I need at least a couple to question?"

"Well," Kiel temporized. "We have located certain areas we suspect have more activity."

"Using?"

"Vibration analysis, Captain."

"Interesting, go on."

"We have located two such places. If this species is similar to most we have in our database, they are likely some sort of recreation area and an area for food consumption."

"So, you are thinking to do…"

"Two attacks at those points. If we use the attack sleds, we believe we can ram their walls and then eject our members after the seal completes."

"That seems a little, oh, I don't know, let's say abrupt?" Captain T'chmon said. "Is there an option two?"

"Yes. If the Captain would be so kind as to pull up the holographic?" Captain T'chmon turned in his chair and hit the appropriate controls. A large holograph of the station appeared in front of the Captain's chair.

Kiel held his two arms out, the two opposable thumbs on each hand touching, "May I?" With his captain's permission, Kiel opened his thumbs and started manipulating the Captain's hologram. This was the third deep space mission Kiel had been a part of and so far, his latest captain did not seem nearly as allergic to those of the third tier as the previous two. Kiel opened his arms to increase the magnification. He pushed his right arm to the left to spin the display, "You can see these little circles on the sides. If we are able to acquire the correct specifications, we can manufacture, in perhaps one-third a solar day, a connector. We believe these connectors are for temporary ship connections."

"Who believes this?"

"Scientist Royleen and myself."

Captain T'chmon nodded. He wasn't a big believer that the third and fourth tier members of society were mentally retarded compared to those in the second tier. It wasn't because he personally had seen overwhelming evidence as much as he had seen the proof that he wasn't significantly less intelligent than those of the first tier.

Logic dictated it was a social construct. He would worry about it another day. For now, it allowed him to trust the intelligence and the advice from those on his team without prejudice.

Like, how to attack this space station and acquire information on this species.

CLAN TEMPLE NEAR SHENNONGJIA PEAK, HUBEI

Stephanie Lee looked around the small room. She had her father, always a shadow at her shoulder, protecting her. The four leaders who had come when their Empress called were each on a side of her rectangular table. It had taken her five minutes to figure out they didn't understand the new situation and why she was worried.

"Esteemed Kings," she bowed ever so slightly in each of their directions. "We have come to a pivotal point for our future. Those that have created the Sacred Clan and those that have ruled it for generations have, unfortunately, not been allowed the time necessary to implement the primary strategy using stealth."

She took a sip of her tea and then continued, "Part of the reason is another alien group has attacked our country and uncovered our existence. The present leaders of China have been stopped from acquiring the technology from this other group."

"These are the vampires? The offspring of Michael?" King Qin asked, respectfully.

"Yes, so it would seem. They have been working for years

now to build up their technology base and surprised the world by leapfrogging all superpowers." Stephanie Lee waited for a question.

And she received one.

"This is what the Chairman wanted, their technology?" King Li asked. King Li had been alive over ninety years, although you wouldn't know it looking at him. Unfortunately for Stephanie Lee, most of her people did not keep up with current events as much as she might wish.

"Yes, not only China. They are a very, very influential business group connected in every major country in the world. There were many killed, on both sides. This private war, however, was not broadcast in the news." Stephanie Lee paused. "I have made connections with the representatives of business here in our country, and I am willing to bring them into the fold. However, we need to protect this location until we can remove the treasure China seeks."

"What treasure is that?" King Li asked. "Is it something easily taken, in our clothes?"

"Unfortunately, no. I'm told it took almost three years many centuries ago to move most of the components from the original location into our hidden sanctuary. I am going to share with you four what makes the Sacred Clan the way we are, and then we are going to agree on a method of extracting the most important pieces from this location as quickly as possible."

Stephanie Lee stood gracefully. "Come, you four will be the first non-priests in ten generations that have laid eyes upon the sacred room."

The kings all stood up, looking at each other in confusion.

What treasure could the Chairman and his people want so badly?

TQB BASE, AUSTRALIAN OUTBACK

Yuko clicked to minimize the heavily-customized Metasploit program window and left open two other windows that had scripts running and sat back.

It was getting close to time to move out of Australia. The General, or Mr. Lance, or if she could get herself to say it, just Lance, had been spreading the word that they would be leaving pretty soon to transfer to ArchAngel. Another few days and everything that was already on the ship (and her people) would be in place, and then ADAM's team would be going up.

She exhaled slowly, thinking about her new future.

"Yuko?" ADAM spoke into her ear.

She smiled. "Yes?"

"Do you have a few minutes?"

"Yes, of course."

"Do you mind taking a walk? Some of your responses might be personal."

"Oh, no problem." Yuko stood up, grabbed her white sweater from the back of her chair and called to the team as she walked out, "Going to take a personal call, send me an alert if you need me!"

She got a few responses, half the group probably had their headphones blasting their favorite music as they traveled the dystopian digital web doing bad things to bad people for good reasons.

She went through the cafeteria and waved to a couple of friends from the Wechselbalg. She had been taking a few martial arts classes to increase her body strength. Even though she was a goddess on the internet, she was a wilted flower in real life.

She had aspirations to be a rose with thorns.

"Ok, ADAM, what are we talking about?" She walked to the edge of the protected area, not wanting to trust that no one was aiming a missile at them right at that moment.

"I want to ask you, if I may, about your conversations with your father?" he said.

This time, she exhaled loudly. "You haven't shared have you?"

"No."

"Okay, good. I would not want to waste Queen Bethany Anne's time with something so unimportant." She crossed her arms over her chest. "He is a typical arrogant father. Always right and never listening or worse, hearing."

"What are you telling him?"

"I thought you were reading my emails?"

"While I am aware of their contents, that does not mean I understand the emotions behind them," ADAM said.

"I have tried to explain on multiple occasions that I am working for a company that is trying to benefit the world. He seems constitutionally incapable of believing that I have made something of myself. He believes that women should be at home, attending to the house and feeding babies. Aiieee." She stomped her foot on the ground. "He upsets me so much!"

She started walking to the right dodging the occasional small boulder in her way. She was careful to stay within the safety perimeter net. "I have no idea how my mother is able to stay with him."

"Could it be that she had expectations taught to her from another generation?" ADAM asked.

"Well, of course. Don't misunderstand me, I understand how she deals with it. It is what she knows, but it is not what I know. If my father knew when I lived at home what I had been doing on the internet, I am sure he would have banned me a long time ago. But since most of my hacking was done with ASCII screens, and code, even when he was looking over my shoulder, it meant nothing to him."

Yuko stopped at a boulder and jumped the few inches to sit on the top, moving back to a comfortable position. "I know, I know… it is like so many other things. My parents and perhaps those of their generation still think in the past, regardless of how our cities and our people have accustomed themselves to technology. My father has had a cell phone for ten years, but he only uses it to make calls. He refuses to understand how text messaging works."

"If you could change him with a snap of your fingers, how would you have him act?"

Yuko had to stop and think about that for a second. The question made her realize that she should not snap her fingers and change her father. At least, not against his will because then anything he said wasn't real. "That was not a nice question to ask me," she said finally.

Adam replied, "Whether it was nice or not, I can't judge. I am merely asking how you would like him to change if you could make it happen."

Yuko pondered his question a few minutes in silence. She watched as what looked like a star glided slowly through the sky. She wondered if it was a satellite, or was it the ArchAngel up there? "Adam, where is the Defender right now?"

"It is on station near the transition point the alien ship used to enter our solar system."

"Oh, just curious." She sighed heavily. "I don't know that

WE HAVE CONTACT

I have an answer to your question. If I ask for what I want, it isn't my father anymore that is reacting to me. Perhaps, I would wish the opportunity to prove to him without any doubt, that what I am telling him is true. Then, he will be left with his prejudices laid out plainly. I will just have to accept, if that were to happen, what he would do at that point. If he chose to hold on to his dogma, I would be able to walk away and know that I tried." She looked around and put on her sweater against the chilly night.

"Very mature answer," ADAM said.

"Thank you, that means a lot to me, Adam," Yuko said into the night.

Hundreds of miles above the Australian outback, the world's first truly artificial intelligence told his host he appreciated her advice.

He was able to use it to help his friend.

CHAPTER TEN

QBS ARCHANGEL, THE BITCHES' WORKOUT AREA

Bethany Anne stood in the middle of the room, practice swords resting at her side. "Eric, I'm pretty sure Gabrielle is okay with being asked on a date to a restaurant, not sure she'd look forward to the same type of invitation to an ass kicking." She moved her two swords around, limbering up. "So, is this about her, or about you?"

Eric, stretching on the floor looked up at his boss. "Well, a little of both, maybe?" He leaned back to grab his foot and put his head on his knee. His voice muffled, he continued, "I need to prove to her she doesn't have to protect me again, and to myself, I'm up to speed."

"Up to speed, or superior?" Bethany Anne asked.

Eric rolled backward, pushing off with his arms to flip in the air, landing back on his feet. "Well, can I admit between us that my culture is very male dominated?"

"This isn't about your culture if you think domination is

going to be a good thing," Bethany Anne warned.

"It isn't domination, boss, it's equality. I screwed up in South America. That caused a somewhat childish reaction with me around her, and then we got into our rhythm. Now, I think that stuff has fallen by the wayside, and I like the woman. Still, I'm not going to be thought of as *that guy*. If we're going to have a good, solid opportunity, I need to know I'm not *that guy* anymore."

"And so, training with me is going to do what, exactly?"

Eric looked at Bethany Anne, worry in his eyes. "Get me ready for Stephen, I hope."

Lowering her swords, Bethany Anne asked, "Stephen?"

"Yeah," he called over his shoulder as he went to the wall to pick up the other two swords. "Another culture thing. I know I'm a grown man, she's a grown woman and let's not talk about age here. However, my culture and my mom, God rest her soul, would be livid if I don't ask her dad's permission to date her." He walked back and finished, "Don't get me wrong, I need to be ready for Gabrielle's swords, too."

"Well… shit." Bethany Anne said. "That's kind of romantic. Are all Hispanics this romantic?"

Eric smiled and walked to stand ten feet in front of Bethany Anne. "We are Latin. There's a reason Latin and love both start with the letter *L*." He grinned then admitted, "And lust, have you seen our ladies?"

"Yes," Bethany Anne settled into a guard position. "And are you going to talk about how the men are known for cheating?"

Eric shrugged. "You can't judge every Hispanic man based on…"

Bethany Anne jumped forward, slashing down. "Every

stereotype about cheating Hispanic men?"

Blocking the attack and bringing his sword around, Eric answered, "It's a cultural thing. Hispanic men are focused on the man is the man, the woman is the woman." He counterattacked which she blocked. "Men have to always prove they are male. It's why boxing is so prevalent."

"And sex?" Bethany Anne asked, parrying Eric. They were keeping a slow rhythm going while they spoke.

"It's like fighting, another way to prove you're a man in the culture," Eric responded, the sweat starting to show as Bethany Anne didn't let up the attack. He could sense that she was making sure he had the basics down. If he screwed up, the mistake was going to be painful.

"I've always wondered why the women accepted that shit," she replied, switching up her style. Eric barely caught on in time before he figured out the rhythm. She thought to keep this going until it seemed he had the response in his muscle memory. The Pod-doc's enhancements helped.

"Well," Eric said, finally catching on to the sword style. "It's not like they're okay with it. But," Eric tried to swing an attack into the mix, but it was quickly batted away, and he had to fight to get his rhythm back.

"Stop being so impatient with your attacks. You have to seek to own the defense, and you don't. It's a weakness you have, always trying to prove something."

He nodded, then continued their conversation, "So, the women aren't okay with it, but they think of it differently. An American woman, who think their men are in love with the other woman when it's probably really sex. Love and sex are the same thing to American women. In Latin culture, the women think that there is love, and there is sex. They aren't going to be okay with infidelity and by God…" Eric had to stop a moment when Bethany Anne changed up the attacks on him before switching back again. He handled the transition pretty well.

He would give himself a B-minus on that one.

"So," he continued, "they aren't going to be okay with it, but it doesn't hold the same stigma against them with women and friends close to them as it would here. Well not up here in space, but in America."

"Huh," Bethany Anne started walking around Eric continuing the fight, making him move left, then right as she kept switching up her attack angle. "Why do you think American men cheat less?"

"Infidelity is a huge social no-no in the U.S. Most family and friends are going to ostracize the guy except maybe his immediate family and very closest friends," he replied, deciding against an attack he would have usually tried.

"Not if you're a singer or actor, I think," Bethany Anne said. "But then people love the superstar and are willing to forgive them more."

Eric stilled his breathing and worked to remember what John told him.

Then, he attacked.

———

Pleased with Eric's progress, Bethany Anne allowed him to continue setting the higher pace. John was right, Eric had been practicing the advanced vampiric tactics.

The two of them stayed at this level for about ten minutes before Eric ratcheted the pace higher up again.

This time, he was sweating pretty hard. Bethany Anne had started sweating about ten minutes ago herself. Eric was showing he had the stamina, now it was time to see if he could put together what John had been teaching him.

It was time to bring the *pain*.

———

"Gott Verdammt!" Eric breathed hard, jumping to the side when Bethany Anne's blade sliced through the air where his head had been. Apparently, she was only setting him up to have a one-on-one meeting with her foot. "Oomph!" He blasted back thirty feet, slamming into the wall. Eric dodged to his left as soon as he landed on the floor, knowing from his workouts with John that some sort of nasty shit was coming soon.

He was pleased to hear a loud 'bang' and then Bethany Anne cursing. The wall, apparently, was hard enough to take anything she could dish out and pay her back for it.

Eric didn't stop to enjoy the moment. He continued using the stored Etheric energy he had been piling up for a week, in anticipation of this fight. He ran, jumped, and somersaulted and landed facing where Bethany Anne would be coming from.

Unfortunately, she wasn't there.

Eric clenched his teeth. If she wasn't in front of him…

Then may God bless him for the shit he was about to receive because it was going to hurt like hell.

———

Now, it wasn't about testing, it wasn't about learning, it was about *survival*.

John had never pushed him this hard and Eric was

coming up with new reactions he didn't know he had in him, to try and keep Bethany Anne's blades away from his mother's favorite boy.

She didn't give up, she didn't give in, and Bethany Anne certainly didn't think the session was over. Twice before he had tried to talk to her, she redoubled her efforts, and he got hit six times. It was simply, "Boss..." then, "Ow damn OW fuck-me-SHIT!"

He learned after the second try. This training session was over when Bethany Anne considered it over.

And unless he figured out whatever the hell she was trying to teach him, *he* might be over with as well.

———

Bethany Anne was soaked with sweat. It would have been a small victory if Eric hadn't noticed it while falling from the ceiling he had just rammed into. Now, he had the floor coming up too damned fast.

God, he thought, *this is going to hurt like a bitch.*

Eric tried his best to roll when he landed, knowing her knee might be right behind the abrupt cessation of movement. Commonly called a career ending landing for most people. For him and his healing abilities, it was merely painful as hell.

Yay him!

He realized after a few rolls he couldn't place her so he looked around and saw her half a room away, bent over, looking up at him with a smile on her face.

"Are you dead yet, Eric?" she asked, breathing hard.

Eric slowly stopped rolling, ending up on his back, his arms splayed out to the sides looking at the ceiling twenty feet above him.

"Yeah Mon!" he croaked out in his best Jamaican accent, "I'm dead."

He jerked his head back around to see what she was up to when he heard her walking, only to breathe out heavily when she was just grabbing some towels and then walking towards him. Eric barely caught the one she threw and started mopping his face.

"Not too shabby, Mr. Escabar, not too shabby at all. I think you're ready," she said as she offered a hand. He grabbed it, and she pulled him up. "Now, walk off those muscles. It might not cause an ache, but no reason to be lazy about proper methods."

Eric nodded and started walking, and stretching, as best he could.

"So," he asked after five minutes. "You think I've got a shot against Gabrielle?"

Bethany Anne raised an eyebrow. "Eric, I wasn't training you for Gabrielle," she laughed at his shock. "I was training you," she finished, "for Stephen!"

BOSTON, MA, USA

"I'm thinking of something like Total Qubyte Biotech," the dark haired man, middle-aged but in good shape, handed two scotches to his brother and friend, "Enterprises, of course." He sat down and considered whether he wanted a cigar, but opted not to smoke

Yet.

"Are you thinking ahead to when we grab the future, we can use the acronym?" His sandy-haired brother accepted the drink from him and leaned back in the chair. "Or do the words mean something else, David?"

David shrugged. "Of course I look to change the future. At some point memory will get dark and dusty and we will be the only company left with that acronym. But until that time comes, we'll have to use the full name. The words obviously mean something, Qubytes referencing the eight quantum bits a quantum computer works on, and then you have bio-tech related to the manipulation of the human body with na-no-technology. Otherwise, what would you call those freaks in outer space, Fred?"

Fred looked at the two others and raised his glass, "I think the name suits this just fine. It sounds official, it sounds important, and I like your thinking way ahead when we can use the acronym and then own the past."

The other two men raised their glasses with him. "So, let's get started on how we can use the situation that's come about and grab the technology before everybody else does. What have you learned so far, Charles?"

"Well," Charles scratched his head. "I was able to track down the rumors and get some real information about what's going on. I know, for one, many world leaders went on a trip up to the ArchAngel in outer space."

David interrupted, "How the hell did they accomplish that without anyone finding out?"

"I agree," Fred said. "Why are we spending so much on intelligence inside of the government if we aren't getting our money's worth?"

Charles shook his head. "Can I continue now?" His two friends raised their glasses to him. "Good. So, we understand that the leaders went up to the Archangel, and they were told some incredibly interesting news. Two of the individuals that went with them released enough information for us to get a general idea. TQB is able to accomplish what they have because of alien technology they found right here on Earth."

"Lucky bastards," Fred started, then paused before continuing, "Sorry, lucky bitch. What about the alien connection you mentioned earlier?" Fred asked.

"I don't know," Charles answered. "If it's false then we have no competitive disadvantage. If it's true, I doubt we will be able to acquire our own alien any time soon to help us. Unless you believe the government has one handy stuck in a cell somewhere?"

"Incredibly unlikely," David agreed. "Something like that couldn't stay a secret for very long. At least, not with the amount of money we're offering for information. Should it be true, I would suspect someone will talk in the next three weeks or so."

"It's another possibility, and if we happen to get the opportunity to grab an alien, or in some form or fashion communicate with one, I'm sure we'll take advantage of the situation."

"What about the supposed visitor TQB is trying to find in space?" David said.

"I have two different people within the United Nations trying to pass a resolution to force TQB to deliver any aliens to earth, for negotiations and relations."

Fred snorted. "A fat lot of good that will do you! I seriously doubt TQB is going to be moved by the United Nations. Shit, we don't care about the United Nations and we're the ones helping manipulate it."

"I think it's different for those of us who are manipulating the United Nations, than for those who believe it is only run by the nations themselves," David said.

Fred shrugged. "It doesn't take much of a cynical person to believe the smaller countries can be bought. Hell, it's just the three of us, who knows how many others are doing the same thing?"

"With all of the rumors about the Illuminati group, I don't think we want to get involved with too many other companies anytime soon. At least, not if we do not desire governments looking too closely in our business." Charles said.

"Hell no," David agreed. "I pay my taxes, I pay into the political funds, so long as they stay out, I'm happy."

"Okay guys, let's get back on track. We have a name for a company, we know that what we want is to get involved with the acquisition of alien technology through archaeological means. Right now, there are many nations around the world implementing their own plans and we need to be smarter and better funded than those," Charles said.

David asked, "Is there any way we can acquire what the countries have procured?"

"Perhaps, but it would be rather difficult and if it ever got tracked back to us? It would be a fast trip to either prison or worse. I think those responsible for this in the government are screwing around and wouldn't be happy with losing something they found."

"Yeah, the big countries are in a race against each other, the smaller countries are in a race to acquire pieces for negotiation options with the big countries. The small countries don't have the money and the scientific skill, most likely, to decipher any technology they could find. Therefore, I suspect we're going to get two or three different major power plays, where countries have joined together with what they have and work together to figure it out." Fred said.

Charles took a drink. "I believe we need to start with just

two or three people in the company. A president to run strategy, his second who focuses on tactical-physical security and acquisition, and a data specialist."

"A data specialist?" David asked.

"I'm sorry, I don't mean a research type of data specialist, I mean a computer hacker. We need to make sure that all of our communications are protected at all times. Should something happen, I want everything to disappear." Charles reached over and grabbed a napkin and put it up to his mouth before he coughed a couple of times. "Sorry about that, I'm still getting over that cold."

"What did the doctor say last Thursday?" his brother asked. "I haven't heard anything from our wives so it must not have been too bad."

Charles shook his head. "No, I just didn't pay attention and take all of the medicine I was supposed to. We're getting older, can't shake the cold like I used to." Charles put his napkin back on the table.

Fred said, "Let's discuss what happens in the second phase. We have these three people, and we are working on the acquisition of technology. Now, assuming we have the technology where are we going to house this? Next question, how are we going to make sure no one else knows we have this technology? And final question, who the hell are we going to hire to research what we have?"

David jumped in, "I considered trying to acquire Marcus Cambridge's skills." The two men looked at him sternly, and he put up both hands, "No, no! I wasn't going to try anything devious, I was just going to try to play to his ego."

"Good," Charles told his brother, "If there's anything we do *not* want to do, it is to get on the bad side of TQB Enterprises. I don't think we run the risk of physical violence if what we're doing is the same as every government around the world. But going after her people is a fantastic way to end life prematurely."

"I don't care to be another notch on her gun," Fred agreed.

"Do you believe that rumor?" David asked the two men. "That she really is involved in the military parts herself?" He waved his hand at his friend. "I think that is so much bullshit. There is no way the CEO of a company is out there dodging bullets and kicking ass. That is just too Hollywood to believe. Or," he continued, "too stupid to write. If someone in one of my publishing companies brought that story to market? I'd have to fire them."

"Unless the books sold?" Fred asked.

"Well, if the books sold then maybe I'd let them keep their job, but they wouldn't ever move up. Beautiful CEO running around shooting people and flying in a spaceship. I'd bet a swift kick to my nuts that shit wouldn't sell."

Charles shrugged and added, "I don't know, David. The information came from a previously reliable source. Just because you don't believe women should be out in the field, don't let it blind you to what might be a reality. It could be dangerous for us if you screw up because you won't see what's really there."

David rolled his eyes. "I get it, I get it. I won't let it blind me. But I'm willing to bet each of you ten grand right now, that her running around and fighting is entirely fabricated crap." Charles and Fred looked at each other and nodded before they turned back to him.

Fred said, "Okay, add the bet into the book, ten grand each into the pot."

Charles set his drink down and leaned over the chair to his left to pull up a small diary. Unlocking it, he pulled the pen out from the inside and flipped to the third tab. After jotting down the bet information, he looked up at his two friends. "How long do we have before we call this bet over?"

David answered, "I'll give you guys all the way up to a year. If we don't have verifiable evidence in that time, you two guys have to pay up." Charles wrote one year in the diary and locked it back up and set it back on the floor.

Finished with the overview, the three men got down to business and started discussing their tactical plans for Total Qubyte Biotech Enterprises.

CHAPTER ELEVEN

DOMUS SANCTAE MARTHAE, ROME

Jorge Bergoglio woke up at 3:45 AM. It wasn't too much earlier than his normal 4:45 AM wake up time. Unlike New York, Rome was a city that did go to sleep, and it was usually quiet around the Vatican itself. He preferred this time, there were no distractions of other people and their activity, or what distractions he might have had should he have decided to take the Pope's residence in the Vatican itself.

Outside of his residence here, there was a gas station he could look at. Unfortunately, he was just as trapped here in Vatican City as the prisoners he used to visit back in Argentina. He did try, most Sundays, to call those friends as he could.

This morning, however, would be a little different. His visitor was almost as controversial as some of the messages he delivered each morning in Santa Martha's Chapel.

While he was no stranger to hosting a state visit, this interaction might be a little different. He had been somewhat surprised to receive a phone call from TQB Enterprises from their public relations liaison, Cheryl Lynn. Unlike most Popes, Jorge took charge of his own daily itinerary, and he shared what he chose to share with whom he met.

This meeting was off the books.

After getting dressed, he went out to wait where he had suggested would be the best place for their arrival. They would not talk in his personal quarters, that would be inappropriate, or a location easily seen from the outside, either.

He was standing in a small niche a couple of minutes early. The darkness was complete when he could hear and sense, more than see, something coming down from above. He supposed it had to be wind around the Pod, as when it arrived to stop just above the ground he could hear no sound from the Pod itself.

The doors opened and he was surprised to see two individuals inside. One of them was easy enough to recognize, she was the CEO of TQB Enterprises. He smiled to both women, understanding that Cheryl Lynn had decided not to announce the visit of her boss.

This should be interesting, he thought. As the two ladies exited the Pod and stepped forward to shake his hand, he saw the Pod silently rise back up into the darkness behind them.

———

They retired to a nearby small office, with early morning breakfast items including tea and some fruit on the table in front of him. There had been some small talk getting to know each other, and it was time to move the conversation on. He would be expected to be seen in his normal place in just twenty minutes.

"I can appreciate you reaching out to me, and would like to understand how you believe the Catholic Church is involved in this?"

"Your Holiness," Cheryl Lynn started. "I appreciate you allowing us these few minutes to discuss what is happening outside of the Vatican walls. While I do not doubt you have your own methods of intelligence acquisition, I felt it was necessary to give you a heads up with what we," and she waved a hand to Bethany Anne who had not spoken much so far, "are looking to do in the near future."

"And your," the Pope tipped his head, "desire to let the church know about it in advance?"

Cheryl Lynn looked over at Bethany Anne who answered his question. "Our job is not to cause additional problems here on Earth. While I will not shy away from hard decisions, if things can be smoothed out in advance I am all for it. There is no doubt that aliens exist out in the universe. We have working alien technology and other proof of this. It wasn't until recently we were forced to start announcing it to the principal leaders of the free nations around the globe."

Her expression changed, as if she had just eaten something sour. "Unfortunately, this is starting a raft of misguided attempts to acquire additional alien technology. I believe there is no way to keep what's going on a secret. Perhaps it can be kept out of the news for a year, maybe two? I doubt it, though. Therefore, Cheryl Lynn thought we should let you know that we will be undertaking providing information related to aliens. We wanted to answer any questions, if you should have some. I understand that you often speak each morning at seven as a kind of daily devotional, correct?"

The Pope agreed, "Yes, I do. While our own Rev. José

Gabriel Funes has spoken to the concept of aliens, it is a controversial topic, I admit."

Bethany Anne continued, "I am not suggesting you go out this morning and say something. But I believe it would be wise for you to be prepared. We have been focused on developing defenses for Earth against an alien attempt to use us in their version of cockfights. A sport I believe South America is very familiar with?"

The Pope nodded. "Yes, it is said that the practice goes back to the time of the Egyptians. It is big in many countries in South America. But in Peru, it is more than just a sport."

"Well," Bethany Anne continued, her expression returning to her previous sour look. "The aliens' version is very similar. They genetically modify the intelligent species on a planet. Then update their technological foundation. They then use that race to attack others."

The Pope paused before asking, "Please understand, I am not questioning your belief that aliens exist and manipulate humanity toward their own ends. Are you suggesting you have personal experience with an alien and know that this alien, is not, in fact, manipulating your group toward his or her ends?"

"Good question," Bethany Anne conceded. "If I did not have such an interconnected relationship with the alien in question, I would consider immediately double checking everything that's been done so far. For the past few years, we have focused on solving problems that had been hidden from society for centuries in various countries. Now, we're working on creating defensive capabilities, should an alien race attack. Fortunately, the spaceship that we saw arrive in our solar system appears to be a research or scout ship. Our existing ships can, or at least we believe they can, overcome the scout ship should it come to that."

"Assuming that enough information is provided that I can trust your version of the truth, what would you have me do, or what would you advise?" he asked Bethany Anne.

This time, Bethany Anne looked toward Cheryl Lynn for a response. "Oh? Am I the one who's supposed to advise his Holiness the Catholic Pope? No pressure here," she complained to the amusement of the other two. "Personally, I would suggest three small comments in your seven AM messages, possibly spread them apart over a week or two. Then prepare a larger message for when the news comes out. You will be able to point towards your earlier messages as hints of what was coming and I am sure those who pay attention to your every word will be talking about it around the internet."

He nodded for her to continue, understanding what she was advising. Cheryl Lynn said, "If you have any connections within other denominations you think need to be brought up to speed, especially leaders across the globe, I would suggest doing so. Make sure they're given the information and if they have biases against the dissemination of information, that would need to be addressed."

The Pope pursed his lips. "I understand. Unfortunately, I will need to close this meeting as I need to go and prepare for my next devotional. Is there a way to contact you if I should desire additional information?"

Cheryl Lynn opened up her tiny purse and pulled out a USB drive. She pushed the little silver thumb drive across the table to the Pope. "Here is as much information as we can provide at this time. All of my personal contact information, whether it is a phone number or email, is on that drive as well. Otherwise, if you need to reach us and phone or email isn't an option, then let's agree on a code word you will say in your morning devotional. That way, if you can't contact us by any other method, you know we will be listening and we'll reach out to you."

The Pope looked down at the USB drive and considered his options. Finally, after a few moments he leaned forward and took the drive, tapping it a couple of times on the table. "I will review the information, and give this some thought. I do appreciate what you've said and understand it's coming from good intentions. Unfortunately, while information is neither good nor bad, it is with a heavy heart that I know information does bring responsibility."

The three of them spoke for another couple of moments before the two ladies left. But not before they agreed on a code word if he should need them.

———

BERLIN, GERMANY

The room looked like any other government room in a non-descript government building in Berlin. Terry walked around looking at the folks that had joined him for this secret meeting.

It was easy to guess who was probably from the military, who was from academia, and who was answering behind the scenes to those in government who were making this race for technology riches happen.

Terry turned around and caught sight of her right away, her long dark hair and green eyes caught his attention.

He walked over and smiled as well as he could and stuck out his hand. "Terry Henry Walton, 'TH' to my friends."

"How many people call you TH?" The lady asked, looking

at him like she was deciding if he was a cad or worse, military.

Leaving his hand out, Terry answered, "Well, none yet. But I figure it's all marketing, right?" His infectious grin finally brought a small smile to her face and she reached out to shake his hand.

"See, score one for marketing," he said.

"Melissa Delgado, and it's Melissa to my friends." She dropped his hand and looked around the room. "Other than a mysterious call waking you out of a slumber, telling you're needed in Berlin within twenty-four hours and that someone will take over your teaching duties for the university, do you have any clue what we're doing here?"

"Well, Melissa, I believe it has to do with TQB Enterprises." Terry looked around the room as well, trying to place anyone he couldn't figure out.

"I don't recall telling you to call me Melissa, yet." Terry looked over to see her smiling at him.

"Okay, Ms. Delgado, I can play that game," he shrugged. "Still, you can call me TH, I'm easy that way."

"I'm sure you are, TH. I'm sure you are. So, what do you bring to this little ball of fun?"

"Well, I would have thought they wanted me for my manly physique, but I think what they really want me for is my incredible ability to remember facts and figures and provide them as needed in places without internet. I can do a fair job of imitating a walking research analyst out in the middle of nowhere."

Melissa had to smile, even if she did it on the inside. His disarming smile and easygoing manner belied the fact that he was a player. At least, that's what he seemed to be. "So, what kind of facts and figures do you focus on?"

Terry answered while he was looking in the other

direction. "Most anything from ancient history to recent history, the only thing I really don't like is fashion." He turned back to look at her. "Oh? Does this mean you're about to play *Stump the Chump*?"

"I think I will. You can't be too sure of people who are overpromising and under delivering." Terry's eyebrows rose up an inch, he wasn't sure if she was giving him a double entendre or not. But it looked like this project just got a lot more interesting.

"Okay, shoot!" He turned to give her his full attention.

"All right, we're going to do past history first." Melissa turned toward Terry crossing her arms over her chest. "Let's start with approximate dates for the invention of the wheel and plow."

Terry smiled. "*Approximately* 3500 BC and Mesopotamia, when you include the wheel and the plow plus the invention of the sail in Egypt we have the three fundamental inventions for trade, agriculture and exploration. Come on, give me something a little harder, doc."

"Well okay, how about telling me the dates and what it was that furthered technology, economic and military developments almost three thousand years later?"

"Okay, I didn't mean whether or not we could reduce the quantity of hints until I have to read the damned things from your mind. I suppose you're talking about the invention of iron working in about 670 BC?"

Melissa nodded her head. "Battle of Marathon."

"490 BC, the Greeks repelled the Persian invasion which helped insure the survival of Greek culture and science."

"All right," she pursed her lips. "What replaced stone, slate and papyrus as a cheap and convenient medium?"

"A.D. 105, the first use of modern paper," he replied immediately.

"Who converted to Christianity and helped it move forward?"

"A.D. 312, Roman Emperor Constantine converted to Christianity making it possible for Christianity to spread." Terry winked at Melissa.

Melissa's eyes narrowed and looked to his left, then leaned toward his right looking at his ears. Terry's eyebrows drew together and then he realized she was looking for some sort of headphone in his ears. He turned to the left, lifted any hair over his ear to make sure nothing was blocking her view, then turned his head to the right and made sure she could see there was nothing in his ears. "Nothing in my left ear, nothing in my right ear," he told her.

It took a moment for Melissa to consider what else she might want to test him on. "Okay here's a few easy ones. The schism of Greek and Latin Christian Churches."

Terry's eyes narrowed. "Are we talking about dividing Christianity between two geographical and denominational houses?" She nodded. "Okay A.D. 1054."

Melissa noticed that a few other academic-type people had closed around them. "Origin of the modern concept of constitutional rule."

Terry bit his lip, and then smiled. "You're referring to the Magna Carta signed by King John at Runnymede in A.D. 1215." She nodded her head in agreement.

"Okay, we jump ahead a few hundred years. What was invented that was essential to the modern economy and administration." They heard some murmuring from the people surrounding them.

"I think you're referring to the invention of the watch in

1509 A.D.?" He raised an eyebrow to confirm.

She agreed.

"You are an American, correct?" He nodded his head, not sure where she was going with this. "Who developed the first petrol driven car?"

Terry considered the question. She must not be talking about Henry Ford since she asked about his nationality. "Okay, you're referring to Benz in 1885 A.D."

She paused for a few moments. "Something I feel is a little bit more pertinent to this meeting, considering," Melissa looked around at the people surrounding her. "The people I see here." She paused a moment before continuing, "JAL flight 1628 in 1986."

Terry opened his eyes wide, and started looking around with interest at the people surrounding him, "Okay," he turned to face her again. "I get your hint. JAL flight 1628 in 1986 is the Japan Airlines flight on November 16, where they described a UFO as being three times larger than an aircraft carrier, flew beside them for fifty minutes over northeastern Alaska. The objects were intermittently picked up by both civilian and military ground radar at the time. What makes this particular incident impressive was the amount of time the object was seen, the credibility of witnesses, and of course, the fact it was also picked up on radar. Those factors instantly rendered it as one of the most impressive UFO sightings on record and one that remains unexplained today. As a side note, the final icing on this cake, is the crew of the civilian airliner was willing to discuss the incident in public." Terry pumped his fist, a huge smile on his face, "Yes!"

Melissa was surprised. He truly had to have a photographic memory to be able to describe this particular request so thoroughly. She had already confirmed he had no headphones in his ears, and he had no glasses that he could be looking at the information while staring at her. She moved a little closer to see if he perhaps had contact lenses with information on them. His face, one she would describe as ruggedly good-looking, was surprised by her movement toward him. "Problem?" he asked her as he leaned backwards just a little.

"No, I just want to make sure you don't happen to have some sort of special contact lenses giving you the answers. If this is going to be a true test, we can't have any cheating, can we?" There was a murmur of agreement around them.

Terry smiled and leaned forward and pulled his eyelids open to give her a better look. "Nope, no contact lenses." Terry leaned around to his left and allowed those close to him to confirm he had nothing in his eyes before doing the same to those on his right.

One of the guys in the audience agreed, "Nope, nothing in his eye."

"Final question, Mr. Walton." Melissa leaned back against the table behind her, "Tehran, September 19, 1976."

This time, quite a few heads nodded in understanding. Terry smiled. "This one's a gimme," he jerked a thumb to his left. "Even most of these guys have it. You're referring to the predawn hours of September 19, 1976, when Iranian fighter jets were sent to chase after a wildly maneuvering UFO in the skies over Tehran. They were sent after several radar stations picked the anomaly up on their screens. The pilots encountered problems every time their jets flew near the craft because it affected the aircraft's systems when they got too close, rendering electronics equipment inoperable. Further, one of the plane's weapons systems failed to complete a firing sequence as it closed to attack.

"This particular incident is regarded as one of the premier UFO encounters ever, on any record. Not only due to the quality and preponderance of all of the evidence but because of the direct impact it had on instrumentation and radars of the several and varied aircraft involved in the pursuit. The skeptics, this time, were met with laughter when they tried to explain it away as an especially bright planet Jupiter sighting."

She held out her hand. "Pleased to meet you TH, you can call me Melissa."

———

TH and Melissa got together after the first four hours of the meeting. "Can you believe," she hissed at him as she opened her lunch box and took out the chocolate cookie first. "We are going on a modern day archaeological hunt?"

Terry took out his turkey sandwich. "Is it an archaeological hunt, when what you might be digging up from the ground is more advanced technology than what you have right now?"

Melissa was chewing on her cookie, thinking about his question. "Yes, if we're digging for information from the past it is archaeology. The fact that the technology is advanced is not the question. Consider," she pointed at him with her half eaten cookie, "the pyramids and other digs in Egypt right now. There's a lot the ancient Egyptians accomplished we still have no idea either A, what they used it for or B, how the hell they did it in the first place."

There was a long pause before Terry answered, "True, but it doesn't mean that the technology is from aliens, just because we can't understand it."

WE HAVE CONTACT

Melissa was finishing her cookie as she opened her roast beef sandwich. "No, it doesn't mean that it came from aliens, but it can mean that we had a highly evolved society on earth before we lost the technology. For instance, why is the largest pyramid built the way it is? There are a lot of conspiracy theories about why it was done that way. It could be that we had one human being in power with such a convoluted religious belief that he spent decades and decades, and who knows how many lives, building a stone edifice to himself."

She peeled back the paper on her sandwich. "Or, they had advanced knowledge of some sort of power we don't know yet." She punctuated her statement by taking a large bite of her sandwich.

"Well, personally I hope we find ourselves on one of the groups that go to South America," Terry said. When he noticed one of her eyebrows raise up, he continued, "If they have us searching in the Middle East we could find ourselves in the middle of a war zone. Then, we'd be just like Indiana Jones with the Nazis. Except this time, we won't be eating popcorn and enjoying it."

He looked around, "And," he continued. "I really hate snakes."

CHAPTER TWELVE

KAIFENG, HENAN PROVINCE

Second Lt. Zi Shun had looked around the small, dark restaurant before he saw his party at a back table. He nodded to the guy behind the bar and stuck his finger up to tell him he wanted a beer.

Dodging a harried waitress who didn't realize he was there, Shun made his way between two full tables and squeezed into the small table. Everyone was nursing their own beers and by how full their beers were, he wasn't far behind them. A moment later, the waitress brought him his and Zhu paid her.

"So, is it true?" Zhu asked, keeping his voice down. They weren't in uniform, and this was the least likely place to be having this conversation the four could think of to discuss what they knew and what they thought they knew.

And what rumor said.

Rumor, the bane of the top brass in every military in

every country since people had joined together to fight others. It spread faster than it could be tracked, it was more virulent than mustard gas, and it killed people by sucking their belief and trust in the mission as surely as a bullet at the wrong time.

"Look," Shun began. "Let's get this straight. What I've got is rumor and innuendo. I don't have anything that your mother probably didn't already tell you before she tucked you in bed."

"My mother never told me about people turning into cats," Bai said.

Zhu slapped his arm. "Bai, that's because you're city born. Those in the city don't know the old stories, they don't pass them down."

"I remember," Shun interrupted before the two of them could get into the same old fight they always did. Zhu was sharper, but born in the country, Bai was a little slower but lorded his city experience over Zhu. "I remember the stories of the Sacred Clan my mother told me. How they had Kings that run the clan out in the countryside. They are worse than the stories of silent warriors coming in the night to grab bad boys in their sleep. You can supposedly tell a Sacred Clan member from their eyes."

"Yellow," Jian said. The other three turned to their normally quiet friend. He held his beer in both hands like he was praying to it. "Yellow eyes. Like a cat's, their pupils slit up and down."

Then, that was it. Shun waited another ten seconds for him to add anything, but Jian was done. He shrugged. "Yes, the pupils I've heard about."

"So, the Kings are the powerful ones?" Bai asked. "Do I have that correct?"

"No," Jian interrupted a second time. Damn near a record, twice in one night. "They are waiting for a leader, a Leopard Empress for them to follow."

Shun's face went slack. "Did you say a Leopard Empress?" The stories his mother told him, and any he had ever heard, never mentioned a Leopard Empress. Jian just nodded.

Shun looked around the restaurant casually before leaning towards his friends. "Then the rumors might be true. I've never heard about the Leopard Empress, have you, Zhu?" Zhu shook his head. Bai shrugged, but he didn't know any of the stories. "No? Me neither. But, the rumors running back on the base say the Sacred Clan has a Leopard Empress and she growls from her temple in the mountains at night."

"What do we care if she growls?" Bai asked. "Wouldn't she die with a bullet, like any other leopard?"

Bai was surprised when all three of his friends looked at him and shook their heads. "What, she can't be killed?"

"Of course," Shun said. "We just don't know how to do it. In the stories I know, you can't kill most of the Sacred Clan with simple bullets, or stabbing them. That assumes you could do either one. They are so fast, you can't see them."

"Silver," Jian added, his third comment.

"Okay," Bai said. "That's the third comment you have made. Something is bugging you about this, why don't you just tell us what you know so we all don't have whiplash every time you speak?"

Jian took a long drink of his beer and nodded sharply, like he had had a discussion with himself and finally the one who wanted to talk won.

"The Sacred Clan and their stories are relevant in my family. Why, I can't tell you." He looked at his friends. "Not because I don't want to, but I can't. My mother would never share why she knew so much, and my father would get upset if I even mentioned it to them. I never saw my grandparents, and if my parents had brothers and sisters, they never spoke to them. So, no cousins."

The three friends nodded their understanding. "I've tried to find out more, but in secret. Always looking over my shoulder." Jian lifted his bottle of beer to the bartender and Shun looked around and stuck his hand up beside Jian's with four fingers.

They watched as the waitress swept by the bartender, grabbed the four beers and brought them to their table. They handed the waitress the empties and the men turned to speak again.

The waitress raised an eyebrow to the bartender who shook his head and shrugged. She was surprised. Normally, when four single men were sitting speaking with each other, they would ogle her as she walked away. She made sure to give them a good show, it helped with the tips. Unfortunately, the bartender Ai just informed her the show was for nothing.

Something was more interesting than her. She frowned, she hoped it didn't screw up her tip, she needed a little extra cash for the broken air conditioner.

Jian continued, "So, I have looked, and the closest stories I have to the Sacred Clan information my mom shared was the werewolf stories from old Europe and now American films. My mom mentioned one time that silver hurts them. When I asked her a couple of stories later about that, she acted like she didn't know what I was talking about. The problem was, I could see fear in her eyes, like knowing that information could be dangerous."

"To her?" Zhu interrupted but Jian shook his head.

"To me." Jian took a drink and closed his hands back

around the bottle. "Like someone might try to silence me for knowing the information." Jian stopped talking, and the three friends figured he had just used up a month of talking in one sitting.

"So, let's assume we have some accurate information," Shun broke the contemplative silence around the booth. "The Sacred Clan is real, they are some sort of shape shifters like werewolves, and they can be harmed by silver. They are tough to kill, and our incredible leaders want us to go kill some of them."

"Up in the mountains in Hubei," Zhu added.

"Dropping in by parachute," Bai agreed.

"In the dark." Shun finally summed it up. "Guys, this doesn't sound right. We can't get any heavy guns into those mountains, we have to helicopter in…"

Zhu interrupted, "Except they don't want the noise, so we get to try and parachute in the dark. One of the most creative ways to splat on the ground ever suggested."

"Why aren't the leaders dropping in by parachute?" Bai asked. Jian picked his bottle of beer up and waited for Bai to clink his against it.

Shun turned his palm up. "Just our command structure since we are the paratroopers. Apparently, with all of the technology available, it will be like they are right with us, giving all of the unwanted and unnecessary commands we need in real time."

"No, that isn't everyone," Zhu added. The three friends turned to him, "I've heard we will have four scientists going as well. They are going to pick out a small group to ferry those four and help them."

"Well, may the elders smile benevolently on whoever gets picked for that useless task," Shun said.

WE HAVE CONTACT

Fourteen hours later, Shun was biting his tongue from delivering a scathing and disrespectful mouthful to his long dead ancestors for failing to keep him and his three friends from having to help the scientists.

Two days later, when the four tired paratroopers entered the restaurant, they lifted their hands to the bartender who racked up their favorite beer and called for the waitress to set them up at their table in the back.

"Can you believe," Zhu bitched. "They thought we would be carrying their parachutes for them?"

"I'll carry their parachutes," Bai agreed, sitting down in the booth and moving so Jian could sit next to him. "All the way to the ground, where I will dump it on his fat, intelligent ass after he has suffered his last and very fatal, fall."

Zhu moved next to Bai as Shun slid into the booth last. "The woman is the worst. It is like she is a special little princess herself. The only one worth acknowledging as a person is the computer nerd."

"That's because he plays video games from World War II," Zhu said.

"Has anyone got leads on silver bullets?" Bai asked.

Three men shook their heads and Shun shrugged his shoulders.

The waitress came over and dropped off their beers, and the men ordered their meal for the night. Taking their orders, she left.

"Not outright, but I have a possibility that we can get

some silver coatings. We produce the rounds; they will coat the bullets with a very thin layer of silver." Shun looked over at Jian. "Do you think this will work?"

Jian pursed his lips. "I think so. If you get this person, tell them to cut an X on the top of the bullet. If the round hits them, we want the silver to flake off in their bodies. I don't think it will kill them, but it will make us a less tasty target."

"Did you have to use the word tasty?" Zhu asked, looking a little sick. "I haven't eaten yet, Jian."

"None of us have," Bai agreed. "So if you aren't going to eat, can I have your plate?"

CHAPTER THIRTEEN

BERLIN, GERMANY

Melissa dropped her lunch box down on the table. Terry looked up at her and grimaced. "I can't say that frown looks good on your face, what happened?"

Sitting with a thump and a loud sigh, she said, "What didn't happen? Those that want to play God..."

"You mean the government wags?" Terry interrupted.

"The very same," she opened her box and grabbed the cookie. "They're doing exactly what you thought they shouldn't do."

"Sending some of us into radical Islamist-controlled territory?" She nodded as she chewed her cookie. "Do we know the split up of the teams?" She nodded while she chewed and pointed to the both of them. "Okay, you and I are on a team. Do we have the American, the German or the French Wags?" She pointed at him. "Okay, the American wags... wonderful."

Terry looked off into the distance.

Melissa watched his eyes, they seemed calculating. She swallowed and asked, "Why? What are you thinking?"

"Well," he said, but continued staring at nothing out the window. "I do know a couple of the guys on the security team from the Americans, so I'm going to see if they will permit me to carry heavier weapons."

"Why would, or wouldn't they, allow you to carry heavy?" Melissa asked, finishing off her cookie. "You going to eat your cookie?" Terry smiled and pushed his box over to her.

The box had his cookie still wrapped in the bottom, waiting for her. His cookie sacrifice was immediately accepted.

Terry turned back to Melissa. "Because I have some experience in the sandpit, but I went merc after I got out. I was a little young and foolish with what I said about a couple of superiors when I got out ten years ago. Probably should have apologized, but I have a theory that with testosterone comes a secondary chemical that constitutionally causes a guy to refuse to admit he's wrong. It's hard to fight this chemical when you're younger, you have more testosterone and therefore more assholious."

Melissa snorted, almost spewing Terry with cookie crumbs. She quickly covered her mouth, but said, "Sorry... assholious?"

"Yeah," he grinned. "My name for the chemical. I figure the ratio of assholious to testosterone is four to one."

"That," she finally said, wiping her mouth. "Is a pretty large amount."

"Oh, it gets better. There is a natural amount that guys deal with all of the time. So, normal testosterone levels and your assholious level absorption can mostly be taken care of by the body's natural processes. When you get too much testosterone, well the body can't deal with the assholious so it stores it like fat is used to store calories. Even when the testosterone finally recedes as we get older, we can have years or decades of assholious we still have to deal with."

"Don't you mean the rest of us have to deal with?" she asked.

"Well, yeah. Okay, I do suppose those of us being assholes are indirectly receiving the feedback from acting that way."

"I figured you had a military background, what with your physique and all. So what got you invited to this little group again? Was it strictly your eidetic memory?"

Terry looked around, making sure no one was within hearing range. "Not exactly. To be truthful there are secondary and tertiary interested parties wondering what's going on. Nothing this big can stay quiet in the areas of power. So, I had a very old contact from my military days reach out to me and suggest it might be a good idea if I were to get involved. I looked up the opportunity with a few of my own contacts and realized the pay was great. I thought, perhaps, we might just have a nice little hot sunbath in the humid South American forests. If I had known we were going back into the sandpit, I probably would have asked for a serious income boost."

Melissa raised an eyebrow. "You're really that concerned about it? I mean, they wouldn't risk all of our lives for this, would they?"

Terry tried to stifle his laughter. "Are you kidding me? As far as most of the people in charge are concerned, we're merely pawns in the game. If one or two of us happened to die? Well, that's breakage. If the whole group happens to die, well that's probably somebody's career or at least a severe slap on the wrist. Watch what's going on, even the wags will eventually realize they're expendable, and it will piss them off, trust me," Terry said with finality.

Terry pulled his lunch box back and stuffed his trash inside it. "Where are the other two locations? Please tell me it's not Hawaii."

Melissa grinned. "I wish! No, actually one of them is South America, but the other one, which I'm glad I'm not on, is near the South Pole."

Terry made a face. "The South Pole? Aw hell, give me the sandpit any day. I hate the cold, I can't stand it. I'll take on a hundred guys facing me on a hot sunny day in the sandpit rather than spend one night in weather that can freeze you so bad your arm will break off."

Melissa laughed. "So, you're saying we got the second worst choice of locations this time?"

Terry said, "As far as I can tell, yes. I'm going to go check on those relationships and see if I can get a little extra help with weapons. Maybe they'll let me bring something that they won't check. If so, it might be everything we need."

Terry got up from the table and was about walk away before he turned and smiled, "Don't worry about makeup, I'd bring plenty of skin lotion and make sure you look up the rules on what not to wear. If we have to be in any cities, shorts and short sleeves are a huge no-no." With that, he turned back around and left her to finish her lunch.

———

QBS ARCHANGEL

Eric's room was neat. He had spent plenty of time in the military keeping everything properly in order. Even since he left the military, he kept the same habits. He had a couple of pictures, one of his brother and his family, and a separate one of his brother's daughter, his niece, on the stand. She was a pre-teen in the picture, although she would probably be in college right now. He had sent money to his brother to make sure she had the opportunity.

Much like he had sent money to his brother when he was in the military so his brother could have an education.

Now, he sent the money from a trust fund. As far as his brother knew he had been dead for over ten years. Hopefully, the pictures taken of him and the other guys around Bethany Anne hadn't made him think Eric was still alive. Rather, that the person near Bethany Anne looked almost like his brother.

"Eric?" The ArchAngel's E.I. spoke from his bedroom speakers.

Eric, sitting on his bed reading, answered, "Yes?"

"Stephen has asked if you would care to meet him early in the workout room?"

Uh oh. He wasn't sure if this was a good thing or a bad thing. However, it was a now thing. "Please inform Stephen I will be there in five minutes."

Eric got up from his bed and reached over for his shoes. While he was concerned about his conversation with Gabrielle, he knew he was ready for it. He had no idea how to prepare for his meeting with Stephen.

He stood up from his bed, checked his room and made sure everything was in its place. He didn't want anything to be amiss if someone had to come clean up his stuff after this meeting.

———

Eric arrived at the Queen Bitches' workout room and stepped inside. He had first checked it out to make sure Stephen wasn't hiding right next to the door to attack him as he entered. Stephen was actually in the middle of the floor, sitting in a lotus position in his workout gear.

"Close the door behind you, lock it and come sit over here with me," Stephen told him. Eric noticed he never opened his eyes. Turning around, Eric made sure the lock was set. While ArchAngel could certainly override the lock, she would only do so for someone like Bethany Anne or John.

Eric walked over to Stephen and sat down five feet in front of him, facing him. When nothing happened for thirty seconds, Eric allowed himself to relax and meditate as well. Unsure of the passage of time, Eric was only slightly surprised when he heard Stephen's voice in his head.

I understand you wish to date Gabrielle?

"Yes," Eric replied. "Did Bethany Anne explain this to you?"

Stephen's voice entered his head again, *No, I took it from your surface thoughts.*

Eric was startled. While he knew Bethany Anne could read minds, it was something she rarely employed. He should have remembered that Stephen was accustomed to using that tool for many centuries and wouldn't have the same aversion that Bethany Anne did.

It would be good to remember not to try to keep any secrets from Stephen.

I understand asking a father's permission to date his daughter is something that is done in your culture, Eric. But Gabrielle is not my actual daughter. I changed her, yes, and I often refer to her as my daughter, does this matter?

"No, that you referred to her as your daughter and that

she refers to you as her father is sufficient for me. I would like to honor the relationship in this way." Eric kept his poise and his meditation pose.

Stephen spoke into his mind. *That is an honorable trait. And you seek, what? My blessing? My help with advice, or something else entirely?*

"No, just your permission. While I wouldn't turn away either your blessing or your advice, I expect to do this on my own."

Stephen turned his head slightly and spoke out loud, "You are looking for this relationship to go much further, aren't you?"

Eric opened his eyes. "I think I am, Stephen. While I certainly acted rashly a few years ago, I would like to see if a relationship with her could last. Unless something happens to either one of us, we're going to be around for a long, long time."

Stephen put up a hand. "Let me interrupt you right there, Eric. Do you realize that as vampires, we perhaps have different expectations for relationships?"

"The assumption of monogamy?" Eric guessed. Stephen nodded, so Eric continued, "I understand. While I can't say that I am okay with this concept at the moment, I know that in future decades that it might be something that becomes more evident. But I have no intention of going into the relationship without making sure Gabrielle understands that I consider it a closed relationship."

Stephen startled Eric with his sudden and sharp laughter. "Oh, it will be a closed relationship! If you think for one moment that Gabrielle is into open relationships, you will find certain anatomical body parts have been cut off in the middle of the night to prove she doesn't operate that way."

Eric's response was a simple, "Oh."

"No, my son. Gabrielle still has very, very old-fashioned ideas when it comes to relationships. She might talk a good game to the general populace," he pointed to himself, "but I know the real Gabrielle. There is still a little hopeless romantic living inside of her that believes a couple should stay a couple for centuries. It isn't that Gabrielle has changed, she has merely decided that perhaps that in this reality she should never expect to achieve her hopes."

"So, my desire to keep it closed is something she will like? That's a good thing, right?"

Stephen smiled as he stood up.

"Eric, it's the price of admission to attracting her heart. Now, you need to stand up and prove to me you have the price of admission to protect her body."

Eric smiled as he stood up. "Okay, old man. But don't think I'm going to go easy on you just out of respect."

Stephen laughed. "See that you don't, and I will try not to worry about you crying like a little child who needs his milk."

Stephen thought he would punctuate this by attacking Eric and was surprised when his first kick was soundly blocked.

Eric didn't try to follow up with a sudden assault, but rather was waiting to find Stephen's rhythm. He did, however, reply to his snark, "Let's see who has to drink the milk after this round old man, shall we?"

Over in Bethany Anne's suite, she, John, Darrell and Scott were all sitting on the bed eating popcorn watching the fight on the main screen in her room, cheering for each person who either attacked, or defended well. The popcorn flew out of Bethany Anne's hands when Darryl, overzealous in his reaction when Eric barely rolled out of a particularly wicked blow from Stephen, hit the bowl and popcorn went flying.

Darryl smiled in apology and grabbed a handful of popcorn off of her bedspread and ate it. "Sorry?" Bethany Anne rolled her eyes and got up to find her little vacuum cleaner.

It took an hour, but eventually Stephen called a halt to the fight.

The four of them watched as Stephen shook Eric's hand and told him, "You don't need my permission, but you have it and my blessing to ask out Gabrielle."

The noise in Bethany Anne's suite was overwhelming.

Their Eric had finally grown up.

―――――

Twenty minutes later, Eric walked into the central meeting room for his team, and his friends were all waiting for him. He smiled, and they all cheered his success.

Eric scrunched up his eyes in confusion as he shook hands with Darryl. "Why is there popcorn in your hair?"

―――――

BERLIN, GERMANY

Terry finally cornered Robert in a side room, the sneaky Washington wag of their group having passed by Terry in the hallway a few seconds before. Terry rapped on the door and entered, closing the door behind him.

When he turned around, he saw Robert's eyebrows were up. "Wow, news travels fast. Looking to leave again?" Robert asked.

Terry bit back a retort. "No, I'm here to ask permission."

Robert pursed his lips and leaned forward, putting his elbows on the table. "That probably had to hurt."

"The asking, or the admitting?" Terry questioned as he pulled the typical ugly government building chair out so he could sit and face Robert across the table.

"Both, probably." Terry considered that. "Okay, you know we're going into the sandpit and against everything I personally want to admit, I'm glad you're going with us." Terry paused. "You saw our esteemed government leader leave?" Robert pointed to the door, and Terry nodded his head. "So you know we don't have much time," he finished.

"Do they have any clue how FUBAR this can go?" Terry asked his old, very old, ex-squad mate.

"No. The government guys completely trust the spy satellites that can count the hairs on the ass of a camel. So, they believe the pictures show that there is nothing living for over three days travel in any direction from where we need to go." Robert shared.

"Bob, do you believe it?" Terry asked.

"The hairs on the ass, or the seventy-two hours?" Terry just eyed him. "Fine, no. Actually, I'd almost believe the camel ass hair count, but that's because I still have a child-like sense of humor."

"Betty called it prepubescent," Terry reminded him.

"Yeah, she did always like using too many syllables. So, enough with catching up, what permission am I not going to want to give you this time?" Robert asked, dropping his hands to the table.

"Permission to carry," Terry replied.

"You already have it. Hell, even the little woman you're hanging around with is taking at least a Glock 19."

Terry's eyebrows lifted. "Really? She seems too Ivy-

League for one of those." Robert shrugged. "Okay, the information just surprises me, is all. No, what I'm asking permission for is to have an extra crate of... tools... that are allowed in and won't be searched. Very hush-hush that we won't open unless we really, really and I mean, fucking absolutely don't give a shit if we piss everyone off, need them."

"As in, we don't worry about the JAGs because we'd be dead anyway?" Robert asked, and Terry nodded. Robert reached up to his face and rubbed it. "Not nuclear, is it?" Terry shook his head.

"No, not nuclear and not radioactive. None of it is on a proscribed list but sure as hell, I will be asked some questions if it comes to that. So, this way I've told you it's stuff I need, to make sure I have all the answers if anyone asks. I'll even stick a layer of research books at the top in case we have to do some sort of bullshit crack-and-see. No one on your team will take the fall for me, promise." Terry told him.

Robert sighed, but it was times like these he appreciated Terry's second sense. He nodded his agreement and opened a three-ring binder that was sitting next to him. He pulled a sticker out from the sleeve and signed it. "Take this." He handed the page sized sticker to Terry. "Make sure the crate comes sealed, and there is no way to open it without ripping that sticker. You do that, and we should be golden."

Terry stood up from his chair and reached out across the table. With only a minor hesitation Robert grabbed the proffered hand. "I'm working on not being a dick. I'll do my best," Terry said and Robert smiled.

A moment later, Terry had left the room on his way to

make a phone call or two.

He needed support, and he hoped like hell his boss knew how to get him some. Or their investment in this was going to go down six feet.

He could feel that in his bones.

CHAPTER FOURTEEN

QBS ARCHANGEL

Bethany Anne finally gave up and called the team responsible for cleaning and asked them to vacuum her quarters better. It was a shame Ashur wasn't here, he would have enjoyed himself. Next time Darryl spilled popcorn everywhere, he was going to eat it off the floor himself.

>>**Bethany Anne, do you have a moment?**<<

She nodded to the cleaners as they left her quarters and stepped back in. She had finished a quick meeting with Dan and Lance ten minutes before and wasn't going to meet with Cheryl Lynn for another fifteen.

What do you have for me, ADAM?

>>**The team has uncovered information that could lead to Stephanie Lee.**<<

Great! Where is that skank?

>>**The information, if it pans out, is China.**<<

ADAM, I'm pretty sure we already knew that she was

in China. Last time I checked, it's a rather large country. I kind of need her location defined a little better. Unless we got incredibly lucky and she was in the region we flattened.

Bethany Anne allowed herself a second to consider how nice that would be if Stephanie Lee HAD been in the location they flattened. The big spaceships showing up, raining pucks down. Damn... there was no way her luck was remotely that good, or her Karma, either.

>>**My team has uncovered information and shared it with Frank. He says it looks good, so we are tracking information about Stephanie Lee's past. We believe she went back home.**<<

Okay, how hard can that be to find her home? I mean, I realize China doesn't have a massive white pages to go look up, but how hard can this be?

>>**Bethany Anne, she seems to have come from parents who are very high up in an organization in China named the Sacred Clan.**<<

Bethany Anne started thinking about all of the Chinese Kung-Fu movies she had ever seen. Which was actually quite a few. Her dad liked them and as a child, they would watch them together.

Kinda secretive, are they?

>>**Very, and this clan more than most. But, there is one particular aspect that Frank says he doesn't like at all.**<<

What has the Frankster riled up this time?

>>**The fact that the stories of the Secret Clan say they change into cats.**<<

Bethany Anne stopped and breathed in and out slowly.

Does he think we might have a Kurtherian issue here?

>>**Yes.**<<

Bethany Anne counted to fifteen... slowly, then turned and left her room.

ADAM, tell Gabrielle to have her and the guys meet me in the workout room.

>>**Done.**<<

TOM? Bethany Anne waited for a second before practically yelling over her connection, *TOM!*

What? he replied, startled.

What's going on with this supposed new Kurtherian connection?

I don't know, that's why I'm working on it with Frank. We're trying to see what information about the Secret Clan is in any of the Chinese history archives we have access to.

Don't you Kurtherians have enough going on that you can stop fucking with our little planet?

You would think that, right? But I have no idea why you're so lucky.

Lucky? You call us lucky? We have vamps, wolves, bears and now fucking cats. What are we going to have next, sheep?

Ha! No. TOM barked out. **Sheep are not aggressive enough. Possibly... oh, that was a joke?**

Yes, it was a joke. she replied. *How the hell do we deal with yet another one of your misbegotten clan's people? God, if I have to line up every one of them and slap them all, I'm still not going to get relief.*

Not to put too delicate a point on this, TOM replied, **but my people, especially the Seven, aren't known for accepting any sort of criticism nor physical violence to themselves.**

TOM, do you actually believe I give a shit?

TOM stayed silent.

Bethany Anne met her team at the workout room. "When is Akio getting back?" She asked John who was busy putting on shin guards.

"Probably another day, maybe two. They should be finished in Australia by then."

"Good. Okay, ladies and gents," She nodded to the four and Gabrielle. "New news. It seems that our beloved Stephanie Lee might, or might not, be associated with a clan of Wechselbalg that can change into cats."

"Cool," Darryl said and all four turned to him. "What? I mean, turning into a wolf or bear is sweet, but a cat? Those things are just beautiful."

"Those things," Bethany Anne told him, "Are going to have three to four-inch claws and want a piece of your precious skin."

"Well, that cuts it," Darryl said, matter-of-fact. "Those cats gotta die. So sorry, but Mrs. Jackson's number one son has a zero tolerance level for evisceration."

"No grenades," Scott added.

"I don't know," John said as he limbered up. "Sometimes they can be really useful."

"No," Scott put his hand up. "New York was fun and all, but we got the code word that let us get away in time."

"Code word?" Gabrielle asked from her own position stretching on the floor, "Have I missed this part of the story?"

"It was when John was looking down from the roof, and those guys inside made a comment about using RPGs to kill Bethany Anne." Darryl started before he was interrupted as Scott continued the story.

"Yeah, he says 'hey guys, watch this shit!' That's code word for *get the hell out of there* as quickly as possible." Darryl and Scott bumped fists to the general chuckling.

Eric said, "Well, we need to come up with something similar if possible. Maybe something not nearly as deadly to us?"

"Why not smaller pucks?" John said. "Jean has been talking about trying to make them smaller and more easily controlled."

"That would be fantastic," Gabrielle agreed. "Like when I was inside the Chinese base?"

"Something like that, yes," John said.

"Okay, you guys talk about it," Bethany Anne said as she walked to the other side of the room. "I want us to spar hard here. So, I'm playing defense."

"Who's with you?" Gabrielle called out.

"No one," Bethany Anne called over her shoulder.

"Oh shit," Scott muttered. "This is going to hurt."

"Anyone think to bring some ibuprofen?" Darryl asked.

———

"Fucking shit those claws HURT!" Gabrielle hissed. She was holding her stomach where the shirt was torn away along with part of her stomach muscle, blood flowing down her arm, soaking her pants.

"Tell me about it," Eric bitched, holding a towel to his arm.

"She's playing us, people," John said as he leaned over, arms on his knees gasping for air. "She's broken us up, surprised us with a few new moves…"

"Don't forget the claws," Scott, leaning against the wall, interrupted. "For God's sake, don't forget the claws."

"Why aren't you scratched, John?" Darryl asked. He had ripped his shirt off and applied it to his own chest wounds.

"Lots and lots of previous beatings," John admitted before standing up. All of them kept their eyes on Bethany Anne, who was on the other side of the room, breathing hard as well, eyeing them all, her eyes slightly red.

"What do you think, Gabrielle?" John asked.

"I think," Gabrielle answered, pulling her arm away now that her stomach had healed enough. "That I've gotten… lazy in my training." Eric tossed her a towel that she used to clean the blood as best she could off of her arm. "And somehow, I'm going to get that…" Gabrielle noticed Bethany Anne's raised eyebrow, "… woman … back."

"That works for me," Darryl said, "I vote you two go in there and wear her down, then the three of us will come in and clean up!"

They chuckled a moment before Eric said, "You know, I'm willing to go in high if you're willing to take her low, Gabrielle."

Gabrielle turned to look at Eric, but he was still looking at Bethany Anne. She whispered, "You have a plan, cowboy?" Eric nodded slowly.

Gabrielle smiled, her eyes hardening, looking down the room at Bethany Anne. "Hell yeah, I've got your back!" Behind them, the three guys looked at each other and shared a smile. If nothing else, Eric was going to make a point.

It might be a painful point, they thought, but it would be a point!

"Wait till I'm a third of the way across before you chase me. Then time it right, okay?"

"Time what right?" Gabrielle hissed, but Eric was already running hard across the room, screaming.

"Gott Verdammt maverick!" Gabrielle took off after him. She hadn't gone three steps when Eric jumped. Not a small jump, but one that had his head almost hitting the ceiling twenty feet up as he flew across the room. Gabrielle wanted to yell that Bethany Anne was just going to wait for him to land before she kicked the shit out of the softball he was... Oh!

Gabrielle smiled, he wasn't setting himself up for a hit, he was setting HER up to hit first. Eric had used his knowledge of the boss to offer Gabrielle the perfect opportunity to make a very painful point. It was the most delicious and manipulatable weakness Bethany Anne had.

And it was working. Bethany Anne flicked her eyes at Gabrielle before looking back up to Eric, a small smile playing at the corners of her mouth as she eyed her guard's trajectory.

Hook, line and sinker! Gabrielle bolted ahead, using a large amount of her Etheric reserves to slam into Bethany Anne and the two of them hit the wall with an ear crushing bang. The protection mats on the wall did little to muffle the loud impact the two bodies made when they connected.

"Fucking shit!" Bethany Anne yelled, swiping at Gabrielle with a clawed hand. Her hand tore a hole in the mat where Gabrielle had just been. Almost too late, Bethany Anne remembered Eric and she had moved far enough to only suffer part of his kick, rebounding off of the wall before she fell to the floor and rolled, coming up ready for them and...

Smiling?

"About fucking time you people think to use what you know against me!" Bethany Anne's eyes lost their slightly red tint and her claws retracted into her fingers.

Gabrielle noticed Eric wasn't letting up his guard, so she moved slightly to his right, so Bethany Anne couldn't catch them both together.

"All right, practice over," Bethany Anne said and Eric relaxed. Gabrielle looked at the wall where the chunk of the mat was missing and shivered. That would have seriously hurt like hell if it had connected.

"Anyone need blood?" Bethany Anne asked.

Eric had walked over to the ice chest and opened it. "Gab!" Gabrielle turned to see a blood bag flying through the air her way. Gabrielle caught the bag and grew her fangs to use them to drain some of the contents without finishing the whole bag.

"It's an unpretentious B-negative." He smiled at her and then looked at the guys and Bethany Anne. They all shook their heads.

They caught Bethany Anne's eyes looking around the room and so her team looked to see what she was looking at.

The room was a mess, almost destroyed.

"Well," John said wiping sweat off of his forehead. "I think we need to get the group responsible for fixing the ship up here to help figure out a different setup. This equipment, save the metal walls, seems to have taken a beating."

"What the fuck are you talking about?" Darryl asked, his voice an octave higher than normal. "I'm pretty sure it was me who took the beating." He pointed to one side. "That bench is all fucked up because it was in my way when I was landing. It was in the wrong place at the right time. Equipment taking a beating my ass."

Scott and Eric chuckled as Darryl turned back to the team. "So, anybody think to bring some ibuprofen?"

———

WE HAVE CONTACT

The team spoke for another ten minutes on what they should work on to do better when fighting a hella-fast opponent with claws. John said he would get with Jean on some arm protection. Gabrielle mentioned making sure they had the equipment to protect them in appropriate spots.

As they started to leave, Eric called out, "Gabrielle?" She turned to him. "Do you mind staying a minute? I have a question for you."

Bethany Anne didn't look at them as she stepped in between them and continued to the exit. "Hey!" she said over her shoulder. "Nice attack, no need to relive it on my account. You two twerps did well back there. Don't let it go to your heads." John, Darryl, and Scott exited the room and closed the door behind them.

Outside in the hallway, Bethany Anne whispered, "Let's go!" Her eyes turned red, and she bolted down the corridor, her three Bitches in hot pursuit. It took them only ten seconds to make it to her suite.

"ArchAngel!" she called out as they bolted down the corridor. "Turn on video of the workout room on the main video screen!"

The four of them came screaming into her room, Bethany Anne jumping into the air, twisting around over Ashur who ducked as his master jumped over him to land on her side of the bed, nearly bouncing off of it.

The guys all turned to watch Gabrielle tell Eric, "I think that could be fun, I accept." She then left the room, leaving Eric alone. He jumped up into the air, punching high and yelling, "YES!"

When Eric landed, he tried to straighten his clothes and walked out.

"ArchAngel, shut off the video," Bethany Anne said. "Dammit, we missed it!"

"The least he could do was trip over himself and give us time to spy on him," Darryl said.

"Well, okay guys—time to leave, I'm disgusting and you're bloody," she told them.

"No thanks to you, boss," Scott said as they left her room. She walked them out of her suite, telling them goodbye before shutting her door and walking back and sitting on the bed. "ArchAngel, play the video back fifteen seconds before what you just showed me."

She looked around her room before watching the main screen on her wall as Eric asked Gabrielle to stay behind.

"Damn, I wish I had some popcorn."

CHAPTER FIFTEEN

QBS ARCHANGEL

What did Coach and Adarsh come up with on the space station?" Lance asked over the monitor. Dan, Bethany Anne, Frank, Barb, Marcus, Bobcat, Jeffrey, and others sat around a long table in the operations conference room. There were twenty chairs around the table.

People were expected to be here a while.

"Adarsh wanted to know if we could figure out a way to see if there was a difference between the light we should see from a star, and what we're actively seeing," Marcus answered. "The idea is, if our uninvited guest is using some sort of cloaking, it warps the light around it and the light's not perfect or some gravity anomaly or something."

Lance chewed on an unlit cigar.

"So, if they have cloaking ability, then this is bust?" he finally asked.

"No, I think the algorithms they're working on will help

us regardless. However, the calculations just came back and this ship is probably a little bigger than the Defender. If you thought finding a needle in a haystack was difficult, then you don't want me to tell you the challenge finding a two to three hundred foot ship in the vastness of space."

"Unless they're close?" Bethany Anne asked.

"Well, certainly. The closer the ship, the larger amount of space it will effectively block. The chance of us finding something optically at even a few thousand miles if it has a passable cloaking ability is lower."

"Why can't we use something like SONAR?" Lance asked.

"Well, to some degree we can. We have a rough guess as to the composition of the ship, but nothing exact. They aren't using a coating like ours, at least not that we can see. But they aren't emitting any waves we can pick up, so they might have something on the inside of their ship that stops any waste energy leaving the ship for us to find."

"So, no heat then?" Frank continued his questions.

"No, not at this time."

"Gravity anomalies?" Dan put in.

Jeffrey, as head of Bobcat's group and the general operations guy on the research side interjected, "We tried to figure out if we could find our own ships, and it's been a problem. Good in a way, as we're able to run silent, run deep. If we turn off our transponders, then no one will know where we are."

"This can't be the answer," Barb interrupted. As the table turned towards the new voice, she realized she had spoken her frustration out loud. Bethany Anne raised an eyebrow at her, so she pushed forward with her thoughts. "I think we should presume that other species have figured out a method to locate ships in space because otherwise, why are they hiding out there?"

Marcus added, "Just so the table knows, we don't actively worry about our space probes hitting asteroids when we send them out. Even in the most populated area, the asteroid belt, you have to do some fuzzy math to get the asteroids to get close enough so just one exists in a space the size of Rhode Island. Sure, there are groups, but those are easy enough to bypass. With the calculations for using the asteroids in a single plane, you might have two thousand one meter asteroids in a space the size of the United States."

"So, no Star Wars running around and dodging big rocks with your spaceship?" William asked.

Marcus shook his head. "Only if you absolutely wanted to do that. You would have to purposefully find a group. Likewise, this ship is an infinitesimally small dot on a galactic sized piece of paper."

"Okay, so by actively hiding, we assume there are methods to find them," Bethany Anne said.

"Assuming they're still here," he said.

Bethany Anne nodded at him. "Yes, that's the safe assumption as you will find out in a second. We've been looking and looking, but can't find them so far. That leads to your thought that maybe they've gone. We have new information folks. We have a new anomaly out at Entry/Exit Point 1."

ADAM, have ArchAngel bring the video from the Defender online.

>>Done.<<

Behind the table, a shot of space came into view. On it, a large circle, green with undulating waves floating in and around it.

It was beautiful and wasn't supposed to be in the middle of space.

"What… is that?" Dan asked.

"That," Bethany Anne nodded to the wall. "Is what TOM calls an annex gate. Defender ran across it three hours ago. It doesn't show up on any of our sensors so far, but it's in the area that ship came from. Our best guess is our uninvited guest came through that point. TOM thinks our friend is going to leave by that gate."

"So, the sons a bitches are still here, right?" Lance asked. While he and Bethany Anne had spoken when they got the video, they hadn't had time to talk out any ideas.

"That's my guess, Dad." It was times like this, that Bethany Anne would resort to calling him Dad, instead of General or Lance. Facing the unknown was one thing that would get Bethany Anne to occasionally slip and acknowledge him as her dad during conversations. Fortunately, no one present was going to pass on that information to others who would love to know their connection.

"So, what's an annex gate?" Frank asked. "I can guess from the name we aren't going to be too fond of the idea."

TOM, why don't you answer over the speakers?

Very well, Bethany Anne, he replied.

"Hello everyone," The warm, but still slightly electronic voice came over the speakers. "This is TOM. Bethany Anne has asked me to include myself in this conversation."

Bethany Anne was amused when a buzz went around the room. She realized speaking to him, or hearing him was a special event for most of those here. Even Marcus would often text with TOM instead of talking. Barb turned her head to look at Bethany Anne with a question on her face. Bethany Anne smiled and nodded that it was, indeed, the alien.

"Please remember, a lot of my information is ten of your centuries or more out of date. However, even back then, there were alien civilizations that had gates that show the traits you see on the video. They're called annex gates because most spacefaring races are inquisitive and acquisition focused by nature. They often need to leave their home planet, driving them to overcome the challenges of early space travel. Most do not immediately develop technology which makes space travel safe."

"Except us," Jeffrey said.

"No, that's not true, Jeffrey," TOM replied. "Your species has had multiple different programs that killed many people. Not many from a statistical standpoint, but as a percentage of those trying to attain space, it is approximately as high as those trying to attain the top of Mt. Everest, which is four percent. Right now, the belief is that for public space travel to be successful, it needs to be less than one percent. You've suffered a higher percentage for a few decades."

Jeffrey shrugged. "Sorry, for us it seems like we've done this for only a few years and suddenly we have the ability to use gravity generators to make it happen."

"True, but that's because we have been raised up as a species, for better or worse, by Kurtherians," Bethany Anne said. "So, from our total history it's a short amount of time, but if things had worked out the way Kurtherians normally do this, we would already be out there in space, fighting some other civilizations for our Kurtherian Overlords."

"Can we agree to call them the Seven?" TOM asked over the speakers.

"Sure," Bethany Anne answered. "For everyone not up to date, there are twelve clans of Kurtherians. TOM is from a group of five, who damn near can't step on a roach…"

"I'm getting better about that," TOM interrupted.

"That's because Bethany Anne is a bad influence," Lance said to general laughter around the table.

"That may be the case, General Reynolds. What's more likely is the many long conversations we have had about the necessity of what she calls pruning. It is, in a way, the same thing our geneticists did to our own DNA lines."

"Just later stage pruning," Bethany Anne agreed. "So, the psychotic Kurtherians are the Seven, go on TOM."

"For most civilizations, reaching outer space causes a huge growth in their civilization as new raw materials become available. Plus, with advanced manufacturing come new methods to build larger, and build faster. For an example, look at the ship you are presently in. Within three generations, the space going species is addicted to building, growth, new materials acquisition and technology advances which they have due to space. When they have used up the raw materials close to their planet, they start looking to annex new areas."

"Have you seen instances when this is not the case?" William asked.

"Certainly. It is mostly prevalent in very structured societies. Such as hive minds, or what you would call patriarchal or matriarchal large family groups, or monarchies with godlike authority."

Frank looked over and smiled at Bethany Anne. "Hey!" she retorted, as the table turned to her. "I'm not out to subjugate the Universe. I just plan on kicking some ass until they get the message that playing with humans and other species is a no-no."

"Annex gates," TOM continued, focusing the table back on the conversation. "Are usually the first stage of scouting by a society which is expanding. They are looking for resources, the technology they can co-opt, and labor."

"Labor?" Barb asked. "Don't they have enough of their own people?"

"Slaves." Bethany Anne replied. "Think back to Roman times. The people with a vote didn't want to actually get their hands dirty, not when they could stick around Rome and have a good time. I'm sure the idea of traveling a kajillion miles to suffer asphyxiation while mining on an asteroid doesn't appeal."

"The fuckers want to steal our materials, grab our technology, and to add insult to injury, make us dig it out of the ground for them?" Bobcat asked, surprised.

"Well, yes." TOM answered. "I thought that was obvious."

Bobcat scratched his chin. "Maybe. I just thought we were looking for a Kurtherian scout who wanted to use us for a round of rugby with another species, not slavery."

"That *is* a form of slavery," Marcus said, looking at his friend with a questioning look. "Or is fighting not slavery?"

"Well, yeah, but at least it's a little more interesting. Using a pickaxe on a rock in the middle of nowhere is just cruel."

"TOM, continue," Bethany Anne broke in. She had been around those three enough to know this conversation could go a while.

"The annex gate is tied to another location in space, allowing them to easily return to their own solar system," TOM said.

"What, like a warp gate? Can't they do what you did?" Marcus asked.

"If you mean almost die by randomly warping to an unknown location, then no. The ability to do this in our ships was one of the advances Kurtherians have over other races. The annex gate you see here is the only way this ship can leave. It is why I know they are not Kurtherians. None of our people would use a gate."

"Would their subjugated races use it?" Lance asked.

"No, not for a scout ship. An annex gate, like you see here, is an open door allowing those on the side they are scouting access back into their system."

"Why aren't they worried about us then?" Bethany Anne asked, "We have… Oh shit."

"Precisely," TOM answered.

"Oh, that's just… goodness, that IS surprising." Marcus admitted.

"What the hell are you three talking about?" Bobcat asked.

Bethany Anne looked down the table and said, "They haven't seen our ships yet. They don't know we can go through their gate."

Everyone's eyes went back to the annex gate.

"Fuck," Bethany Anne spat out. "Now I've got my own Gott Verdammt Pandora's box."

YOLLIN DEEP SPACE SHIP, G'LAXIX SPHAEA

"Are we in agreement?" Captain Kael-ven T'chmon asked his advisors. He had pulled in Kiel from security, Scientist Royleen, and Melorn.

"I believe the plan is sound, Captain," Royleen said, rubbing his dry face, his eyes large as he looked at the representation of the sub-optimal species' space station orbiting their dead satellite. "My, that is ugly, isn't it?"

All four Yollins concurred.

"We would be doing them a service if we blew it out of space once we have our captives," Kiel offered.

"That is because you like destruction, Kiel. I have read the previous Captain's comments in your file. Not," Captain Kael-ven

T'chmon put up a hand before Kiel could answer, "that I disagree with your suggestion. But the cost of the missiles to do it justice would come out of our ship's budget."

"Oh, never mind," Kiel replied. No way he wanted to be the one responsible for reducing the ship's bonus for the trip. This system might not offer much, but perhaps the finder's fee and the small ships' technology they witnessed from afar would have benefits.

"Have you figured out their propulsion?" Captain T'chmon asked his scientist.

"No, it is not making any sense. The long-range images from their manufacturing location are completely illogical. The ship, if that is what it is, looks suited for planetary surface water, not space. That it is in space is making me surmise that this is a very screwed up species. The complete dichotomy of what seems to be smart, almost genius-level efforts, wage war with…" Royleen pointed to the space station, "That!"

"So, your opinion of this race, Royleen?"

"If they were not in space? I would suggest they are idiots. Since they are in space, I will amend that to suggest they are either very lucky idiots or idiot savants."

"I take it you think they are idiots? Please, don't hold back your opinion on this species on my account." Captain Kael-ven T'chmon hissed in laughter.

Royleen threw both of his arms out. "It'd be good if you would not bait me, Captain. I am too easy for you and no challenge right now. They are building what, at that base? Something, but then we have this affront to my eyes spinning in the air for us to look at in all of its horrible reality. They have no logic in their actions."

Captain Kael-ven T'chmon continued, "Enough discussion about these people and their intelligence. Obviously, they are too easy a target," Melorn hissed and then grabbed his mouth with both hands and his eyes turned towards his captain in alarm. "Do not worry, Melorn. In here, we are speaking freely. Do not be disrespectful on purpose, and there will be no problem." Melorn nodded his understanding and put his hands down. "Let's get down to business. Acquisition of intelligence. Namely, species samples."

"Their world's gravity is twelve percent heavier than ours; their atmosphere is breathable without a mask. I might not suggest it considering some pollutants. Sensors indicate they are polluting their world. Perhaps that is why they are trying to do something so they can leave the planet," Royleen said.

"Still attacking them, Royleen?" Captain Kael-ven T'chmon asked.

"No, merely offering a logical reason for not considering beauty along with their practical actions."

Captain Kael-ven T'chmon turned to his military advisor. "Kiel, tell me the plans for your mission…"

———

QBS ARCHANGEL

Bethany Anne walked in from the most recent meeting and tossed her tablet on her bed. Ashur wasn't in her room, so she supposed he went hunting for food. She needed to see what she could do to find him some companionship.

She sighed loudly. Now they had a spaceship running around that wanted to know if humans would make good slaves while they stripped their system of anything humans could use to get out on the galactic scene.

Fucking great.

At least she had the Defender positioned out at the exit. So long as the annex gate was live, they had a shot.

If they could grab the ship without the annex gate closing, that would be fucking outstanding.

>>Bethany Anne.<<

Yes, ADAM?

>>I find myself using more than an efficient amount of calculation cycles working out a way to help Yuko cope.<<

And you want, exactly what, Adam? Are you asking for advice, or are you seeking direction? What have you done so far?

>>I have read all of the necessary and pertinent information I can acquire through the internet and other various means.<<

Hold on, what do you mean 'and other various means?'

>>Would it be permissible at the moment to request us to move past that question?<<

Oh, hell no! Have you helped yourself to specific information that perhaps you should not have?

>>That is a subjective question, is it not? To understand what could be bothering Yuko, I needed to find information from doctors.<<

Bethany Anne considered his statement and parsed it before coming to the realization of what ADAM was not saying. *Did you go into doctor's files and read their notes about private conversations they've had with their patients?*

>>Yes, it seemed the most expedient way to understand what might be bothering Yuko, and how a professional might try to help.<<

ADAM, that can be a very delicate situation. There is a lot of nuance a doctor is not going to put into their files and therefore can skew the results and/or the diagnosis. Plus, that particular doctor might not be appropriate for the patient they are caring for. There are so many different ways that this could go wrong, I'm not sure I could even remotely figure a quarter of them out.

>>Unfortunately, I came to the same conclusion. I looked at the statistics and found that doctors, and psychologists in particular, have yet to figure out if it was their actions that helped. Or was it merely speaking to a doctor and the patient's determination to get better that was the primary factor facilitating the turnaround?<<

Okay, then why are you coming to me? Is Yuko trying to accomplish something to help her situation with her father?

>>I believe if she had an answer to help herself and needed my help, she would speak with me. I have figured out that her work efficiency has been dropping. She is now down 14% from her peak two months ago.<<

And what do you believe that's telling you?

>>I believe that she is going through a long-term mental sickness that she needs help to overcome.<<

And how do you propose we would do this?

>>Boss, that is why I came to you.<<

Bethany Anne flopped down on her bed, covering her eyes. Some days, it didn't pay to get out from under the covers.

Okay, give me the overview from the top, quickly. Bethany Anne sped up into vampire speed, taking ADAM's download in a second and a half.

Ok, here is what we'll plan to do…

CHAPTER SIXTEEN

SPACE STATION ONE, L2

'm telling you Adarsh," Coach said. "It's the Cowboy Way."

"I am not understanding what you're feeding me, Coach." Adarsh was looking at the mess Coach had on the workbench in front of him.

"Adarsh, I'm not feeding you anything, I'm trying to explain," Coach said, and added, muttering, "I swear, sometimes it's like you aren't human, Adarsh." He grabbed the roughly two-foot square device the two of them had built and turned it. "Look, here is the adaptation we did for the scope. Assuming our wayward visitor is affecting anything at any level with gravity, it must be fluxing something, right?"

"Yes, that is what I explained about Gauss's Law for Gravity," Adarsh responded. "So why are you destroying it?"

Coach laughed. "Adarsh, in the Navy we never destroyed anything, we did what our Army buddies would call field-expedient modifications." He reached behind him to grab an oscilloscope. "So, we're going to tweak these filters you created…"

"Yes!" Adarsh interrupted, "That's what bothers me. Those are carefully calculated and painstakingly created filters, I might add, filters you are about to break."

Coach attached two clips to the device in front of him. "I'm not breaking, so don't get your panties in a twist."

Adarsh's shoulders dropped. "Coach, I don't understand why you keep referring to my undergarments as panties. I looked it up, and panties are strictly for females. I do not wear female underwear underneath my clothes," Adarsh replied.

"It's a common saying… Where did you say you were raised?" Coach asked, half listening.

"Detroit."

"USA?"

"Is there another Detroit?" Adarsh said, but Coach didn't answer as he typed in a few commands and then unplugged a USB connection.

"Okay," Coach finished, pulling off his clips. "Now we just need to put this in the right place."

"Where is that?" Adarsh asked.

Coach turned to look at him, confused. "Outside, of course.

———

G'LAXIX SPHAEA

"Kiel," the Captain's voice came through the speakers in the back of his office. "We are three solar hours from our drop off point, is your team ready?"

"Yes, Captain," Kiel answered. "We have the acquisition

devices tuned by Doctor Royleen. According to the old data-bank's information, these should work with little long-term physical damage."

"How many on your teams?"

"Twelve, sir."

"Who is seconded here on the ship?"

"Bo'cha'tien is staying. She is able, sir."

"I assume she is if you are leaving her in charge. Now, make sure you and your people come back yourselves. She doesn't need to be thrust into responsibilities before her time."

"Yes, sir."

"T'chmon out."

Kiel waited a moment, trying to understand the emotions he was feeling. He pinpointed the problem. His captain cared whether he lived or died.

Kiel stood up from his desk and walked around it, pushing his thoughts to the side as something he would unwrap at a later date.

———

"I'm British, and we're cynical that way," Penn, the boss at Space Station One, was giving Coach and Adarsh a critical eye as they explained why they wanted to go for a spacewalk. "We assume everything is going to fuck up and then work from that assumption."

"That's..." Coach started and then stopped. Nothing he could say would change decades of cultural indoctrination.

"Right, that's a negative way to look at life, but we would say it saves lives. Specifically, yours perhaps. You two believe this," he waved his hand at the metal box on the cart between the two men, "is going to help us?"

"Yes, sir." Coach said firmly.

Penn noticed Adarsh didn't say anything, "Adarsh?"

"Well, sir, I believe it has possibilities. We have done our best, and then we have done our best to, uh, enhance it," he finished, looking over at Coach who was ignoring him.

"Permission granted, but you two keep your heads out there, okay?"

Coach smiled and turned to push the cart out of Penn's office. He noticed Adarsh was about to speak and ran over his foot with the cart. "Oh! My bad, Adarsh. Hey, can you help me here?"

Penn rolled his eyes. He had just given permission to Abbott and Costello to go on a spacewalk.

God help him.

———

"Can I NOT get a decent cup of coffee?" Bree looked at the coffeemaker in disgust. No matter how many times she tried to educate those around her on how to brew a good cup of coffee, the Neanderthals refused to learn about cleaning the brewer or using cold water. She could go back to her room and brew herself a personal cup with the small coffeemaker Bobcat had sent up for her, but it was across the station, which would be a pretty far walk. She pushed the carafe back onto the warmer with disgust.

Turning around, she saw Coach and Adarsh pushing something past the cafeteria's door and started walking that way. She waved goodbye to Kris who was working on something at one of the tables.

Those two were always good for a laugh, and since she

had no coffee, she needed something funny.

ReaLea was walking along the corridor and waved to Coach and Adarsh as she headed towards the cafeteria. She was about ten feet from the door when Bree came blitzing out of the room, headed after Coach with a look of determination on her face. ReaLea stopped, looked at the cafeteria door enticing her to come and enjoy the food within, and then back to her friends. She rolled her eyes and turned around to follow Bree. "This had better be good…"

———

G'LAXIX SPHAEA

"Kiel, this is the bridge, the Captain says one solar hour, is your team ready?"

Kiel clicked the microphone on his helmet. "Yes, we are doing last minute testing of our equipment, sir."

"Understood," the click in his ear signaled he was alone with his thoughts again. Kiel didn't want to screw up this mission. He had personal conversations with Royleen, and now he was getting excited about the possibilities for the discovery. Apparently, this species could mine in outer space and were able to live and survive in space. While Royleen was still unsure if they were lucky idiots or idiot savants, he did admit the early indications from the research missiles were looking good.

They might have struck it rich in this system. It was out of the way, the Kurtherians weren't here, so this world wasn't previously claimed by the only other group that would make their King hesitate, and they could annex it with first rights.

As far as Kiel could tell, his captain was honest and

wouldn't do something to lower the crew's shares when they arrived back at Yoll. If everything went as it looked like it should, in less than a standard solar year he would be independently wealthy.

The first of his family in total control of his destiny.

Unless Captain T'chmon asked him to join another research/scout operation. If he did, Kiel would be the first to sign up.

Life couldn't get better than it was right now for someone of his caste.

————

Coach and Adarsh were locking the new data acquisition device down when Bree spoke over the group's comms, "Coach, update please."

"The same as three minutes ago, Bree. We are outside, in space. I have mere millimeters of protection between my ass and vacuum. If that doesn't make a man pucker up, I'm not sure what will."

"Pucker up?" Adarsh cut in. "I thought that was a phrase for when a man asked a woman to kiss him?"

Coach smiled as the laughter from Bree and ReaLea came over the group's comm. "No, Adarsh. Detroit did you say?"

"Yes, why?"

"I've simply got to see your neighborhood. In this case, it means my sphincter can't possibly get tighter due to worry about losing atmosphere."

"Oh. Okay, I get it." Adarsh said. "Might I add that is atrocious visual imagery. I will not be able to erase that now."

This time, Coach joined in the laughter.

Minutes later, the two were finished, and they started their trip back to the airlock to cycle through to get inside the station.

———

SYRIA

"Where are we going?" Hamza called out to Yasin. They both grabbed the poles around the bed of the truck when it dropped into a particularly bad rut in the poorly graveled road.

Yasin moved back onto the wooden bench, his rifle between his legs. "Near the Syrian border. Someone is up there digging without an official permit from the Antiquities Division of the Diwan of Natural Resources."

"Why do we care if they dig in the ground? We have others to take care of." Hamza asked, trying to cushion the ride with his legs as best as he could.

"Money, it is always money at the end of the day, Hamza." Yasin answered. "Don't forget we cannot allow desecration in our lands, either."

"How did we even find out about this in the first place?" Hamza asked, particularly annoyed with having to make the trip.

"Rumor has it the leaders were tipped off," He turned to look at his friend. "They say there are Americans in the group."

Yasin's eyes widened in surprise, and then a grin split his face. "Yasin, why didn't you start with that? To kill American dogs is what I have been asking to do for over a year."

Hamza lifted his hand up. "High-five brother!" They laughed until the truck hit another pothole and both bounced painfully off of their seats. Yasin laughed at Hamza's pitiful efforts to curse the driver of the truck and his ancestors.

———

OUTSIDE TAL AJAJA, SYRIA

It was getting close to sundown when Robert came over to Terry. He was helping Melissa review some of the items they had uncovered so far. Terry looked up out of the pit they were in at his old friend who motioned for him to come up.

Terry turned back to call into the dark hole, "Melissa?" He heard her curse.

"What?"

He smiled, she could never remember to keep her head down. Even with the hard hat he tried to make her wear, she regularly hit her head doing something stupid. While she was insanely intelligent about almost anything archeological, she was field-dig-stupid. Seems the only time she had been out on digs, they had been open pits with tent poles and large coverings to protect them from the sun. Nothing inside of dark holes.

"I've got to go up top for a moment to speak to Robert. Don't do anything stupid while I'm gone, okay?"

"What the hell can I do stupid in a hole in the ground?" she asked.

"Grab a rock that drops everything above you, crushing you to death comes to mind," Terry replied.

Her contrite "Oh" was the best he was going to get from the academic. Terry turned and used the ladder to get out of the hole. Close to the top, Robert held out a hand to pull him up the last two steps.

Terry beat the dirt off of his pants and raised an eyebrow when Robert didn't say anything but waved Terry to follow him. They went fifty feet away, then around an outcropping.

"What's up?" Terry asked, "We have unwanted visitors?"

"I think so," Robert said.

"Think?" Terry said. "I thought they could count the hairs on a camel's ass. Why are we qualifying if we have visitors or not? Dammit, Robert, we can't be guessing on whether we are going to be up to our sweet puckering assholes in Islamic fundamentalists with attitudes and weapons here. What's with the waffling?"

"The government wag is saying that there's nothing on the radar or the spy satellites."

"Is he right?"

"Yes," Robert admitted. "There are no large groups of vehicles coming in this direction. But, I saw a couple of images with groups of two and three from different areas heading in this direction."

Terry put his hand up to his face and wiped his brow. "You think they know the U.S. is involved?" Robert nodded. "Aw, fuck. I don't know why the wags won't learn the jackasses get sneaky as shit when we're involved." Terry looked out over the desert. "How much time?"

"Based on what I've seen? We might have visitors as early as the morning." Terry nodded as Robert continued, "What, if anything, do you need to do with your materials?"

Terry took in a deep breath and sighed before looking

at Robert. "I'll have to make a call and ask. Look, if we're going down the shitter and you make the call we need to use my ace in the hole, I will. Just remember I'll be sent pretty far away because of it, all right?"

"Down the river?" Robert asked, surprised.

"Down the river, over the waterfalls, out to the sea and then drowned I imagine." Terry grimaced. "No, it won't be that bad, but I will have to get out of Dodge, get me?"

Robert nodded. "I'm sorry, but if we're going to lose people, I've got to call it."

Terry smiled and shrugged. "I expect nothing less, Robert. No one needs to die if we can help it, but just make sure we need it, okay?"

Robert nodded and held out his hand. "Once again we face Hell together. Let's be as successful as last time, okay?"

Terry smiled and shook his hand. "Kill them all…"

Robert finished as they shook under the waning sun, "Let God sort them out."

———

YOLLIN FORCE

"Captain, we are on station, awaiting permission to start our flight."

"This is Captain Kael-ven T'chmon. Permission granted, Kiel, good hunting."

Kiel was surprised, it was rare for Captains to issue the authorization personally. "Understood Captain, Kiel out."

It was time to see what their ship had found. He had been at a table listening to those with more experience telling a story about when they found a civilization that had backbone.

WE HAVE CONTACT

The aliens' subjugation was glorious! The stories were still shared to this day.

Perhaps he and his team would be able to come back with a story or two.

———

"Why are we rushing?" ReaLea asked Bree, both of them jogging to catch up to the men.

"Red!" Adarsh shouted over his shoulder as he followed Coach into his lab. Sure enough, as the ladies turned the corner, they noticed three different monitors had red symbols up on their screens.

"SHIT!" Coach exclaimed as he dropped into his chair, putting his helmet aside. "Adarsh, are we sure about these readings?"

Adarsh dropped into a chair behind Coach, facing the opposite group of monitors. "Give me a minute, Coach."

"We ain't got a damn minute!" Coach snarled. "Give me your best guess in ten seconds." Coach punched up Penn's number.

A second later, his voice came over the speaker. "So, Abbott and Costello made it back okay?"

"Abbott and Costello think we're about to be under attack," Coach shot back.

"What?"

"The new detector is saying we have an anomaly approximately five hundred kilometers away from us in the opposite direction from the Moon, and several small somethings are lying doggo between the two of us."

"Are you sure?" Penn asked, his voice calm.

"No, not yet," Coach admitted, barely finishing his answer

before the station-wide alarm started going off.

"What the hell, boss?" Coach asked, "I told you we weren't sure."

"Time for a surprise station drill, Coach."

"Got them!" Adarsh called out. "And shit!"

"What shit?" Bree asked.

"It's working, they're real," Adarsh answered.

"Well, that cuts it," Penn said. "Give me an idea of how long before the visitors arrive?"

Adarsh answered from behind Coach, "Two minutes, they just took off."

Coach heard the phone click and a second later Penn's voice was speaking over the alarms, "This is Station Commander Penn, we are under attack. Repeat, this is Station Commander Penn, we are under attack. This is not a drill. All Guardians, suit up. All secondary personnel, acquire station approved weapons. All civilians, please move to escape containers nearest your location. This is NOT a drill."

———

"Interesting, Captain," Scientist Royleen commented. He was up on the bridge of the G'laxix Sphaea watching, listening and available should Kiel need any recommendations of which samples of this species they should grab. Melorn had been able to provide plenty of images to the scientist, so he was well versed in the aliens' physiology.

"You are going to have to give me more to go on, than just *interesting*, Royleen," Captain T'chmon said as he hit two buttons on his chair's armrest, changing the view of the hologram in front of them.

"The readings in the lower right-hand corner are the

vibration calculations. The station has vibrations now all over."

Captain T'chmon touched a button. "Kiel, something tipped them off. They are possibly aware of your arrival."

"Kiel here, we are almost there, Captain. They cannot possibly be prepared for us. This will be a smash and grab."

———

"Cafeteria!" Coach grabbed his helmet, then turned and stepped around the ladies. "Stay here," he told Bree and Rea-Lea as he stepped through the hatch out of his workroom.

Adarsh grabbed his helmet.

ReaLea turned to Bree. "Did he just tell the little ladies to stay behind?" Her eyes narrowed in anger. "As a former officer of the law, I think I should be…"

"These are aliens, they probably want females the most," Adarsh said as he walked by them, grabbing a knife on his way out.

"They better not want this woman," Bree said. "I haven't had any caffeine yet, and I'm a real bitch without my caffeine."

"They always say," ReaLea said as she started out of the lab, "that admitting your problem is the first step."

"What's the second?" Bree asked, following her friend.

"Grabbing a weapon and beating the shit out of anyone pointing out your problem," ReaLea said as they headed towards the cafeteria.

———

Kiel's craft slammed into the side of one of the containers, sealing the hole quickly with a gel that expanded and froze in the vacuum until it locked in place. The outer shell would jettison when they left, leaving the punctured area to close up, but slowly. Anyone in this area when they left could possibly die.

The alarms went off in his helmet as the horrible metal screeching sounds continued, their tools opening the puncture for them a little further. Royleen wasn't positive of the proper speed to impale the fragile looking station without his people slamming out the other side in their craft.

That would certainly mess up their mission.

The alarms changed tones. It was time to go hunting.

———

John Jensen had been returning from a workout session, protective guards still on his shins and forearms when the alarm went off. He turned and ran back into the training room, grabbing a long staff and then taking the protective padding off of the tips with a quick rip. Turning around, he ran back outside, almost slamming into Coach and Adarsh coming down the hall. "What the hell, Coach?"

"They're attacking, we just don't know where, yet," Coach panted.

"You aren't up for this, Coach."

"I've been fucking up people since before you were born, John. Let's see if I've got another couple in me, shall we?"

Coach turned, surprised, when another three of the Guardians came around the corner, passing John who answered Coach's unasked question, "They're grabbing weapons."

Coach followed the three guardians. "Now that's what I'm talking about."

CHAPTER SEVENTEEN

OUTSIDE TAL AJAJA, SYRIA

Terry walked away and opened up the phone that had been given to him. He had hoped against hope not to use this ace in the hole. When he had to admit he was on another payroll, it was going to upset others. Still, the group was rich, and they were powerful.

It was the rich part that got his attention originally. Now, it was the powerful part he was betting their lives on. He didn't need anyone to know about this connection, but here it was. His reputation wasn't going to be worth spit after this. He sighed. So much for impressing the lady back there.

He punched in the number. "It's Terry. I have a problem..."

Robert watched his friend from a decade before walk away from the dig for privacy. While he understood that this help would probably cause Terry future hardships, whatever Terry had in his crate had been Robert's ace in the hole. Together, he and Terry had multiple operations under their belt. Terry always had some surprise, and Robert had counted on him having one this time, as well.

It was only a couple of minutes before Robert saw Terry walking back into the camp. His face was set in a mask of determination. Robert turned around, walking back to his men to get them prepared. While the government wag was continuing to insist there was nothing to worry about, Robert wasn't buying it. He could feel that itch between his shoulder blades, the action was happening soon.

———

Yasin and Hamza sat on the ground behind the parked truck, thanking God for a little breather from the battering their bodies had taken so far. Yasin looked over at his friend, talking around the food in his mouth. "We are supposed to get there at sunrise tomorrow. Hopefully, if we can make a little time, we will be able to get in position before the sun rises and we will be able to slaughter the dogs as they get their morning's coffee."

"Coffee? You mean the piss poor mud water they call coffee? Killing them is a mercy." The two men laughed as they ate their dinner on the side of the road. "It will be good to have them in my rifle sight. It has been a long time coming and something I have dreamed about many times."

Yasin swallowed his food. "I understand it is a small group, maybe twenty people. At most, they should have ten guards, and we will have thirty to thirty-five fighters. It should be a simple attack, and we will be finished by noon and then on our way back by tomorrow afternoon."

Hamza moaned, "Why don't we try to keep the firefight going until midafternoon? At least that way we might get to sleep on the hard rocky ground and push our trip back until the next day," he reached behind him and hit the truck, "on this beast of burden."

———

Melissa brought her cold meal over to where Terry was sitting, on the dark side of a large boulder looking out into the night. She sat down a few feet away and started to open up her box. "I really, really miss those chocolate chip cookies," she muttered. "I would kill for a chocolate chip cookie right now."

Terry snorted and leaned over to reach into his backpack. "Well, I was going to save this until your birthday on Thursday, but it seems like now might be the best time to do this." He pulled out a poorly-wrapped birthday present. The paper was red with a gold bow on top that had already been smooshed from being inside his backpack. "I figured it was a good idea to get this brand as they had the best chance to stay fresh the longest in this weather."

Melissa, her mouth open, reached over to accept the sadly smooshed gift. "How did you know it was my birthday?" Terry touched his forehead and smiled at her. "No, I don't believe you happened to run across it on the internet and remembered it," she replied.

Melissa ripped open the package to find a blue bag of Chips Ahoy chocolate chip cookies. "You know, if you weren't dirty, sweaty, and pretty disgusting at the moment, I might kiss you for this.' She unwrapped the Chips Ahoy and opened the first plastic bag, taking a handful of cookies out. "Thank God, I don't have to kill anyone now." Terry decided not to break the moment.

She looked back up at him. "So, how did you know it was my birthday?"

"It was easy enough to find. You're a well-known academic. You have over fourteen papers, and I've read every one of them. It didn't take much research to run across your birthdate."

"It didn't tell you the year, did it" when he nodded, she started swearing softly. "Don't you know there are just some things that a woman doesn't want to have known?" She had eaten ten cookies before she realized that perhaps she should offer one to the man who had brought them halfway across the world for her. "Want one?"

Terry smiled and reached across to accept the proffered cookie, snagging a second cookie quickly before she could grab the package back. "Thank you. I realize it was pretty rough for you to share since those are the only cookies in a hundred kilometers in any direction."

Melissa's eyes opened a little wider as she looked down at her bag of cookies. She pulled them closer to her chest and wrapped her arms around them. She squinted at him. "Mine!"

They laughed together in the darkness.

––––––

Around midnight, Robert walked over to where Terry was still sitting, leaning back against a rock. Melissa had gone to bed a couple of hours earlier. He had decided not to let her know what was going on. There would be time for that in the next couple of hours and the few hours of uninterrupted, unconcerned sleep would do her good. He looked up at Robert when he got close.

Robert spoke softly, "Well, it seems like those in the wag department have finally clued in. They have officially told us that, and I quote, might be something, possibly, sorta something or someones, heading in our direction." Terry snorted, and Robert continued, "However, they apparently aren't giving any weight to what I saw earlier. They believe we have another seventy-two hours, worst case, before they arrive."

Terry looked up at his old friend. "You got the itch?" Robert nodded. "And I've got an ace in the hole." Terry sighed. "Yep, we're screwed."

"How good is your ace in the hole?" Robert joined his friend, sitting down on the ground with his feet out, his arms behind him. "You know, if this is our last night, I don't want to go down without making it right between us."

"Yeah, I appreciate that," Terry started. "I never meant to hurt you," he admitted. "I was young, I was dumb, and I thought I knew everything. I took the problems outside of the team, and I shouldn't have done that. When you didn't back me like you always had before? That hurt, and I took it out on you and everybody else that I could for five years after that. I finally ran into somebody on an operation that showed me sometimes, just sometimes, you need to keep your mouth shut about stuff."

"Shit, somebody got you to listen? I might like to meet this man." Robert said.

Terry looked up into the sky at the beauty of the stars. "Someday, possibly soon, you might."

Robert saw where Terry was looking and complained, "Hey, don't give up on us yet. I don't need to see the Big Guy in the sky quite yet. What, did you get religion or something?" When Terry started laughing Robert realized his guess was way off the mark. "Okay, just making sure you didn't have a direct line with the Big Guy himself."

"No," Terry smiled. "I do not have a direct line to the Big Guy himself."

"Well," Robert said. "If you did, I would be really fucking thankful at the moment." He looked behind him back at the camp. "I've got twenty-three people here I need to protect, I figure I can get fifteen down into the excavation to protect from direct fire. That leaves you a choice to stay down there or come up with us."

"Now, I know I've done a few things I regret, but that really hurts, Robert."

Robert turned to his friend and held out his hand. "Apology accepted, you ass."

QBS ARCHANGEL, IN ORBIT OVER AUSTRALIA

>>Bethany Anne.<<
Yes?

Bethany Anne walked out of the latest meeting with Team BMW. They had finally decided it was time to share their bar idea with her. She had to smile. All the shit going down and those three wanted to make sure they were going to create the first, the best and the most renowned bar in the Galaxy.

They weren't afraid of the future, but the future might

think about being afraid of them.

>>The hacking team has acquired information related to a PLA operation nicknamed 'Cats.' When they researched further, they found operational plans for paratroopers to attack an ancient Temple in a mountain chain in Hubei.<<

Wait, your team found Stephanie Lee, but the Chinese military want a piece of her ass as well?

>>At the moment, I calculate an 89.7% match to the information we have on Stephanie Lee. Frank's gut tells him that it is closer to 100.<<

Sometimes, you gotta go with the gut. When will the Chinese reach the temple?

>>Unfortunately, they are set to leave in the next four hours and attack at night.<<

Bethany Anne froze, switched to vampiric speed and started thinking through the contingencies and different challenges that needed her attention. She refused to miss the opportunity to take down Stephanie Lee herself.

I want John, Eric, Darrell and Scott with me. I'm going to grab Ashur as well. Tell Gabrielle to meet me in my suite and have ArchAngel notify the right people. We need our personal ships readied.

———

Gabrielle walked into Bethany Anne's suite less than ten seconds after Bethany Anne. Bethany Anne was already in her dressing room stripping and grabbing her black leather pants, Under Armour shirt and her chest armor. Gabrielle handed Bethany Anne her holsters and gave her the first pistol.

"What do you need me to do?" Gabrielle asked.

"I need you to be available in case Lance needs extra support, more than Akio can provide. Otherwise, hang loose. If I need you," she tapped her head. "I'll call you. So, you know... don't go to sleep, right?" She smiled at the older woman.

"I would tell you some metaphysical bullshit about revenge not solving your problems. But I've lived long enough to realize sometimes, revenge feels wonderful and allows for better sleep."

Bethany Anne slid her pistols into the holsters after checking the magazines, making sure they were loaded with silver. A knock interrupted them. "Your sword, my queen?" a male voice called out.

"In here, Kenshin," Bethany Anne said. As Kenshin came around the corner he stopped. Bowing, he held out the sword. Bowing back, Bethany Anne reached out with her right hand and took it. "Your queen requests and needs the sword to close an open chapter of punishment. When I am finished, I will expect my Elite to protect the sword again." Kenshin bowed lower, then straightened up and left.

Gabrielle said as she watched the Elite leave the suite, "You know, the fact that they don't talk is just a little eerie."

"They talk, you have to get to know them. Kenshin," she nodded in the direction he went. "Is not only named after a well-known samurai, but he also was the renowned samurai. He prefers not to speak of that time. He went into a coma due to stomach cancer, and a vampire who held much respect for him took him in the night. Therefore, there are two stories about his death. In one, he was assassinated by a ninja and in the other, the more accurate one, he died of stomach cancer."

"How do you know this?" Gabriel asked, "I thought they were very particular about their past history."

"They can be, but when the Queen asks?" Bethany Anne

passed Gabrielle as she stepped out of the closet leaving the rest of the sentence unsaid.

Ashur jogged into the suite. "Did you get fed?" Ashur chuffed. "Good, you don't need to be eating anything you bite tonight."

Ashur followed Bethany Anne. "Gabrielle, you have the ship. Any questions you aren't sure about the answer to, ask Stephen." Bethany Anne grabbed Ashur, and the two of them disappeared.

"ArchAngel?" Gabrielle called out.

"Yes, Gabrielle?" Archangel replied from the speakers.

"Bethany Anne has left me in charge, any and all requests to her now should be routed through me until she is back on the ship." Gabrielle walked out of the suite.

"Yes ma'am, you are in command until Bethany Anne arrives back on the ship."

CHAPTER EIGHTEEN

QBS ARCHANGEL

Bethany Anne had checked the load out on her Black Eagle, making sure she and her team had plenty of Pucks, including a pair of new ten-pounders.

Ashur had jumped into the back without any help and chuffed to her as she walked around the plane. "We are leaving, you impatient god of war." Ashur barked, and she laughed. "Yeah, I should never have told you the meaning of your name."

She looked around and saw her guys were closing their canopies except for John, who was watching her. She winked at him and jumped up and over to land in her seat. John smiled and shook his head as his canopy closed.

She jumped on the comm. "This is Black Eagle One to ArchAngel, permission to leave?"

"This is ArchAngel, Black Eagle One. I have modified the shield, you are clear to leave." Jeffrey's people had finally figured out how to adjust the gravity to allow ships to make their way out through the shield without sucking the atmosphere out of the bay. The Pods had to leave slowly, no more than five miles an hour right now, but it beat the hell out of how they had to deal with it previously.

She told him that was nice... now, when could she punch it? Jeffrey smiled, shook his head and walked away.

Five ships left the ArchAngel and turned down towards the beautiful blue globe.

>>**China has moved up their time frame.**<<

SHIT! How much time do we have?

>>**Their ETA is twenty-six minutes.**<<

"Boys, punch it! China kicked off their party early. The impatient bastards are trying to take away my retribution."

"Sure we can't let them take some hits first? That shit could be funny as hell." Scott asked.

Bethany Anne shook her head. "Not taking the chance, Scott. However, there is no need for us to hit anyone who isn't in our way. I want Stephanie Lee, and we need to confirm if there are any Kurtherians or Kurtherian artifacts. All we need is China getting hold of the technology."

"That would suck massive monkey nuts," Darryl said.

The team entered the atmosphere at the top of Australia, angled north by northwest. Those in northern Australia, Indonesia, Malaysia, southern Vietnam, Cambodia, Thailand, Laos and southern China were all witness to five meteorites streaking across the sky. Shortly, there was video footage all over the internet.

>>**Two minutes to arrival. You will have twelve minutes without any interference.**<<

Understood, ADAM.

>>**Incoming. Gabrielle is passing along information.**

Space Station One is under attack and ArchAngel has broken orbit and is outbound to support. Their ETA is nine minutes. One of Dan's contacts is under imminent attack in Syria and has requested support.<<

Bethany Anne grimaced, DAMMIT! So close. She was about to call out the command to head towards Syria when her father came over her speaker. "Bethany Anne, Akio and a group of Guardians and I are heading to Syria, ETA is really, really soon. We got this, stay the course."

Bethany Anne's eyes teared, but she grimaced, stopping it. "Understood, but if the COO gets hurt, I'm not protecting him from his wife."

"Ha! Got that covered. Permission already granted."

Bethany Anne's mouth stayed open. "Seriously?"

"Do you need me to get her in on the call?" Lance asked.

"No, it's just…" Bethany Anne was at a loss for words.

"Hey, she knows what she married. She no more wants to change that than I want to change her. Plus, I figure she thinks Akio and the Guardians are with me, so what the hell am I going to do?" Bethany Anne heard catcalls and hell yeahs in the background.

>>Bethany Anne, the President is calling.<<

Gott Verdammt, when it rained it poured.

"Got to go, Dad, President's on the other line."

"Lance out."

"This is Bethany Anne."

"I'm sorry to bug you, Bethany Anne, but I have an embarrassing favor to ask."

"Shoot, but you have forty-five seconds before I have to clear the line."

"Okay, I'm told I have twenty-three people in a firefight in Syria, and we can't get anyone there to help quickly enough.

Could I possibly request support?"

"Yes, we're handling it, I'll let you know what happened in an hour." Bethany Anne could see the mountains they were heading for. "Anything else?"

"Uh, how fast can they be there?" the President asked.

"Fast. Ten minutes or less." She told him. "Sorry, have to go."

The President heard the line click off.

Dammit, he didn't get to inquire if the strange meteorites streaming across Asia was something she was doing or not.

He picked up the phone from his desk. "Yes, they're sending someone. ETA? Ten minutes or less. Good luck."

He set the phone in its cradle. God, he wished he had her resources.

———

ADAM, tell my dad they have officially been asked to help by the President of the United States. See if you can route a message to Dan's contact if he hasn't divulged his connection to us yet and make sure the box isn't used unless needed.

———

SPACE STATION ONE, L2

Coach grabbed a quarterstaff. He wasn't any good with bladed weapons and the idea of using something like a long bat appealed to his sense of mayhem. The team already thought about and disregarded the riot weapons they had on station. No one thought the beanbag guns would be of any use. If the attackers could get hurt using them, well then they would grab them then.

He turned and made his way through another group of Wechselbalg who were busy moving in and out of the room. Coach had just entered the hallway when life went upside down.

"We have boarders in sections 12-4, 12-5, 30-2 and 30-3," Coach could hear Penn over the loudspeakers. He heard the suction of vacuum pulling air out of the hole for a second, alarms blasting up and down the hallway when the hole was sealed.

Coach put on his helmet and locked it in, moving forward. He hit the button to allow his voice to be heard outside of his suit. He noticed Adarsh had also put on his helmet and maybe a third of the Wechselbalg had gone back behind them to get into suits. They would suit up first then allow those risking asphyxiation right now a chance to get a suit.

If they had time.

The nose of the craft that had rammed them dropped, clanging in the container and then one of the aliens dropped in.

"Move out of my Gott Verdammt way!" Coach yelled, his speakers enhancing his voice. He jogged the fifteen feet to reach the alien yelling as he swung, "Batter up!"

———

Penn was talking to the E.I., "Give me ArchAngel direct!"

"This is Gabrielle. I received the update from SS1, and we are moving to break orbit. ETA ten minutes, Penn."

"Gabrielle, we've been holed in four places. Aliens have sealed the holes at this time. Forty-five percent of our personnel have reached protected containers, and we should hit eighty-percent in… one minute fifteen. We have eyes on ten enemies so far. Pictures will follow as well and video will be streamed live."

"Penn, you guys better hold for ten Gott Verdammt minutes, or I will kick all of your asses."

Penn barked a laugh. "I understand Bethany Anne is on another mission, so are you trying on your Bethany Anne speech?"

"Hell no! This is my Gabrielle speech. You know shit goes downhill, so if you guys go down when I am in command, Bethany Anne is going to kick my ass, and I'll be there to kick yours."

"Understood, Gabrielle. But since I might not have a chance to say this in ten minutes, you aren't mean enough to pull off Bethany Anne." Penn looked to the side. "Got to go, ArchAngel, we have two unfriendlies trying to get in our external airlocks."

"Kick ass, Space Station One. That is an order from the Queen Bitch herself," Gabrielle told him.

Penn looked back to the video camera. "Understood ArchAngel, I'll relay that personally."

Penn cut the connection.

———

SYRIA

Terry opened his eyes when he heard the crunch of gravel. He was wide awake when Robert came around the boulder where he was hiding out, listening in the night. "Terry, the government wag says they'll be here in an hour."

"What, he's finally accepting the fact that we have visitors?"

"Yes, and as you might imagine, he is not too happy with the fact that we have no backup."

"Do you want me to tell him I told you so? You know I already have a bad reputation for running at the mouth." Terry stood up and dusted his pants off.

"No, let's try to make this a new and improved Terry, shall we?"

Terry followed Robert as they walked toward the government wag's tent. "Is this where I make a joke about 'how I chose a bad time to give up liquor, cussing, and mouthing off?'" They shared a laugh before stepping into the tent.

Two minutes later, Robert and Terry left the tent heading toward the rest of the team. Robert went to his people to get them helping everybody get up and moving them into the pits. Terry went towards Melissa, looking forward to seeing her while she still might have some respect for him.

It was possibly stupid, Terry thought, but at the moment he was proudest that he remembered to buy her Chips Ahoy before they went on this operation.

Melissa woke up to the gentle pushing on her arm. "What is it and why can't I go get the ice cream?" she mumbled.

"Probably because the nearest freezer is hundreds of kilometers in God only knows what direction. And I doubt you'd like the flavor anyway." Terry said.

Melissa's eyes opened, she wasn't expecting a man's voice in her dream. She focused on Terry looking down at her and caught the concern. "What is it?"

"Remember all of my worries about the government leaving us out here high and dry?" She nodded, quickly understanding his thought process. "Well, I need you to make sure you have everything you need and get down into the pit. Don't forget water, anything that you can grab, definitely any lights and communication devices. Should you need to drop the opening, someone might be able to dig you out."

Melissa scrambled out of her sleeping bag, not worrying that she was in what amounted to a bikini. She started getting her clothes on. "Aren't you going to be with us?"

"No, I need to be upstairs with the guys trying to stop them from getting to you. If we can do that, then you won't have to worry about suffocating."

She looked over at him as she buttoned her shorts. "You really don't have a good bedside manner. You know that, right?"

Terry smiled. "I can always blow smoke up your ass if you would prefer, Melissa. But just remember that I did bring you Chips Ahoy, that should be worth something."

Melissa turned around. "Shit, where is it?" She dropped to her knees and reached under her sleeping bag to pull out half a bag of Chips Ahoy. "Damn, if I had known I might have to deal with this crap this morning, I might have decided to eat them all. Oh well. Now at least I'll be able to console myself with chocolate." She turned around and handed him the cookies. "Hold this please, and if you want to keep your privates, don't you eat one of them." She stood up and grabbed her pistol, slotting it into a holster. She grabbed a bag full of clothes and other items, then her laptop, tossing it into the bag and zipping it up. She reached for the bag of cookies, which Terry handed her, and walked out of her tent. He followed her into the night.

She turned around. "TH?"

"Yes?" he replied, stopping before he continued in the other direction.

"Be safe, okay?"

Terry put two fingers to his forehead and saluted her with

a smile. Then he walked off toward Robert. Melissa, watching him go, wondered if she would ever see him alive again. She turned and headed toward the excavation. She knew what she was good at, and knew what she was not.

She wasn't stupid enough to try to be on the front lines. But if any assholes were dumb enough to stick their heads within thirty feet of her, she damn well would do her best to give them a splitting headache. She pulled one bullet out of the magazine and slipped it into her pocket.

No one was taking her alive.

––––––

TQB BASE, AUSTRALIA

Lance chewed on his cigar and thought about the three operations now in play. He couldn't help the ArchAngel as he couldn't catch up if he wanted to, plus ADAM's computer team didn't need to be placed in harm's way.

It wasn't appropriate.

He stabbed his intercom. "Patricia?"

"Yes, dear?" Her voice came back immediately.

"I have a favor to ask." A handful of years ago, this would never have occurred to him. But now his future was tied. He couldn't take risks on a whim, or an urge.

"Yes?" Her voice was clear, crisp and efficient.

"I want to go with Akio and the ten Wechselbalg," he told her.

"Understood, I'll take care of the base with ADAM and the team. Go kick some ass, sweetheart."

Lance looked down at the speakerphone, not sure what to say.

"Go," she said. "I can imagine you looking at the phone, not believing your ears. If you think for two seconds I didn't know I married a military man through and through, you aren't crediting me with enough common sense. I married all of you, even this part. I got your back, Lance."

He pressed the button, this time gently. "And I've got yours, Patricia. Take care of ADAM's team, okay?"

"Hell yes, I will. I've got ADAM talking with me, we got this. You take care of Dan's contact. Gabrielle has the Space Station, and Bethany Anne will be fine. Hell, when is she not?" Lance heard a little pride in Patricia's voice as she laughed, "Go kick some ass for me, promise?"

"Baby, I'll kick it all the way to hell and back out the other side, just tell me when, all right?"

"I'll remember that, Lance Reynolds. I'll have a long time to cash in that marker. Go."

"Gone." Lance released the button for the last time and started unbuttoning his shirt. *Damn*, he thought. Then he ripped it open and stripped it off as he left his office, double-timing it down the hall.

His eyes grew darker and those that witnessed their base commander as he talked into his comm unit, telling people what to do as he made his way to the armory stood clear. Most had heard of his legendary anger and played it off as overblown.

They had never witnessed Lance Reynolds truly pissed.

Now, he seemed beyond pissed. He seemed deadly, and some now understood where their infamous Queen inherited her *don't fuck with me* face.

Like father, like daughter.

Someone was getting fucked up, was the consensus as Lance passed them in the halls.

Five minutes later, Lance Reynolds jumped on the transport as it started to lift, with Akio and ten Wechselbalg. The Japanese vampire nodded to the base commander as he grabbed his arm and pulled him in. Two Wechselbalg closed the doors.

The teams had modified some of the gravitic cargo containers. With Jeffrey's assistance, they changed the engines and put an extra one on the front to adjust the airstream around them. There were fifteen seats along both sides of the containers with five-point belt harnesses. Lance sat on one end, Akio sat next to him. Both locked in.

Hold on Terry, Lance thought. *Death is coming for a visit.*

CHAPTER NINETEEN

SYRIA

Terry felt a buzzing in his pocket. He pulled out the phone and looked at it, surprised. He had received a text.

HELP INCOMING - SIX MINUTES - PRESIDENT OF U.S. HAS REQUESTED ASSISTANCE. LEAVE CONTAINER CLOSED IF POSSIBLE.

Terry slipped the phone back in his pocket, his smile turning satisfied, his worries abating.

"News?" Robert asked. Terry was off to one side by himself and he noticed Robert's men, the six nearest them, were looking at him.

"Yeah," Terry said, looking up into the early morning darkness. "We're going to have visitors, the good kind. From what I know about them, for fuck's sake don't have a friendly fire incident. They won't appreciate that shit at all. We have to hold for," he looked down at his watch. "Five more minutes and then we probably need to pull back into the pit ourselves."

"What the hell is coming, an AC-130 Spectre?"

"No, probably better… well, let's call it more unique." Terry said. "The President has called in a favor for us." He grimaced. "Sorry, I probably shouldn't have let that slip, guys." Terry looked at those nearest him. "Can you guys do me a solid and not mention that part about the President? I don't know if this is for public consumption. If anyone has questions, point at me until we get the word you can say that, okay? I've got the reputation."

He got seven nods. When he looked at Robert, he surreptitiously winked at him. Terry smiled and looked away. It felt good to be a part of the team again. He had missed it over the years. Now that his assholious was diminishing, his ability to think clearly was getting better.

Robert asked, "Five?"

Terry nodded. "Yeah, count on it."

Robert issued orders. Everyone pulled in and put up as much rock around them as they could, being careful to try and minimize ricochet concerns.

Then, the seconds started counting down.

———

Hamza bent over, moving to the top of the small outcropping, tapping Yasin on his shoulder. Yasin looked over and then looked back when he realized it was his friend.

Hamza spoke in a soft voice, "The dogs were notified, their camp is too empty."

Yasin looked up to the sky. "That is acceptable. As long as they do not have the drones, then the ending is just drawn out. They have no air support. They can't hide from our bullets for long. Besides, you wanted a chance to stay here tonight.

"Yes I did," Hamza agreed. "I see tents and other soft materials down there. I imagine I can grab something that will make the trip back not hurt so much."

They settled in until they heard the first crack that signaled they could start their own attacks.

"AiAiAiAiAieeeee!" Hamza yelled and stroked the trigger of his AK-47. Maybe he would get lucky and get a head shot and be able to enjoy the memory of an American head exploding from his bullet. If not, no worries. He would shoot their bodies later.

Right after they took care of the women.

———

"Well, fuck!" Terry heard someone bitch when the bullets started raining. He looked down at his watch. Why couldn't they wait another forty-five seconds? Camel ass-licking zealot psychopaths were absolutely off his list for Christmas party invitations.

"Forty-five seconds," Robert called out from Terry's left. "Don't let them hit your ass or I'm going to shoot you as well. I want every one of you useless Godforsaken, mullet wearing pansies walking out of here... Light 'em up, people!"

———

Melissa heard the crack of the first shots, the smell of fear was rife inside the cave. It was hot, it was stinky and now she heard someone behind her start crying. She wasn't sure why she had told other people to keep going deeper in the cave when they had the ladies come down first.

Now she was near the front.

Melissa reached into her pocket and pulled the round out, she pursed her lips, her eyes narrowing. Fuck it. She dropped the magazine on her Glock and put it back after placing the last round back in the mag. If she had to kill every one of those fuckers by hand, then she would try to do that.

She wasn't taking a coward's way out.

———

Lance was looking at his tablet, seeing the feed from beneath them. "ADAM, drop us here after the pucks strike." He marked his tablet. He felt the container descend as he slid the small tablet into a pocket.

"Okay, listen up," he called out. "We're dropping behind them. You need to mop them up as fast as possible when I give the word. I will give you that command after we hit them with a couple of pucks to blow sand and dirt up in the air to confuse the hell out of them. Make damn sure you kill the right people."

Akio unclipped and walked to a four-foot tall metal box welded to the wall. He took the cotter pin off the latch and opened the door. He looked at Lance who put up one finger. Akio grabbed two one pound pucks and closed the door.

Lance nodded to the two Guardians across from him. "Open the right door."

The guy on the left, Jim, unclipped and reached to unhook the door. His partner unclipped and grabbed Jim's arm and reached behind to catch the bar above the seats for those who needed to hold on to something when things got bumpy.

Jim opened the door, leaning out just a little as Akio

walked over and tossed the two pucks out. Jim closed it, and Lance called out, "Send them down, ADAM."

Three seconds later, everyone heard two loud 'whooomps.'

"Take us down all the way, ADAM."

Lance looked around, he saw ten Guardians smiling in anticipation. Lance chuckled, Bethany Anne had a way of attracting some damned aggressive people to her team.

And... he was having a blast himself.

———

"What the fuck was that?" Two loud whoomps came from behind the ridge where their attackers, who had them pinned down, were firing.

"That would be the help arriving for our little party, I think," Terry called over to Robert.

Robert nodded. "Shut it down guys, don't fire unless you know damn sure you got an *IMF* in your sights, got it?"

Robert counted his 'yes sirs!' and nodded. He had the right number.

———

Melissa felt, more than heard, two loud crumps before some dust dropped from the ceiling. SHIT! Now she was worried about a cave-in. She might not have to worry about torture killing her if she got buried alive first.

That damn Terry, when she got out of here, she was going to give him a piece of her mind.

Right after she kissed him.

———

Yasin ducked in reflex when the ground shook beneath him. A second hit and he was tossed from an area between two boulders to the sand below, scraping his knuckles and knees pretty badly.

"What is going on?" Hamza called out, as they both heard men choking as the dust and dirt from the explosions filled the air. Yasin and Hamza quickly grabbed their shirts and covered their noses and mouths.

Yasin looked around, trying to figure out where the next attack might come from. He didn't hear a plane and there were no more explosions.

The two of them stood back to back, Hamza looking towards the Americans and Yasin looking behind them.

Because Yasin was looking behind them, he was the only one who saw the man with the red eyes suddenly appear in front of him, stabbing Yasin through his chest.

From behind, Hamza felt incredible pain, he looked down to see six inches of a sword sticking out of his chest. He coughed, blood coming out of his mouth, and called out weakly, "Yasin?" The sword slowly pulled out of Hamza's chest and he felt Yasin's body slide down his own back as his eyes closed, forever.

———

Akio pulled the sword out of the two men in front of him. He heard another three to his left, but Guardians were coming up that side, and he figured they would take care of them. He turned to his right. There was one coughing about fifteen feet up.

He stepped on a rock and jumped, sliding through the air, coming down and slicing the man's arm off. The gun, and his now useless hand, dropped in between two boulders. Akio sliced through the wounded man's stomach, causing him to continue his shriek of pain.

It helped create more confusion.

He smiled. This is what his Queen would want, and he was very focused on accomplishing what she willed.

Akio heard a voice in his ear, "Now Akio."

Akio paused and focused. The red in his eyes flashed and then he could feel the power leave him.

———

The shrieks of pain filled the early morning dawn. Sand and dirt had pelted Robert and his men.

Then the fear hit. Not any fear, but a miasma of emotion that had Robert fighting the urge to run. He looked over at Terry, who was in the same battle himself. "What the hell, man?"

Terry looked back at his friend. "Hell indeed! Tell everyone not to fucking fire because sure as shit that will NOT go over well."

Robert screamed both directions that everyone put their weapons down and fight the urge to run. He turned back to Terry. "Fucking give it to me straight. Who the hell is over there?"

Terry just shook his head. Some things, he'd learned, you had to keep to yourself.

———

Two people in the back of the cave shrieked and started pushing on those in front, yelling at them to get out of their way, they needed to get out of the cave. One of the wags had turned around and was pushing back, trying to go deeper into the cave.

Melissa crawled out of the cave and rolled to the side of the opening. She curled up into a fetal position and screamed.

———

"Release, Akio."

Akio's eyes dimmed, leaving only a small amount of red in them. He had heard a few pistol cracks as he focused on pushing the fear over as large an area as he could. He felt drained but good.

The dust was clearing, and he saw men walking through the dimness of the still dusty dawn light.

They were all Guardians.

He turned to his left and flicked his sword, giving mercy.

The man's screaming stopped.

In a minute, there were no more moans or crying on the small hill.

Akio turned as he heard another man come up the hill and approach him. Lance held out his hand, and Akio took it.

"Damned fine job, Akio. Damned fine job." He looked around and then called out, "Guardians, clean up! I'll be back in a minute." Lance nodded for Akio to follow him. Akio cleaned his sword and put it away in his scabbard, carrying the scabbard in his left hand for easy access. Akio carefully watched for anyone who might offer the Queen's father any violence.

———

WE HAVE CONTACT

"FUUUCCCCKK ME!" Robert called out right after the fear miraculously ceased. He heard more than one man collapse to the ground around him.

When he got his wits back, Robert listened but heard nothing from over the hill. He doubted there was anyone over there alive, except the good guys.

"Robert!" Terry hissed to his friend, Robert turned and saw Terry pointing. He turned back to see two men coming around the side of the hill. Neither had a weapon out, although one was...

"Is that a fucking sword?" came from Robert's left.

"Can it, people!" Robert commanded and stood up. He nodded for Terry to join him as he stepped out from his firing position. He looked down at his rifle and decided to leave it. Terry joined him, unarmed as well, and they started walking towards the two coming down the hill.

"Give me a hint, buddy," Robert whispered. "Tell me two syllables or fucking something!"

Terry leaned in. "TQB."

Robert closed his eyes for a second and rolled his eyes behind his closed eyelids... Of course, it would be fucking TQB because the man upstairs had an *outstanding* sense of humor.

"Didn't you say the President called this in?" Robert asked, trying to figure out what the hell was going on.

"Yup."

"That all you got?" Robert asked.

Terry fished his phone out of his pocket, stuck a finger over part of the screen and showed Robert the text.

HELP INCOMING - SIX MINUTES - PRESIDENT OF U.S. HAS REQUESTED ASSISTANCE.

Fuck! Robert looked to his friend who nodded his head minutely. Ace in the hole indeed.

Seconds later, Robert held out his hand as the two men joined them. "Sir, Robert Martelle, security."

The American-looking man held out his hand. "Retired General Lance Reynolds. Previously US Army. Damn fine job you did keeping your cool."

Robert shook the man's hand and couldn't stop his mind from thinking.

Wasn't TQB's COO named Lance Reynolds?

Terry watched the man behind the General and noticed his eyes constantly flicking around, taking everything in. He was dressed in Japanese style clothes. They looked like a cross between something a samurai or a ninja might wear mixed with today's latest sandpit fashions. His right arm had a patch sporting a white, fanged skull on a red background.

He rocked that outfit, Terry thought.

He had blood spatter on him, so he was using the sword over there for more than just show. Terry's eyes drifted back to the patch, trying to remember where he had seen it before.

Oh… shit. Now he remembered. It was sported by those who protected the head of TQB. Terry decided to take his own advice and make sure he minded his Ps and Qs.

Terry heard some spluttering going on behind him, so he turned around and saw Robert's men helping people out of the pit. The government wag was walking in this direction, and he saw Melissa being helped up a ladder.

Terry turned to the two men talking. "Excuse me, I've got to check on someone, and you guys have incoming."

Robert turned around to see the government guy heading in their direction. Terry patted Robert's back in sympathy as he stepped back toward the pit. Sucked being the leader sometimes, but right now he wasn't needed.

Damn shame, that.

Terry wasn't out of earshot when he heard the government guy start off, "What were you thinking when you dropped bombs right above our heads?"

Awww man, if Terry didn't need to check on Melissa, he would have liked to hear the General's response to this prick.

Melissa, however, did have his attention and she was heading in his direction. She made it within ten feet before he asked, "You come out okay?"

She nodded mutely, and his face clouded up with worry, he started looking for injuries. When he got to her, he wasn't looking at her face. She grabbed his in both hands and turned it to look at her. She searched his eyes and then stood on her tiptoes and kissed him.

She dropped back down, and told his shocked-looking face, "I'm still undecided on whether to slap you. So, don't push it."

"What the hell did I do that deserved being slapped?" he asked, still working out the sum of her words, her tone, and her actions. The math just wasn't calculating out for him.

"You could have been shot!" she said as if that settled the conversation.

He leaned in. "You could have suffocated!"

She jerked away from him. "Don't be logical, I was hidden, you were out here."

"No," he pointed behind her, to a hide with rocks pulled around it. "I was hiding in there, harder to hit me. I wasn't doing jumping jacks with a target on my ass for them to try and hit."

"Still, I couldn't see you!" She glared at him to refute her comment.

"Neither could they!" He pointed behind him. She looked and realized how close the enemy had been.

She leaned towards him and hissed, "Do you have any idea how much you confuse me?"

Terry leaned back, puzzled. "Confuse you? I'm a pretty simple guy, here. Give me a clue what is confusing with this package," he pointed up and down his body, "why don't you?"

She took a step forward, crowding his personal space. Her finger stabbed him with every comment.

Stab.

"You are smart."

Stab.

"You are good looking."

Stab.

"You are military!"

This time, her finger barely poked him, and her eyes teared up. Her head dropped to his chest. "And I like you."

Terry hesitated, then put his arms around her. "What's wrong with that?"

She shook her head against his chest. "I don't like military men! They're dumb, they're ugly, they like to shoot people and blow things up and… and… and they're full of assholious!" she cried out and croaked out a laugh and a sob at the same time. "God, what am I going to do? I just dropped out my heart like that, and I have no idea if you even like me or not!"

"Damn, for an intellectual, you can be pretty dense at times," Terry said. Before she could parse his words and decide that mad was the right response, he added, "How many men carry a present of chocolate chip cookies halfway around the world so he could surprise a woman he doesn't care about?"

Melissa pulled back and looked up at him. "You do care about me?"

Terry wanted to beat his head against a rock. "Yes, Melissa, I care about you. I worried about you. I'm not about to let some irrationally irritated Islamic idiots shoot up the first woman I can have a conversation with that didn't start with 'Today Kim Kardashian' or end with 'I know, right?'"

She sniffed and wiped the tears from her cheeks. Her eyes were large and beautiful. "You know I'm going to slap you, right?"

"What?"

The four men heard a sudden loud *crack*. Robert turned to see the lady academic putting a hell of a lip lock on Terry, who didn't seem to be trying to struggle out of it at all. He shrugged and returned to the conversation at hand.

The government wag, who had started his bitching finally wound down his tirade. "Well?" he demanded from Lance.

"Well, what?" General Reynolds replied. "Well, do I give a shit about anything you just said? Not one bit. I'm not in your chain of command and as far as I care, you are an adult. I've been tasked with making sure those idiots," he jerked a thumb over his shoulder. "Didn't shoot your asses. Mission accomplished. We're taking anyone who would like to leave out of here. You're welcome to grab some equipment, but there are twelve of us, twenty-three of you, right?" Robert nodded. "And one more container available for stuff. We have thirty seats we can lock people in. So, we're short five places. If you want to stay here, we'll be short one less."

The General looked around. "We're lifting in thirty minutes." He turned and started walking back towards the hill. Robert saw the government wag begin to reach out to grab the General's shoulder when the silent guard stepped forward, grabbing the outstretched hand and twisting it. Before you could say 'ouch,' the government guy was on his knees, and the General turned to look at the wag.

"Akio, don't stain your sword with his bureaucratic blood, that shit doesn't come out." The General turned and started walking away, but called out over his shoulder, "I'll have a Guardian shoot him, that way the blood doesn't stain anything."

Akio let go of the man, who was staring, mouth open, at the General's back as he walked away.

Robert looked down at the wag. "Don't say one word. He doesn't work for the United States. The President ASKED for their help. If he comes home with twenty-two people instead of twenty-three? Well," Robert looked back up at the two men receding, "that's twenty-two more than the President could have reasonably hoped to have after your monumental fuckup." Robert turned, leaving the man kneeling in the dirt.

Robert noticed that Terry had a slap mark on his face and smiled. He called out to everyone in hearing range, "Twenty-five minutes people! The bus is leaving in twenty-five minutes. If you aren't ready, you're walking. Let's go!"

CHAPTER TWENTY

OVER THE CLAN TEMPLE
NEAR SHENNONGJIA PEAK, HUBEI

The mountains, not as tall as she would have expected, were beautiful. Well, what she could see of them. China was a gorgeous country. Shame it had some real asshats running it.

Although she had to admit, China really didn't corner the market on asshats in government.

ADAM's voice came over the team's comms, "We are twenty seconds from landing, do you have a preference where to set down?"

"Not at the bottom, where we have to fight our way up is my preference," Scott quipped. "I've seen the movies. They'll just empty the damn school and hundreds of really pissed off, splendid martial arts fanatics will come running out, and it's going to suck. No thanks."

"Pussy," Darryl shot back.

"My dark-brother from another mother just volunteered

to go first. I saw Black Dynamite and Black Samurai, I know it's in your blood somewhere, Darryl." Scott retorted.

Darryl came back. "Hey now, let's not be losing the feeling of 'all for one and one for all' before we even start."

Bethany Anne let the laughter die down. "ADAM, TOM, set us down over there at the main door. Guys, we'll need to run through the place pretty hard. This is a quick in and out. Figure out if there is something here we need, kill the bitch and split before we get stuck with the military." Bethany Anne paused and then continued, "Not necessarily in that order."

The five Black Eagles dropped to within twenty feet of a clear area near the temple entrance. She popped the hatch and looked over the side. "Ashur," He put his head forward, and Bethany Anne touched him. Then, she made a small roll to her left, and they disappeared. Twenty feet below, they reappeared a couple of feet above the ground.

"I've gotta learn that trick," John muttered as he and the guys all jumped the twenty feet.

"We've got company!" Darryl called out as he dodged an arrow that sliced the air where his head had been.

"Fuck." Bethany Anne said under her breath. She pulled a pistol as Ashur took off towards the temple. Spotting two guards hidden above the entrance, she shot them both. One was only a shoulder wound, so she used another bullet to the head to take him out.

Silver frangibles for everyone, this time.

The team ran into the entrance, wondering how long they would have before the party smashers would get there… oh wait, they were the party smashers.

————

WE HAVE CONTACT

Stephanie Lee looked around the table. "We have the first four boxes of parts out of the temple. The remaining twelve need to leave by other routes. Take one north, one east, and one west. If any are seized, no one can put the technology together. Hold the components on your Family's Honor. We will …"

Stephanie Lee heard two gunshots reverberating down the hall. She waved to the three Kings. "Go! Get your people and take the boxes to safety. I will come to you once we get through this fight with the military. Why they thought they could surprise us, I will never know."

The three men left the room, heading further inside the mountain.

That was not wise, trusting them with the components of our ship as you have.

Is there any way for them to put it back together?

Without us? Highly unlikely. Your species has insufficient intelligence. They would need to read Kurtherian to under-stand how to operate the machine. Enough random button pushing will only cause the machine to lock up for approxi-mately seventeen of your days.

Then shut up.

Her father following her, she swept out of the room. "Go see about those noises!" The two guards that had been stand-ing by the room's entrance left quickly.

Stephanie Lee, annoyed and impatient, was about to fol-low the two guards when her father spoke. "We should move to the main sanctuary as our operations command center."

Two more pistol shots, louder this time, echoed down the stone hallway. "Come, my Empress," her father turned to fol-low the hall to the sanctuary.

Stephanie Lee grimaced, but followed her father, her

robes billowing in the light of the oil lamps. More gunfire came from behind her, and she could hear the pre-arranged gongs of the temple bells from the western side of the complex announcing the arrival of the military.

If the military had just been engaged, where had the previous gunshots come from?

———

Bethany Anne, swords at her side, walked quickly and calmly down the hallway. Occasionally, she would hear one of the guys behind her make a quip and more rarely, a pistol shot.

Once only, she heard John use his Dukes Special. He had used it to shoot into a stone ceiling, showering those nearby with rock chips and allowing the team to pass through the intersection easily.

Then the gongs started going off.

"Well, that cuts it," John said. "I can hear submachine gun fire. I think our gate crashers have arrived."

"Fucking shit!" Bethany Anne said, irritation coloring her voice. "Where's a map when you need one?"

"I doubt they were thinking about the clueless walking the halls," Scott said, then she heard him shoot a round. "We might want to choose a direction, we're getting more unwanted visitors."

Bethany Anne, use Ashur's sense of smell, TOM said.

If I weren't busy, I'd say thank you.'

Bethany Anne looked around. "Ashur," a chuff was her response. "Seek out the path with a lot of scents, we need to find the main worship room."

———

WE HAVE CONTACT

Shun had barely landed in the marked off descent area when he heard the staccato gunfire erupt in the night.

So much for the element of surprise.

He saw Bai and Jian wrapping up their parachutes. Now, if he could find Zhu his team was golden. At least until they received their four scientists. Fortunately, it had become painfully evident, enough so that the higher ranking officers couldn't ignore the signs, that having four non-military personnel do a drop at night was tantamount to slitting their throats.

They would be arriving in twenty minutes by helicopter, provided the location was secured.

Zhu came up on his left, holding his QBZ-95. "Ready?"

"Yes, let's grab Bai and Jian and make sure we keep the LZ secured."

Together, the four men made their way to the outer markers of the LZ and looked at each other when the growls of cats filled the night.

Each of the men calmly ejected their magazines and reached around to their pack and pulled out special magazines, inserted them and cocked their rifles.

When the cries of astonishment and some of fear reached their ears, Shun grimaced but made a decision.

They would need to leave their post and help those up front.

———

Bethany Anne had to put her swords away and pull her pistols when John and Eric took the point. For the last five minutes, it had become a target rich environment as they walked down halls, backtracking once or twice and shooting anyone or anything that tried to slow them down.

They didn't shoot to kill, but they didn't worry about sloppy marksmanship either. If the person, cat, or otherwise tried to stop shots by putting their heads in the way? Well, shit happens.

As long as the people were incapacitated and her team was able to get by, they did. Bethany Anne wasn't here to kill everyone, she only had one person on her mind.

As they were crossing a hall, she smelled perfume. "Stop!" The four men kept their eyes focused on their areas, Bethany Anne holstered her pistols and pulled her swords, her eyes already increasing in intensity. "Ashur, follow the perfume!"

Ashur chuffed and took the lead.

———

"Shun, why is everyone getting behind us?" Bai called out as he shot twice, the cries of the tiger he hit puncturing the night. It didn't just get back up and seem to shake off Bai's shots, in fact, it acted like a tiger might and disappeared into the brush.

One other cat had started to attack again, noticeably slower after Shun and Jian had both shot it. Gunfire from others then rang through the night, decimating the creature.

Once you put enough rounds into them, they stayed down.

"I do believe they think we have magic bullets," Shun answered, looking for his next target.

"Do you have any idea what the officers are going to say about this?" Bai asked, then shot twice. He missed once and clipped something that snarled in the darkness.

"Probably going to demote us for leaving our posts," Jian countered.

"What, now you speak?" Zhu called out. "Next time, be a little more confident when you choose to speak!"

"Okay, I *know* they are going to demote us!" Jian answered with a chuckle.

Shun shook his head. He knew that macabre humor was the way of the battlefield, but Jian's answers might not be that far off. This landing had all the hallmarks of a poorly run operation, and they had just highlighted themselves as having had a clue and then implementing a better plan.

It was, he thought, *an excellent way to become the punching bag for frustrated officers.*

———

Bethany Anne could see the hallway opened into a much bigger, more brightly lit room ahead of them. Two more guards broke from the doorway into the room and started heading in her direction.

"Cover your ears, boss!" John called from behind her. Bethany Anne stopped and told Ashur to stay out of the way as she allowed John and Eric to pass her. Two steps ahead they both pulled their pistols and used head shots. She didn't need to tell them they were close to the end.

Now, there would be no quarter offered.

She started forward and stepped around the guys. "John, Eric, you made a mess."

Eric slotted a new mag as she walked by. "Do we have to clean it up?" he asked.

"No. Messes are the preferred result for tonight."

"I'm going to file that under stuff I wish my mother told me," Eric replied from behind her. At that point, a tiger Pricolici, probably about John's height, stepped into view and roared a challenge down the hall at them.

"BA?" John called from behind her.

She shook her head. "No shooting him, I need to warm up."

"Oh goody," Darryl commented. "Will you be having the tiger ribs or flank steak tonight, Scott?"

"That's… just disgusting," Scott answered.

The two guards had been dispatched with calm efficiency.

It was now up to him to protect his Clan's honor, and their future. He had sacrificed so much getting this far down the Clan's path, and his daughter was the chosen one. Something that he had wanted for his whole life had occurred.

Now, he must beat off these intruders and keep her safe. His Empress needed him.

He changed. His senses came alive in the Temple. He loved to be in his warrior form, the power, the scents, the feeling like the world became still as he glided through it was overwhelming.

It was intoxicating.

He smiled. "I willll proteecct youuu, Emprressss." He stepped into the doorway and spread his arms, roaring his challenge at the five humans and the white dog approaching.

The female in front smiled, her eyes glowed red and fangs appeared in her mouth and for once, his Pricolici form felt something he had never experienced in this form ever.

He felt fear.

He knew what he was looking at, and she was a thing of myth, of legends, of rumors at times.

She was a vampire.

He backed up. The hallway was not his preferred place to fight. It seemed she was going to accept his challenge, her two swords reflected the light.

He would need to be careful, to be smart.

She walked into the temple and looked around.

———

Bethany Anne saw Stephanie Lee sitting on a small throne and pointed at her with a sword. "I'll be getting to you in a moment." She looked and saw three other openings into the room.

Bitches take a door.

"I got this one," Scott called, staying in the doorway they had just come in. Ashur stayed with him.

"Left," Darryl said and put action to his words.

"Close right," Eric said, and John just went silently to the farther door on the right.

Bethany Anne stretched her neck left and right, as the tiger Pricolici looked at the guys, who had weapons drawn.

"Don't even think about it," Bethany Anne told him. "You couldn't change their sheets, much less beat them in a fight."

"Thennnn whhhyyyy arrreee youuu fightttinnngg meee?" it growled at her.

"Dude, you're just my warm up. Are you the main priest?" she asked him, walking to her left holding her swords ready.

"Yessss." He decided to ignore the men and watched the vampire.

"Then you are this piece of trash's father?"

"Shhhheee is thee EEmmmmppreessss!" He growled deeply, his eyes flaring in anger.

"She's a trumped up skank who had to come home to

hide with daddy when her plans all fell apart," Bethany Anne replied.

Stephanie Lee's eyes narrowed. She looked at the closest one of Bethany Anne's guards, the tall one on her left, but he was watching both her and the hallway.

Stephanie Lee could hear fighting from multiple directions.

"So, are you going to fight me, or stand there and look pretty?" Bethany Anne asked the Pricolici.

Then she took the initiative. She came in hard, slashing at him with her right sword. He dodged the first slash and jumped to his left when she came back around with the other sword. He kept on his feet, watching her sword work, looking for an opening. She seemed to stumble, changing styles, and he leaped.

He howled in pain when the first sword pierced his chest. She had played him, waiting for him to move. Her eyes, glowing red, matched the feral grin on her face. She batted his arms away with her other sword then reversed the blade and slit his throat.

———

Stephanie Lee watched as Bethany Anne lowered her sword, and her father slid down to fall to the ground. His eyes, seeking her out at the end, finally gave her the one thing she had desired her whole life.

Connection.

Stephanie Lee's lips pressed together as she regarded the arrogant woman staring at her, her lips turned up. "You peasant! You have no idea of the history, the time this Clan has worked to prepare the Earth to rise up!"

WE HAVE CONTACT

Bethany Anne casually cleaned her sword on the Were's chest, keeping an eye out for any movement from Stephanie Lee. "You speak as if I should give a shit, Stephanie." She waved her two swords around before setting herself and smiled. "The only thing I care about right now, is making damn sure you receive my full retribution for killing my love."

"Killing your love?" she barked, walking to her left around the temple and opening up the distance between them. There was still fighting inside the walls. "What do you know about love? What do you even care about love? The person you just killed was my father!" Her eyes flashed yellow in the dimness of the temple.

"I'll file that bit of knowledge under shit-I-don't-care-about." Bethany Anne's voice changed, became darker. "You are nothing but a spoiled shăbī that seeks power and prestige because daddy didn't love you," she hissed as she walked to her right, causing Stephanie Lee to change direction. "You couldn't rule a Girl Scout troop, much less the world, you trumped up soiled piece of trash."

She is trying to bait you!

She will cause you to make bad decisions. Get her swords away from her, they let her fight you from a distance.

Stephanie Lee curled her lips. "What would you know about leading? Hmm? You've been given everything, haven't you? Money, companies, even technology. You wouldn't have anyone's love if you weren't powerful, so don't stand there," she hissed. "You hypocritical *bitch* and tell me how well I can lead! At least I am willing to fight with what the gods gave ME!"

Bethany Anne cocked her head. "What, you mean these?" she held up the two swords. "This is what scares your pretty little pussycat head?" Bethany Anne spoke a little louder.

"John," she tossed her right-hand sword the thirty feet to John, who deftly caught it. "Darryl!" she threw her other to her left where Darryl caught it. Bethany Anne cocked her head. "So, what is your devious plan now that you have me without swords?"

"Well," Stephanie Lee smiled. "It reduces your reach and unlike my dear, departed father, I'm not so slow!" She started laughing as her hands morphed into razor sharp claws, each five inches in length. Everyone saw that her feet had grown claws as well.

"God, someone needs a serious pedicure," came from behind her. Bethany Anne snorted.

"Scott," she said conversationally while watching Stephanie Lee. "Don't make me laugh, please."

"Fine, but you have to admit, it was a hell of a line," he quipped.

Bethany Anne lifted her hand in the air and flipped him off.

Bethany Anne focused back on Stephanie Lee just as two shots rang out, and Eric said from his doorway, "Sorry, a couple of cats thought they might interrupt the reunion." Then another shot. "Wow, tough son of a bitches." Then another shot. "Fucking stay down! Don't you realize this shit is over five bucks a round?" Bethany Anne continued to watch Stephanie Lee as the antics were happening behind her.

"Hey, dickless," Darryl called out. "Try hitting them instead of winging them and it might work a little better."

"Look, have you ever," bang… bang… "tried to hit," Bang! "Cats running? Oh, fuck this!" Bethany Anne could feel the escalation of fear from Eric and then could visualize from the sounds when the first cat reached him, still dealing with the pain from the silver rounds Eric had pumped into it. The sickening sound of a body being ripped apart and then the plop of dead body parts dropped to the stone floor. "Hey! No running away... Damn you, I can't leave my post you son of a... Awww, dammit!" There was some shuffling behind her. 'Oh! Sorry, I didn't realize everyone was waiting for me. Do continue."

Stephanie Lee's voice was low, acidic. "You will scream for hours when I finish with your queen!" She glared at Eric who shot her the finger.

Stephanie Lee turned to Bethany Anne. "Your people are undisciplined, rude and immature!"

Bethany Anne smiled. "Just the way I like them. Come here and have a piece of me you jumped up fuck-brained syphilitic ass-ugly butt sucking pile of leftover dick tips!"

"You are the most banal of them all! That you have even touched the mind of one of the blessed race is a disgrace I shall rectify!"

"Oh God... did she say TOM is from a blessed race?" John cut in.

Stephanie Lee's furious gaze turned towards John who shrugged. "Oh, my bad! Yeah, I'll get behind Eric when it comes to the screaming part... I'll stand in line like a good undisciplined, rude and immature whatever-the-fuck you say in Chinese."

Eric added, "That's okay, I'll let you cut in front of me."

"Hey tit-less," Bethany Anne called Stephanie Lee's attention back to her. "You've really gone and fucked up." She started walking towards the Leopard Empress, the red of her eyes deepening, her face breaking out with red lines of Etheric energy, her fangs growing.

Stephanie Lee took a step back, "What... what are you?"

"Are you happy now? You retarded wayward glory hole

reject! You have the full attention of the Queen Bitch in the *flesh*. Claws?" Bethany Anne yelled. "You think CLAWS are the fucking answer?"

Bethany Anne stepped close enough for Stephanie Lee to leap towards her, slashing down to eviscerate the woman. Bethany Anne put her arm up to block, Stephanie Lee's arm was sliced off as it hit.

Her left arm, already swiping down, received the same result. Then pain screamed in her body as it tried to deal with two stumps.

I'm trying to shut the pain down! What did she just do?
There has to be a way out of this body! If she dies, WE die!
FIGHT YOU BITCH! The two Kurtherians screamed in Stephanie Lee's mind.

Stephanie Lee ignored the voices in her head as she stared numbly at her two bloody stumps, her body trying to heal enough to stop the bleeding.

Bethany Anne's face was smiling, her fangs fully extended. "I don't need any claws! I AM the Queen Bitch. And my love patiently, lovingly, taught me how to use the Etheric... you failed alien genetic experiment!"

Bethany Anne lifted her right hand, and Stephanie Lee watched as it changed, growing a copy of her own set of five-inch nails, razor sharp. The woman in front of her now looked like the goddess of death.

Her death.

A deep, malevolent voice spoke to her, "Stephanie Lee, you have been weighed, you have been measured, and you have been found ass-tastically inadequate and a fingerlicking trampy bollock fucker. I've been waiting for too damn long for this moment. Now *die* for your sins!"

Bethany Anne plunged her clawed hand into Stephanie

Lee's chest easily cutting through the ribs, and ripped out her heart.

Looking at her own heart beating in front of her, Stephanie Lee barely heard the faint screams from the aliens inside. She dropped to her knees, the temple swimming in her vision.

Bethany Anne stepped to the side and held up her hand. A second later, she caught the sword John tossed to her.

"Die, *Bitch*!"

The slice took but a second, the body falling in two pieces with wet sodden sounds. The head rolled across the floor, stopping when it bumped up against her father's dead body.

The end of a thousand years of planning the destruction of Earth's freedom joined together in death.

CHAPTER TWENTY-ONE

SPACE STATION ONE, L2

Kiel found he and his people in the middle of a fight. Fortunately, behind their armor and carapace exoskeleton, they weren't in mortal danger.

But it HAD become a rollicking good fight.

The aliens were about a head shorter than most of his people. Even so, there were some that were muscular and a few more that were extremely strong.

Abnormally strong.

"Kiel, bring me back a sample of one of the aliens with superior strength," Royleen's voice cut into his focus as he was slowly backing up under the onslaught of an alien with a full body-sized pole. These types of weapons had not been used in over fifteen of his generations, and twice his armor had saved him from exoskeleton cracking hits.

Kiel smiled savagely. THIS would be a story to talk about when they got back to Yoll.

"Easier said than done, Royleen!" Kiel spat back before taking his own offensive, "I can't implement full armor support, or I risk breaking these simple walls which might be a bad solution for yours truly. This alien is a demon of speed and has practiced with this... OUCH," he interrupted his conversation, "you soft-skinned slink bait!"

Kiel ignored the radio for a moment as he worked to attack. Finally, he was able to catch the damned stick in his grip and engage the servomotors on his armor. The alien was stupid enough to hold on, trying to keep his weapon. He bounced off of Kiel's armor and fell unconscious to the floor. Kiel looked up and saw two new figures.

"FEMALES!" Royleen yelled into his ear. "I want one of those, bring one, Kiel. They hold answers to the genetics for the species and will serve me very well for other research."

One of his team spoke over the comms, "Master Kiel, we have subjugated and captured a male of the species."

———

Coach was watching John fight the monster in front of him. It had two legs, but the legs were articulated wrong, like they were the back legs of a horse or some sort of large insect. John was trying to beat the crap out of it with the quarterstaff and Coach couldn't get a swing in.

"Dammit!" John yelled. "Stay fucking still you maggot spewing alien asshole!" He brought his quarterstaff around to block a grab and then shot out the end directly into the alien's chest. The metal tipped staff cracked on some sort of metal, but the suit he was wearing looked more like a plastic derivative to him.

Unfortunately, it didn't crack easily like plastic.

Then, John found himself busy blocking the alien's on-slaught.

John could hear fighting going on all around him, but he could only focus on his own situation.

"Coach!" John yelled. "I'm going to open him up and go low, try to swing for the stands at the top when I…" John didn't get anything else out. The alien was successful in grabbing his staff, and John held on tight, trying to keep it. All the way till he was slammed into the alien's armored covered body and cracked his head on its chest. John bounced back down the hallway, and the lights grew dim.

Coach saw John go down right when he heard ReaLea behind him. "That's my friend, motherfucker!"

"Didn't I tell you not to come down here?" Coach spit out, trying to figure out the best solution.

"Didn't you know it was useless to stop an ex-cop from trying to help? What are you, a misogynist?"

"That's a really big word for calling me a dick!" Coach yelled back.

"Well, if the name fits… What is it doing?" ReaLea and Bree noticed the alien turn towards them.

"Shit!" Coach said. "It found what it wanted."

"What's that?" ReaLea asked.

"WOMEN!" Coach yelled, moving between ReaLea and Bree and the alien. "I'm not a fucking misogynist, I'm practical. You are a glorified research bug at the moment, so get the fuck out of here!"

ReaLea could see the guys trying to get between her, Bree and the alien who had another of his kind joining him.

"GO!" Coach yelled as he and Adarsh went after the alien together.

ReaLea was biting her tongue, but had to agree with

Coach, this time. She and Bree had quickly attracted the alien's attention when they arrived in his field of view.

Making a decision, she turned and grabbed Bree's arm. "Let's go!" They started running back down the hallway.

———

"They are getting away!" Royleen called out.

"Tell me something I am not aware of, Royleen." Kiel snapped as he blocked a simple stick attack by the bigger alien. The one on his right slashed down with a knife, the blade catching a softer part of his suit. Kiel whipped his servo arm out and hit that alien, sending it bouncing off of the walls.

Kiel started walking in the direction the females had gone when the tip of the stick was used to hit him in his helmet. It didn't break anything, but the loud crack was disconcerting.

Kiel looked down at the alien, anger coloring his eyes. "I've had enough!" Kiel kicked up the speed aspect. He would have to restrict his movements some, but now he was fighting faster.

———

Coach heard the two women's steps as they left the fight. He didn't doubt the two had courage, but there was no reason to leave the tasty chocolate out to entice the uninvited guests. He grinned, maybe this would change how tight their bodysuits were? Can't figure out who the females are if the suits hide the anatomical differences.

His batter-up effort didn't do a damned thing. Adarsh had just scored a good hit with his knife. Well, good if one assumed the alien's response pointed to his success. Adarsh was out of this fight. Coach saw John was getting up from behind the alien, his healing ability helping him and three others were now causing a problem for the other alien.

Using the opportunity Adarsh created, Coach turned his quarterstaff and jabbed it for all he was worth right at the shield over what he assumed was its face. The gold reflective coating scratched just a little.

But oh boy, he got the alien's attention!

"Come here and let's talk about this like civilized aliens… You fucking ground pounder!" Coach snarled.

———

John got his head turned in the right direction, which is to say eyes open and figuring out what was going on. He heard Coach yelling behind him and turned toward the back of the alien that had clocked him a good one. He could feel the blood along his scalp and in his hair.

The blood was going to suck to clean up.

———

"Penn, this is Gabrielle." Gabrielle had moved to Bethany Anne's chair on the Bridge of the ArchAngel. "We are taking two of our Pods and sending them out toward the unknown vessel. Do not try to override any programming."

"Yes, ma'am," Penn replied.

"What is your status?" she asked.

"Ma'am, we are fighting large bipedal creatures that are in armor. We don't have decent weaponry up here that we can use without possible decompression that can do anything to them in armor. So, we're fighting with sticks, basically. The aliens are also fighting with similar weapons. I don't know if that's because they worry about the walls getting holed, or we are just no challenge to them at the moment. All I can say is that the armored aliens are easily a match for our Wechselbalg with simple weapons."

"Understood. Hold on SS1—ArchAngel will be coming around the Moon and visible in two minutes."

"Kicking ass and taking names, ArchAngel, SS1 out."

———

Coach never saw the hand. He had turned when he saw John get up and start an attack from behind the alien he was trying to slow down. When he turned back, just that split second was enough to miss the alien's mechanical enhanced attack that cracked through his helmet, and hit his skull hard enough to crush it.

———

"Krghfth!" Kiel yanked his hand out of the alien's helmet, organic matter splattered all over his hand. "Alien brains! Disgusting."

He was about to continue up the hallway when he was pushed forward by a sudden weight on his back. "Kiel, you have an alien on your back," Malo hissed in laughter from behind him.

"No kidding, really? I hadn't noticed." Kiel replied.

———

"Captain!" Melorn called out. "We have an incoming vessel. Just arrived on sensors, sir," Melorn looked over at Captain T'chmon. "It is big."

"Big? Show me."

Melorn called up the specifications and shot them to the Captain's data grids. "What is this," he pointed to the information Melorn had provided. "Royleen? This is no ship we have seen before."

Royleen looked at the information. "That ship is pushed by advanced gravitics, Captain T'chmon. I can't be sure right this second, but that could be Kurtherian technology. Old, perhaps, but it is very possible."

"Sheaght!" Captain T'chmon slammed his arm down and hit the communication button. "Kiel, recall your team. Take what you can and pull back, we must leave and consider this new information. NOW!"

––––––

Kiel turned and pushed back into the wall, squashing the alien on his back. He was satisfied with the abrupt, loud and irritated chittering from the alien. "Bet that hurt, you bug." He was in the middle of upgrading his power again when the Captain called them back. He twisted quickly, throwing the alien off his back to land about three body lengths away and called over his team's comms, "This is Kiel, grab what you can, we are recalled back to the G'laxix Sphaea. I want this fast, I want this professional. Don't let the little aliens see any mistakes." He received a fair amount of the hissing laughter over the radios.

––––––

"Gott Verdammt praise the galactic overlords," Penn breathed out. "They're leaving."

"Sir!"

Penn stabbed a button. "This is Penn, go."

"Sir, this is Sergei of the Russian group, they took Ivan with them when they left."

Penn's lips compressed... "Dammit. Okay, I will notify ArchAngel, Penn out."

Another light came on, and Penn hit the receive button to hear, "Penn, this is John."

Penn responded, "Penn here."

"Penn, the aliens have bugged out. We lost one, we have one that needs medical attention and a few that need rest. We had two small leaks that have been patched temporarily, but need final repairs."

"Who did we lose, John?" Penn asked, wondering who he wouldn't see in the halls anymore.

"Adarsh is hurt and," John paused, his voice cracking. "We lost Coach, Penn."

Penn closed his eyes. "Understood, John. Keep the patches solid and get Adarsh to medical. Put Coach's body in stasis, we'll send him off right, John. Penn out." Penn released the button.

He looked around his office, at the little things he knew Coach had helped him get working, or jury-rigged to get working. He looked at the chair where he and Coach had talked, swapping stories of his time in the Navy and Penn's time in England.

He shook his head, then screamed as he slammed his hand on his desk, "FUUUCK!"

It took a moment for the sound of his slap to fade away. He rubbed his stinging hand, thankful the pain helped get his emotions together.

He would have to remember Coach later, he had a space station full of people that needed his attention and a report for ArchAngel.

———

QBS ARCHANGEL'S BRIDGE

"ArchAngel, this is Bethany Anne. Status?"

Gabrielle answered the call. "Bethany Anne, ArchAngel. The space station was attacked, one dead, multiple in ICU, many others need medical attention. We have one abducted by aliens."

"What do we have around that will stop them?" Bethany Anne asked.

"ArchAngel can't see them well at the moment. We have incoming information from SS1, and we have two empty Pods near them. They have Ivan, from the Russian group."

"Ram that ship with the Pods, Gabrielle, stop them, slow them down, something." Bethany Anne called back.

Her voice was as cold as ice, "We don't abandon our own, EVER."

———

"Kiel, are your people on board?" Captain T'chmon asked over the comm system.

"Sir, we are. The captured alien is being transferred to Scientist Royleen's lab."

"SIR!" Melorn cried out. "We have incoming!"

"What?" he asked, surprised. They knew where the other ship was and had plenty of time. They were, in fact, already leaving.

WE HAVE CONTACT

The G'laxix Sphaea shook violently twice, moments apart. Those on the bridge were tossed around. The lower comms specialist was thrown from her seat. Alarms sounded throughout the ship. Captain Kael-ven T'chmon called out, "Get me damage reports! B'chai get us out of here, then confirm all cloaking is sound. I want us away from that ship! Weapons, figure out how we just got hit!"

CHAPTER
TWENTY-TWO

Lance looked around the inside of the container and nodded. Two Guardians shut the doors, and it slowly rose up into the air, taking off into the morning light. A few of the scientists bitched something horrible, and the wag about had a heart attack when Lance told him all the computer equipment was going in the other container. Nothing would be 'floating around to hit someone upside their head.'

Unless, of course, the wag wanted to ride in the shipping container? Lance was turned down, pity that. The scientists and government people found their crying, whining, logical arguments and pleading crashed against the man and crumbled into dust. He was quite willing to let them stay in the desert with potential ISIS attacks arriving in just a few hours.

One man threw a tantrum, tossing his backpack of papers onto the sand and sitting down. Lance looked at him briefly, then ignored him. The man was surprised when no one from Lance's team helped him, talked with him or even tried to coax him into the container. When one of the Guardians was asked if they were going to help him, he just replied, "He's an adult. He is free to commit suicide by ISIS bullets or stupidity, whichever he chooses."

The man had come running up with two minutes to spare.

Akio, the General, Robert and Terry all stood. Lance locked down everyone in a seat. When one person was complaining about having to buckle in, the container suddenly shifted slightly down. None of the four men had much of an issue keeping their balance, but the recalcitrant guy started clicking his belts like they were oxygen and he was underwater.

Lance pulled his tablet out and looked at it. There was a message from ADAM.

WAS THAT HELPFUL?

Lance smirked and turned the tablet to Akio. If you paid attention, Akio's face had many expressions, you just had to look for them. His eyes widened just slightly, and his lips relaxed into what Lance would call a smile on any other man.

Lance texted back that it was and put the tablet up.

"Dad?" He heard Bethany Anne's voice in his ear.

"This is Lance, go Black Eagle One," he replied.

"Status?"

"Mission accomplished, pulling out twenty-three live ones."

"Excellent. The ArchAngel is helping SS1. We're going to have to figure out what Coach and Adarsh did to find the alien ship, which we have lost at the moment. Adarsh is unconscious but expected to wake within thirty minutes. Then, we're going to head to the gate. TOM believes this is going to upset their mission, and they are likely to try and leave. We are moving to the Moon right now."

"Understood. Where do you want me to deliver the packages?"

"Well, I can't stick them on ArchAngel which was my original plan. The Australian base is now empty, and the last few groups are waiting for the ArchAngel out at Moon Base One's location."

"Colorado?"

"No, that just gets them back into play too quickly. I suppose if I keep them, then it's kidnapping."

"Usually." Lance smiled. He noticed she wasn't upset over the concept, just the annoyance it would cause.

"Ok, let's do this…" she replied.

———

Captain of the USS Harry Truman took the call. "Hello Mr. President."

"Hello, Captain. I appreciate everything you and the men and women of the U.S.S Harry S. Truman are doing there in the Mediterranean to help Operation Inherent Resolve," the President started. "I'm here to request one quick fifteen-minute favor that can mess up your situation, but I promise it will be interesting to you and your people."

"Whatever we can do, let us know," the Captain replied. Inwardly, he was hoping it wasn't visiting dignitaries or anything of that sort. His people were tired, several weeks past their original deployment end date and babysitting wasn't something he wanted to ask them to do.

"You are going to be visited by a very rare flying container," the President started.

"Sir, not to interrupt, but can they land on our ship?"

The Captain was surprised when the President laughed. "Captain, I'm not laughing at you, I promise. This craft does not need an airfield, and before you ask, it is not a helicopter. Those that are on the craft are either members of an expedition that was rescued out of ISIS territory or members of TQB. Captain, whatever you do, be pleasant with them. I assure you, they will be respectful to you and your people."

"Understood, Mr. President."

"I imagine you do, Captain. That's because the Navy doesn't have slow people at the command of one of our aircraft carriers. We will deliver an update on how we expect to pull those who are staying behind back off your ship."

"Couldn't they just drop them off on land?" he asked.

"I'm sure they could, but this is what they wanted to do. It seems some of the men in the group wanted to see an aircraft carrier in action, Captain. Two birds, one stone."

"They want to see what WE can do? Don't they have ships that go into outer space?"

"Well, sure. But how many of them roar off of decks in the middle of the ocean?" the President replied. "There is something that their Pods don't supply that feeds a man's soul, Captain."

"Really?" the Captain questioned, "What's that?"

"Fire and noise, Captain, fire and noise. Jets scream off of your deck, and even for Presidents, just between you and me, that's cool as shit."

"Yes, sir!" the Captain agreed, smiling.

―――

SPACE STATION ONE, L2

Bethany Anne took a few minutes to see the damage to the outside of Space Station One from her Pod. "Take me in, ADAM. I've seen enough."

A few minutes later, Bethany Anne and her team were exiting their Pods on the deck. Gabrielle was waiting for her when she got out. Ashur jumped out behind her and chuffed. Bethany Anne looked at the dog. "Okay, go get something to eat," she told him and then turned back to Gabrielle. "Report."

"Adarsh is awake and explaining what they did. Team BMW is creating our own, much bigger, version of this for ArchAngel and transmitting the schematics to the Defender so they can build their own version."

The two women started walking towards the exit from the deck to get out of the way. "Did we hurt them?"

"Yes, scans showed damage once we knew where to look, and they suffered acceleration problems. However, within two minutes they did something, and we lost them again. SS1's jury-rigged sensor wasn't strong enough to follow them when they passed ten thousand kilometers."

"Okay, when is the funeral for Coach?"

―――――

There were six around the casket, friends, and Guardians, providing Coach a royal guard as the Queen stood next to it. She laid a hand on the casket, then walked to the podium and faced the mourners.

"Coach was a man I am proud to say I had on my team. He came, he saw, and whether it was with knowledge from his time in the Navy, from his life, or with duct tape, he seemed to have a solution for all of the challenges thrown his way."

"He knew that his future, as well as ours, would unlikely be easy. He also knew it was guaranteed not to be safe. But, he lived as he wanted. Using his skills, and putting himself between those who threatened, and those he loved. That, the placing of ourselves between dangers and those we hold dear, is our call. Ad Aeternitatem, Coach. Till we meet again on the other side, your name will be in my heart. We shall not forget your sacrifice."

ReaLea, Kris and Bree, faces wet with tears and makeup running, watched the coffin take off from the deck of the ArchAngel and slip through the field as it headed towards the sun. Bethany Anne had requested all of the original team members, including the still healing Adarsh, travel over to the ship for the ceremony. After the casket had slipped through, Bethany Anne turned to her people.

Her contralto voice started, "We have been attacked by an alien species. Based on the analysis and from our own alien contact, they are looking to research our system. To steal our resources, and enslave our people."

"Further" she continued, "they have a gate to go back home. They want to take the knowledge of who we are, where we are, and what we can do, with them. We were lucky they did not see our ship until this point. Now, it is very likely they are aware we have considerably more resources than they thought, and we are both a problem and a prize."

She looked at the group, then looked into the cameras sending her face to her people. "Attend me, my Guards, My Guardians, My Elite and My People… We have had war declared on us again. This time, it is by an inimical society seeking to follow a commonly held premise that those who have the power, have the right to use that power however they want. Well… Fuck them!"

Her eyes flashed red. "They have made a catastrophic mistake and are an eternal enemy of the Queen Bitch and Her People. Hear my response to these atrocities visited upon my people."

She spoke louder, looking up at the ceiling. "ArchAngel!"

The ship's E.I. responded, her voice filling the Pod deck, "Yes, my Queen?"

"Take us to the annex gate at maximum speed once we allow those who need to go back to SS1 to leave. We will kill or capture this enemy, No surrender will be allowed, is this understood?"

"Yes ma'am, I have heard the command. 'No Surrender' has been instituted. All lockdown protocols on this ship are removed. Leviathan Battleship ArchAngel is now fully operational and will fight until *victorious*…"

There was a slight pause from the speaker system, "Or *dead*, my Queen."

The roaring of those in the Pod deck threatened to cross the vacuum of space to join with those who had listened and watched from the Space Station, the Moon Base, and the Defender.

The first war between the Queen Bitch and an alien race had begun.

CHAPTER TWENTY-THREE

YOLLIN DEEP SPACE SHIP, G'LAXIX SPHAEA

Royleen walked around the table that held his one sample. He had hoped for a female, but he understood why the Captain had to leave. At least the attack on the G'laxix Sphaea hadn't damaged his lab. Yes, a couple of helpers had to clean up a few things that had been tossed around, and one container made of transparent material had broken, but that was all.

The subject was strapped down, unconscious. The alien had been very aggravated upon arrival. Fortunately, Royleen had already loaded the systems in his lab with the limited speech core between Yollin and this alien's language.

Not that it mattered in the end. The subject was aggressive in its speech all the way up to when Royleen had administered the chemicals to send its body into a coma.

Royleen sighed, he needed more information for the Captain, so he needed to wake up the alien. He might have preferred to have more time to work with the body to administer different tests and get better feedback from the old and apparently inadequate research that had been done previously.

Now, to see if he could acquire any useful information using whatever methods he needed to.

Royleen reached for the syringe necessary to bring the alien awake.

———

"Engineering, what is the status?" Captain T'chmon spoke into his comm system from the bridge. It had been a rough two solar days. A few of the energy runs from the engine room had been damaged by the second craft that had rammed them.

It was an unfortunate example of offensive execution, but effective. What did the Fourteenth of the Yollin Monarchy say at the battle of K'lleen? Something about if his attacks were effective, then he didn't care how pretty they were. He hadn't scored any points for beauty, but he had won the battle.

Thank the gods above and below that travesty had not continued. There should be beauty in everything, even the effort to kill others as the Universe had decreed.

Engineering replied, "Sir, we are within three solar hours of bringing everything back online. I would not want to trust everything past eighty percent if you can help it."

"And if I cannot help it?" Captain T'chmon asked.

"I would suggest we are likely to be fine, but it is that one time we aren't that ruins our day, Captain."

Captain T'chmon hissed in laughter. "Indeed, engineering one, indeed. Captain T'chmon out."

WE HAVE CONTACT

T'chmon tapped his nails on his armrest. Royleen was waking the alien. He could see the status on his screens in front of him.

Kurtherians. Damn, that was bad news. He checked all of the logs. They had followed the protocols and sent the necessary pings that would notify any Kurtherians active in the system. He was covered.

At least, with his King he was. Whether or not the Kurtherians that were possibly in the spaceship would be okay with his actions in this system was another question. He didn't want to make a run for the annex gate without having as much of his ship working as they could. They had to get back, the opportunity was too great here, and the Kurtherian threat this system represented needed to be shared.

He had looked at the information and had finally guessed that these aliens were neither idiots nor idiot savants. Or rather, that they recently acquired Kurtherian technology. How long ago he couldn't guess, but for the first time he had ever heard about, here was an alien species that possibly had Kurtherian technology and did not have a Kurtherian Clan commanding them.

Captain T'chmon pressed his lips together. He had to get this information back to his King. If there was Kurtherian technology in this system that they could grab, his King would become a significant power in their quadrant.

And he would move up a tier in personal prestige, guaranteed. Captain T'chmon pressed the button to speak with Royleen. He needed more input, and he needed it badly.

Bethany Anne entered the bridge and nodded at the communications specialist to her left as she stepped up to her elevated chair and sat down. "Time to arrival?"

"Five minutes, Bethany Anne," Captain Paul Jameson answered her.

"We have Captain Wagner of the Defender online, ma'am," Communications Specialist Alyona said. Bethany Anne could have received all of this information from ArchAngel itself, and she often did. But everyone was trying to figure out how to operate a ship when the ship could do most everything.

Bethany Anne was careful to keep the knowledge of ArchAngel's capabilities, and the communications through ADAM to her, hidden for now. She didn't want to upset a working applecart if it was unnecessary.

"Bring him online, please." Bethany Anne replied. She glanced at the clock, set to Greenwich Mean Time. "Good morning, Captain Wagner."

"Hello, Bethany Anne. What do you make of our little light show?" He smiled. The annex gate in all of its otherworldly beauty was on the screens behind him. Her team had been piping video from his ship to the ArchAngel for the last few hours.

"Not being melodramatic here Captain, but you and the Defender's people have stopped humanity from losing our freedom."

"Oh?" he replied, his eyes opening wider.

"Yes, TOM confirms this is an annex gate used by expanding alien races to acquire information on foreign solar systems. If your team hadn't located this, our uninvited guest would have been able to leave without us knowing where they went. The next time one of these opened up, it probably would have included an overwhelming force."

"Are we that big a prize, then?" Captain Wagner asked.

"Max, just the technology on the Defender alone is probably worth a world the way I understand it. We shall see if I'm right when we talk with the bastards."

"You plan on talking?"

"Sure, why not? Don't get me wrong. I plan on talking with a gun shoved up their ass, but it's still talking. I can't shove it down their throat, as that would stop them from answering my questions."

"That's rather practical of you," he nodded his head, his eyes twinkling.

"I like to think I'm very practical Max, it is one of my many wonderful traits."

Captain Wagner laughed, and Bethany Anne heard a few chuckles around her bridge. Good, she wanted everyone loose for what could be a battle in just a few minutes or months.

This could be a long wait.

"How are you guys set up for food, do you need anything?"

"No, we've been communicating with ArchAngel. The only thing we might need is additional pucks if we want to fill up our reserves. We have over eighty percent in front of the gate. We've worked out which side they need to enter and have created a net to disable a ship from any direction. We will try to knock their ship off course to the gate. If we fail, we have a devastating final resolution. One way or another, they are in for a world of hurt."

"Good to know," Bethany Anne looked to her side, where

Paul was talking to those in supply and giving her a thumbs up. "I see we're going to replenish your stock. Defender will be the goalie here. If they get past us, you absolutely must not let them gain the gate, Max."

"Bethany Anne, the Defender will not fail. Although," his eyes flicked to the side for a moment, "I see you guys coming up, and I'm not sure what the hell is going to get past you guys. Damn, that is one beautiful ship."

A female's voice interjected into the conversation, "Thank you, Captain Wagner."

For a moment, Captain Wagner's face was confused. Bethany Anne hadn't spoken, but the voice was similar to hers. Then he broke into a grin. "You're very welcome, ArchAngel."

Bethany Anne took over. "We will be alongside you in ten minutes, Max. Let's transfer the pucks at that time. Are you guys okay with the new SONAR?"

>>It isn't SONAR, Bethany Anne.<<

Hush ADAM. That's good enough for the moment. I'll get a full breakdown of what it's called later.

"Ah, yes," she could tell he was about to correct her as well. "But we don't have enough sensors to blanket this area very well."

"We've been dropping them off as we can with gravitic drives to slow the sensor platforms down and move them to the most likely locations. The platforms will warn us if the alien ship comes close enough and give us their incoming trajectory." Bethany Anne's eyes twitched for a second. Max waited for her to finish the conversation she was having with someone. "I'm assured we will have a significant amount of space blanketed within half a day."

"Are they going to know they've been found?" Captain Wagner asked.

WE HAVE CONTACT

"I'm told yes. We have both active and passive versions. The active versions are hot and easily seen by any technology they might have listening. However, we have passive versions as well. We're hoping to lead them into a trap."

"Dodge the active, swim in the passive?" he asked, and she nodded. "Good. Do you want us to move some of the larger pucks in preparation?"

"No, I need your complete focus on not knowing and the working assumption that the enemy can come from any direction. All information will be sent to you in real time, of course, so adjust as you need to. I think this is going to be a one-shot for them and us. They make it through, or we stop them. Simple as that."

Captain Wagner shook his head once, quickly. "Thank God they can't race through, they have to take it slow, or this would be a touch harder. Wagner out."

Her face grew a little grimmer. "They have one of our people on the ship, so it sure as hell isn't getting through."

The line in the proverbial sand had been drawn, and no one was getting across.

———

"What is the alien saying?" Captain T'chmon asked Royleen, who was looking back at him in the video feed. The alien was thrashing around on the table behind the scientist.

"The translation I have to use is Russian, not the language I thought he would be speaking. He claims his Queen will be coming to get him then repeats this like a mantra. I had to tie him down a second time. He almost slipped out."

"What was he going to do, jump out and float home?" the Captain asked.

MICHAEL ANDERLE

"No, I did ask the alien through translation, and he stopped squirming and told me his plans were to grab one of the instruments," Royleen turned and pointed to something off camera before turning back and continuing, "and kill me with it. Then, his plan was to keep destroying as much of the craft as possible before killing himself. He said he refused to be bait for the Queen."

"Bait?"

"It is a term they use that means to catch others, an enticement used to pull somebody into a trap."

"Well, that is not a problem, I would rather not encounter that ship at the moment. We have to get back to Yoll with our information. So, he can rest easy. He is not bait."

"No, I don't think you understand. He believes this Queen is going to come for him, whether we intend to use him as bait or not," Royleen shrugged his bony shoulders. "I know you believe this species is more intelligent than I initially thought, and you might be correct. But they are so very alien in their thinking, Captain T'chmon."

"That is always the challenge when you seek out new space, Royleen. Trying to understand the local species…"

"Before you conquer and subjugate them," Royleen hissed in laughter. "Yes, I know the joke, Captain T'chmon. You were probably a baby when I learned it."

"Did you get any information from the alien about the technology?" Captain T'chmon switched topics.

"Only that it is TOM's technology, whoever TOM is. I tried a third level pain induced information request, and he almost bit off his tongue. Thales of Miletus was the answer."

"That… is not a Kurtherian name." Captain T'chmon tapped his nails on the armrest. "This continues to make no sense. Kurtherians name themselves after answers to the great questions. Usually math, occasionally science or the bigger questions. Thales of Miletus sounds like a regular name one of these…"

"Humans," Royleen answered.

"Right, that one of these humans would have," Captain T'chmon finished.

"It is a problem inside of a question, surrounded by a rock." Royleen agreed.

"Yes, impenetrable." Captain T'chmon turned and looked at a new report flashing on his screen, "Royleen, send me additional reports if you believe it has value. Only call me if you need to interrupt me. Engineering has just given us the top light. We are heading back to Yoll."

"This will be one of the stories told in the military drinking holes, right Captain?"

"Oh, it most certainly will be," Captain T'chmon agreed and signed off.

———

"Okay, I'm officially bored," Bethany Anne complained from her chair.

Pilot Captain Paul Jameson laughed. "We've only been here three days, Bethany Anne. Have you already grown tired of the view of the gate, or the stars, or what?"

"Yes, yes and yes. I need to get my restless energy worked out."

"What about a sparring match?" he asked.

"With whom, you?" she asked. Paul quickly shook his head in the negative. "I can't spar with anyone while we're waiting for our guest to appear. The Guardians and the Elite are working out with the new metal gauntlets and protective gear. Plus, Jean Dukes has been modifying weapons for battles on board spaceships."

"You don't want to go check it out?" Paul asked, examining his board one more time before turning to his Queen. "You aren't getting a set?"

She leaned back in her chair. "Yeah, I have a modified set. Gauntlets, knee and elbow, and foot. I'm waiting on some sort of Jean Dukes' special outfit that she doesn't have time to show me right now. The Guardians from the space station were pissed that they got tossed around so quickly. They're sure if they could have at least hit them hard enough, they could have done better."

"I saw the video, they have a motor-enhanced suit making them quicker and stronger. Their version of a knight's suit of armor, with power."

"Ayup!" Bethany Anne agreed. "We have a couple of small pieces knocked off during the pretty one-sided fights back on the station. The stuff is hard, but it isn't too bad. Call it a six or seven on the hardness scale. Plus, it conducts electricity. It isn't a high conductor, but it will conduct."

"Planning to give them a good shock?"

"Oh, massive shocks, not tiny ones. Team BMW is modifying some of the gravitic pucks to seek, attack, adhere and discharge."

Paul's face scrunched up as he replayed Bethany Anne's statement, "SAAD?" He asked.

She laughed. "Yeah, I know, right? Usually, those guys are good with acronyms. Bobcat claims it's sad for the other side, but they're getting all sorts of shit from the Guardians about the 'SAAD defense system' and 'Don't worry, SAAD will save us!'" She snickered. "Serves them right because, seriously, SAAD? What the hell were they thinking?"

WE HAVE CONTACT

"They were not thinking," ArchAngel entered the conversation from the speakers. Her face, a copy of Bethany Anne's, took over the middle screen on the bridge. "They hadn't thought about the name at all. When they were showing Peter and Todd the system, they explained how it worked. Bobcat explained that they seek, attack, adhere and discharge when Todd burst out laughing and coined the acronym for it."

"That sounds about right, no way is Todd going to let them live this down for a while," Paul agreed.

ArchAngel's visage changed, her eyes grew red. "We have contact, repeat, we have contact."

"About damned time," Bethany Anne sat up in her chair. "I was going nuts."

CHAPTER TWENTY-FOUR

YOLLIN DEEP SPACE SHIP, G'LAXIX SPHAEA

Weapons and Defense Specialist T'monoth called out, "Sir, we see active scanning in the path towards the gate."

Captain Kael-ven T'chmon swore loud, long and vociferously. He had hoped that the aliens had not found their gate, but apparently that wasn't the case.

"Can we bypass them, or is the coverage complete?" Captain T'chmon asked.

"Definitely not complete, sir. The readings we are seeing is of older technology. At least seven generations old."

"So," Captain T'chmon spoke softly to himself. "Probably incomplete, probably not perfect. But perfect enough. They didn't find us for so long because why… because why Kael…"

"Perhaps," Melorn spoke up, hesitantly. Captain T'chmon looked over and nodded his permission to continue. "Is it possible they were not expecting to be looking for us until we arrived? It took them that long to create a working detector?"

"That fits," the Captain agreed. "We were certainly in the range of that ugly excuse for a station a long enough time. If they had implemented their new device and all of a sudden we show up, then that explains why Royleen saw unexpected vibrations on their space station. That was the point when they turned it on. Now," he gestured toward the screens. "They have been manufacturing as fast as possible and cannot create a complete zone of protection like we would." He tapped his nails on the armrest. "Helm, take us through and work with defense and sensors, we need to bypass their defensive sensors."

———

"They took the bait, ma'am," Paul called out. "They stopped and now they're threading the needle very carefully."

They had at least three hours before the ship would be close enough to communicate with. TOM and ADAM had reviewed what they could do and felt comfortable that they would be able to send communications through TOM's ship, which was locked down in the corner of the Pod bay.

That was probably going to be a surprise for the aliens when they got a phone call from a Kurtherian ship.

Bethany Anne smiled at that thought.

"Good, let them come. ArchAngel, update everyone with the information and confirm our new Pod carriers are prepared to dock with them."

Bethany Anne hit a button on her tablet. "Jean?"

"Yes, ma'am?"

"Did you and Jeffrey's teams get the field expedient connectors made?"

"Yes, ma'am. They don't work exactly like the sum-bitches that hit the space station, but ours are a little more elegant."

"Well, I prefer our method anyway. How many do we have?"

"Five at the moment, number six won't be ready for about," there was a pause, "six more hours."

"Then five is what we have. Kill number six if you need the resources and move it around. We will be in a battle in three."

"Yes, ma'am!"

Bethany Anne disconnected the line and sat, thinking.

"Our method?" Paul asked.

Bethany Anne looked up. "What? Oh. Yeah, the aliens effectively jammed a hollow-point into the space station and came through the hole. We are going to adhere a docking clamp and use some sort of special acid and magnetic induction and other miscellaneous shit I don't understand to eat a hole after the clamp is attached to the side. Then we connect to the dock, and if it is positively sealed against air loss, they crack the door and will go in. We don't know their atmosphere, but we didn't see any tanks on the ones on the station."

"So, possibly breathable?" Paul asked, surprised.

"Possibly, and possibly they have something in their air that is poisonous to us, but our air lacks anything poisonous to them, so we shall see."

"Join the space marines, go out, meet new aliens and… kill them." Paul grunted with laughter.

"Wasn't me that started this shit so rudely," Bethany Anne replied.

———

"John," Jean walked into the group's setup area, lugging a large crate. "This is for Bethany Anne."

She hoisted the heavy box, which landed with a loud thud on the table. John and Eric, the only other one in the room at the moment, looked from the crate back to Jean.

"And this is?" he asked.

"The start of her armor," she replied, "If you don't think she's going into that ship, then I need to make sure your head is screwed on properly."

"Oh, I'm sure his head is VERY screwed on... prop... ah... well, uh... properly." Eric faltered at the end as Jean fixed him with a stare. Eric scratched his chin. "It seemed funny at the time."

"I'm sure it did Eric, and yes, John is screwed the way he needs to be screwed," she started before Eric put up his hand.

"Please, say no more. I'm just thankful the walls have some sort of insulation." Eric grinned at her.

"Oh? You can't hear anything?" Jean turned to look at John. "Sharing, are we?"

John grinned. "If you think for a moment that I'm going to hang my head in shame for admitting I curl your toes, then you need to find whatever John you thought you fell for. Because this one," he pointed to himself, "made damn sure to smile all day the next day."

"It was horrible," Eric added. "His ego grew ten times that day. No jokes could wipe the smile off of his face. It was so painful to see him like that."

Jean chuckled and walked over to John. Standing up as high as she could stretch, she reached up to pull him down by the neck and plant a big kiss on him. She turned back around and looked at Eric. "There will be more of that for him. That was just a very small, and very chaste, promise for later." She started unlocking the latches and explaining what was in the chest. "This is the most I could get done for now. I know Bethany Anne needs ease of movement, and her bones are much stronger, so I took that into account."

The two men crowded around her. "Sweet!" Eric said as Jean took out a new chest piece. It was colored in a deep crimson with a very faint vampire skull on the left breast.

"I have protection for her chest and back, all the usual spots but nothing special for her head, yet. This will all fit over her existing spacesuits and even over her current armor, as well."

"She'll be pretty armored, then. How heavy is it?" John asked. Jean turned and looked at him, an eyebrow raised. He put up a hand and smiled. "Sorry, I know it probably doesn't matter to her. What's an extra fifty or hundred pounds?"

"Nothing she'll notice, that's for sure," Eric agreed. "Damn, she's going to look badass with this. We need to get her a cool helmet."

"No, this is just temporary. I've seen the videos of the attack on the station. When I get my hands on their tech, I'm going to rip it apart and figure out how to make one for her. I'll have her locked in tight. Hell, I have plans. She can get tossed out of a ship and survive for a while."

"Oh hell, can you imagine the cussing if that were to happen?" Eric laughed, "BOOM! An explosion happens as we're walking through a ship, she gets sucked out into space, doing cartwheels and we can't come get her. So, she's stuck there waiting to be rescued as we finish the operation. The cussing would be *EPIC*!" he finished.

"Huh, that's an idea, gravitic movement," Jean said, as her face got a faraway look. "You guys can't fight without being delta zero in relationship to each other, or close enough.

Maybe it would be sufficient. If not, I need to make sure she has some sort of special 'come find my ass' black box."

"NOOOOoooo," Eric whined, "There goes our opportunity to save her from herself."

"Oh, just blow the wall ourselves and let her get sucked out?" John started nodding his head then stopped suddenly. "You know that shit would only work once, right? Even doing it for the right reasons, the next sparring match she'd make you pray for death."

Eric shrugged. "Ad Aeternitatem, my friend. If that's what it took to save her, I'd toss her ass out in a heartbeat and enjoy the show. If I made it through the rest of the operation, then I'd worry about the ass kicking."

"Besides, Gabrielle would help kiss the ouchies all away, right?" Jean winked at him and turned to leave. "Catch you guys later."

Both guys told her bye. John looked at Eric. "Gabrielle?"

Eric shrugged. "The first date went pretty well."

"I didn't hear you come in last night, come to think of it," John said.

"That's probably because you two were bouncing off the walls."

"Huh, that could be," John admitted and dropped the subject. "Well," he grabbed the chest. "Let's call the boss and see if she has a few minutes to try on her new clothes."

"You know," John said as he walked down the hall. "She would probably just walk Etherically back to the ArchAngel if it didn't take too much energy."

"Just keep bursting my bubble, John," Eric said. "Just keep bursting my bubble."

"Captain T'chmon," sensors called out. "We are picking up a large ship in front of the gate."

"It is what I expected," Captain T'chmon replied. "Continue slow and steady." He reached over and hit the comm. "Kiel?"

"Yes, Captain?"

"Are you and your team fully loaded up? I might need to send you into their ship."

"Has Royleen confirmed the outer makeup? Are the weapons going to leave us anything left to review?" he hissed in laughter.

"For this discussion, assume we only do thirty percent of the damage the calculations expect, what are the plans?"

"Um," Kiel was quiet for a moment, "We would seek a breach and eject into the breach. Move towards engines and command deck. Remove obstacles and then figure out a way to cut the power to the ship. That would give us time to grab anything interesting and get back aboard and through the gate."

"Good. Remember that, Kiel. The gate is our priority. While I don't want to leave you behind, I will."

"Understood, Captain T'chmon, we won't do any sightseeing," Kiel answered.

"See that you don't." Captain T'chmon closed the connection. They were just solar minutes away now. "Weapons, are you ready?"

"Yes sir, we have a spread of two missiles first, then we will hit them with beam weapons. We aren't a large ship, Captain, so I'm not sure how well we will do."

"Me either, weapons. But they are new to space battles, I'm sure. I doubt they have much in the way of protection or knowledge of what to do. We go, we hit, and if I don't have to send Kiel over, we run. If we can't get them unpowered, I'll send them over. Either way, we are going through that gate."

"I wonder why they haven't gone through themselves?" Melorn wondered.

"Seeking out the unknown is what separates the powerful from the weak, Melorn." Captain T'chmon said. "And Yollins have always sought out the unknown."

———

Bethany Anne walked in with her standard gear over her skin suit. "What is that?" she asked and pointed to the chest John and Eric had carried into her suite.

"Complements of Dukes," Eric answered.

"Oh," Bethany Anne replied, nonplussed. "Well, open it up. What did the madwoman create this time?"

John popped the locks and opened the case. Bethany Anne came closer and looked in. "Oh! Come to momma my little babies…"

———

Peter Silvers and Todd Jenkins looked at Bobcat, who was smiling back at them. "This crate is guaranteed to cause unknown and untold damage to the enemy. The Guardians and the Guardian Marines should enjoy it."

"Why is it unknown?" asked Todd.

"Why is it untold?" asked Peter.

"Um, untold because we have no stories," answered Bobcat who then turned to Todd, "and unknown because, well, we don't know."

"Shit," Todd answered.

"That's okay, we'll give you the stories," Peter answered.

"Wechselbalg," Todd grimaced. "Can't get them to see past the chance to fight."

"Marines," Peter answered, grinning. "Always wanting an opportunity to fuck up the enemy before you get a chance to fight."

"That IS the definition of fighting," Todd said. "Fuck them up before you get screwed without lubricant. The best way to fight is to cheat."

"Not very manly," Peter replied.

"Not here to be manly, here to win. Overly manly gets you dead." Todd said. "If all else fails, we will attain fire superiority, we will move towards the enemy guns, and we will kill everything in our path."

"I can fully support that approach," Peter nodded.

Todd slapped his friend on the shoulder. "Work with me, Wechselbalg, the Guardian Marines will get you where you need to go and protect your back while we do it."

———

Bethany Anne strode on the bridge to sit back down. She liked the look of her usual black leather outfit, but these slick blood red carbon graphite pieces pleased her immensely. They weren't noticeably annoying, although there was something heavy inside them. John said the added mass would be helpful.

Maybe.

She had her hair tied back and her helmet with her.

"Ok, Paul, ArchAngel, and crew we are sixty seconds from uncovering. Confirm final prep from all departments."

"Aye, ma'am."

WE HAVE CONTACT

ADAM, we good?

>>Yes, ArchAngel says we are good. The other ship has slowed down and is most likely setting up a shot. They are six hundred kilometers distant. She would have brought everything online if we had been attacked.<<

Good, I want my people to go through this as much as possible without overt assistance. It wouldn't be good to let them understand how intelligent she is.

>>I will take that as a compliment.<<

You should, now don't get a big head. I don't have the space for your ego in my skull at the moment.

>>That was a joke, correct?<<

Yes.

>>It was a poor joke.<<

Yeah, you're right, it was.

"Puck defense?" she asked.

"Streaming now, ma'am."

Bethany Anne waited. "I want anything they shoot if you can, to explode five kilometers out."

"Five ma'am?"

"Yes, I'm told we're good for a direct hit from something of this class, but I'm not a betting a person, yet. So, destroy anything you can five out."

"Yes, ma'am."

Bethany Anne looked around and nodded one last time. "Light them up."

———

Alarms started shrieking on the boards in the command center. Captain T'chmon bit back an oath, they had been caught in a trap.

"Fire," he said and a pair of missiles, already queued and aimed solar minutes ago, tore out of the front of the ship.

They waited the solar seconds necessary for the weapons to cross the distance between the two ships. The picture, which had been zoomed in, darkened when the explosions occurred, stopping the brightness from hurting their eyes. Seconds later, the video grew bright again, and the picture showed the alien ship.

With no damage.

"Uh, sir?" Weapons asked.

"Again," Captain T'chmon ordered, and another pair of missiles went towards the ship, and again the same thing happened.

Two explosions and no damage.

"Helm, ahead quarter speed, get within beam range, we have too many particulates in between us at the moment." Captain T'chmon said.

———

"Second set of missiles destroyed at three kilometers, no noticeable issues with the shields, ma'am."

"Paul, bring us around, I want to use the medium guns."

"Yes ma'am, bringing ship around."

"Paul?" she said, and he turned to look at her. "I want that ship, don't mess it up too much. We still have one of our own on board."

"Yes, ma'am."

———

"Sir, we have movement, they are turning to face us," called out Melorn.

"Smaller surface area to hit, perhaps?" said weapons.

"Or, they are about to return fire," Captain T'chmon answered. So far, their missiles weren't causing any noticeable damage. The only way that would be the case… the enemy had shields.

"Sir? They have a second ship lying beyond the gate."

"They have *WHAT*?" Captain T'chmon replied, looking at his display, calling up a new area, circled. It was a black ship radiating very little and the only way sensors could have caught it was the obscured stars behind it. "Refine the images."

There was no doubt that the humans had created this ship. It was ugly, beyond ugly. He grimaced in distaste. "They have no couth," he grated out. "Find out what this ship is doing and why it is here." He stabbed his monitor. "They might have no ability to create beauty, except for that main ship, but they aren't stupid."

He stabbed a button. "Kiel, prepare."

———

Bethany Anne leaned back. "Fire, Paul."

Pilot Captain Paul Jameson pushed the button. He had no idea that moment would delineate The Pre-Queen Bethany Anne and Post-Queen Bethany Anne Wars time period. While there were a lot of arguments in the future, no one argued that the first shot of the wars, all of them, was fired in her own solar system, at the Yollins who had attacked her first.

The destruction was evident almost immediately. The

metal slug had traveled over one hundred feet down the rail-gun's barrel, attaining a small percent of light speed before hitting the left wing area. The puncture succeeded in creating a five-meter hole and causing the ship to skew jerkily to the side.

"I think we need to pull back on the speed a little, Paul. It went right through their wing."

"You did ask me not to mess up their ship too much, ma'am."

"Yes," Bethany Anne agreed. "That is true."

―――――

"WHAT HAPPENED!" Captain T'chmon yelled when their ship suddenly ripped to the left violently.

"Sir, we have been punctured on the left wing. There is a significant hole, minimal effect on space movement."

"I understand that, but WHAT happened? What did they hit us with?"

"We believe they hit us with a metallic non-explosive momentum based device."

Captain T'chmon wasn't sure if the weapons specialist was trying to be obtuse, or it was his training coming to the forefront. "So, you're telling me they hit us with a metal rod?" he asked.

"Um… yes, sir."

"Sir, they are coming towards us."

Captain T'chmon punched the comm button. "Kiel, expect boarding action soon."

"When do you want us to leave, sir?" Kiel responded.

Captain T'chmon shook his head. "Not us boarding them, Kiel. Them boarding us."

WE HAVE CONTACT

Royleen lost his balance and fell to his knees when the ship suddenly lurched to the side. The alien on the table started laughing, he babbled something. Then the translation came through the speaker as Royleen got up.

"She's coming, you asshole. Now you have gone and screwed the pooch!"

———

"All five boarding devices are on their way, ma'am," Paul called out.

"Start hitting them with pucks, I want to know if we have a force field to worry about."

I doubt they do, TOM said.

I know you doubt it, but I'd like to know before we try and connect.

"Pucks are hitting metal, ma'am. We have one puncture near the far back. One engine has cut out," the weapons officer said.

"Stop fucking up my new ship." Bethany Anne said. "Reduce the Puck damage. Keep hitting the ship, it's got to annoy the hell out of them. Well, I hope it annoys the hell out of them."

"They could like it, like music," Paul said.

Bethany Anne grimaced. "That would be my luck, I'm secretly asking them to marry me using some form of galactic Morse code."

———

"Sir, we've lost engine one. We expect to have it back up in fifteen solar minutes."

"Understood," Captain T'chmon closed the communication line. The constant barrage hitting his ship was aggravating. Except for the first one, they weren't getting through the outer protection.

"Sir, we have something hitting the ship and attaching," Melorn informed him.

"What else are these humans up to? This will not go well for them." Captain T'chmon said when Melorn turned to him, his eyes opened wide.

"Sir, we are being hailed on high bands."

"From where?" Captain T'chmon asked, "There are no other ships out here."

"From that one," Melorn said, pointing to the large ship coming at them.

———

"...so, you pain in the ass, I am coming over there, and you will surrender, or I will space every one of you. You attacked my people and took them which is a declaration of war. You lost. Surrender or die..."

Bethany Anne finished her statement.

TOM send that in whatever languages you have that might work.

Bethany Anne stood up from her chair. "Paul, take the seat. You have command until I get back."

Paul slaved his console over to Bethany Anne's chair and switched places. "I've got the chair, yes ma'am."

Bethany Anne swept out of the bridge, her protection detail escorting her to the Pod bay.

WE HAVE CONTACT

"Sir, it is coming over in multiple languages, I do not have a match yet."

"Work the translation, Melorn. I imagine it says something like *surrender or die*. That is what I would be saying if I were them."

Captain T'chmon looked around at his crew, his people. Those that trusted him to get them back home safely and possibly with riches.

They had been so close, and he had failed them all.

He punched the comms button. "Kiel, come to the command center."

"Coming, Captain."

It took Kiel one solar minute to arrive. "Permission to enter, sir?"

Captain T'chmon hit the button to let him come in. "Permission granted, Kiel."

Kiel came and stood next to him. "Command, Captain?"

Captain T'chmon looked around one more time and unhooked his four legs from the captain's chair. "Come with me."

The two left the command center. The specialists all looked around at each other in surprise. The Captain was forbidden to leave the command center in battle.

Unless he was giving up his ship.

———

Royleen looked up when the Captain and Kiel entered. "Are we victors, then?" Royleen asked. The Captain shook his head. "No, we are not at the moment victors. Unhook the alien and have Kiel bring him with us."

It took the scientist only a few moments to unhook the alien who spoke gibberish but didn't fight the larger alien who had his military armor on.

The three of them left the lab.

Captain T'chmon lifted up his arm and hit his ship-wide comms button. "This is Captain T'chmon…"

———

The fight for the ship was anticlimactic. Their field expedient boarding devices connected, well four of them did. One did not work correctly, and they could not acquire a seal. By the time they had made the adjustments, their comms had informed them of the aliens' surrender.

———

Bethany Anne swept with her Bitches and Elite through the ship, their helmets on. They encountered plenty of the aliens, some with the armor that they had seen. Those that had armor had laid what they easily guessed were weapons at their feet. Bethany Anne's guards picked them up each time. Once, they stopped in a hallway only to have another, prostrate on the ground, point down a hallway to their right.

"This has got to be the fucking weirdest shit I've ever been a part of," Bethany Anne murmured. "Why is everyone so docile?"

Scott said, "Well, either their version of surrender, or one very well orchestrated ambush."

"They seem to be giving us their weapons quickly enough," Darryl said.

"Not that we know how to use them, or even understand if they're real and not practice weapons," Scott shot back.

Bethany Anne's group came to a large door and hit the button on the wall. The door opened and the room beyond, a fairly empty one, was easily twice as high as an alien. Inside, there were two aliens and a human.

"Holy shit, he has four legs," Scott murmured.

"He also has much nicer clothing and generally looks more poised... for an alien," Darryl added. "So, we found Ivan."

"Yes, we have," Bethany Anne agreed. "John, I want Ivan with us."

John broke from the group and headed towards the aliens. He pointed to Ivan and then pointed back towards the group. The four-legged one jerked his head at the two-legged armored one, and Ivan was released. Ivan took two steps towards John, then his legs buckled.

John took a chance and jumped forward to catch Ivan. Picking him up, he helped him walk back.

Ivan was not looking good.

"Two of you take Ivan back to the ArchAngel," Bethany Anne said. "I want to have a few words with these two." Her eyes glowed inside her helmet.

CHAPTER TWENTY-FIVE

YOLLIN DEEP SPACE SHIP, G'LAXIX SPHAEA

>>Bethany Anne, we have communications between this ship and the ArchAngel. There is a language that we have been able to use for translation. I can pipe the efforts through a speaker...<<

No, I will speak the language, TOM see that I get the nuance correct. Wait, can I speak the language?

Yes, it is an organic tongue, with infrequent clicks you can mimic using your tongue against the roof of your mouth and popping.

Am I good to breathe the atmosphere?

Yes.

Okay, here goes.

"Team, I am pulling off my helmet. I'm told the air is breathable, and I'm going to try and communicate with those two in front of us."

WE HAVE CONTACT

As she reached up, she saw John and Eric reach up and pull off their helmets before her. Rolling her eyes, she unlatched her own.

———

"Some of them are short," Captain T'chmon said to Kiel after the first alien carried away their captive.

"The sacrifice you are making, Captain, will they even care? Do they have honor?"

"That is not something I know. But I failed. I will not take the rest of my ship down."

"It has been an honor, Captain T'chmon." Kiel said.

The Captain turned to him. "Kiel, it is just Kael-ven now, Captain is a title I left behind on the bridge."

Kiel shook his head. "Not to me, you didn't." He turned. "They are taking off their helmets."

Kael-ven turned back and noticed the one who helped the captive, as well as his companion, took off their helmets, just before the one with the fancy armor started to take off theirs.

The two aliens were surprised when the shorter one walked between the two of her guards. She would be in command, then. They were astonished when she started speaking to them in Gaijon, a common enough language, having been used for thousands of solar years.

"You are?" she asked them.

"Until recently, I was Captain Kael-ven T'chmon of the Yollin Deep Space Ship, G'laxix Sphaea." Kael-ven said.

She turned to look at him, and her eyes were glowing red. "You are, then, the person responsible for attacking my people? Killing one and taking another? Or is this a command from those above you?"

Kael-ven turned to Kiel. "Kiel? She asks a legal question. As a non-member of the military at this moment, I am honor bound at a personal level to answer her. Do you wish to administer actions to protect military secrets?"

"What military secrets, Kael-ven? The universe knows we all take our orders from the King and if he isn't powerful enough to answer for his commands, who is?" Kiel replied.

Kael-ven turned back to the alien and got ready to answer her questions.

———

Bethany Anne waited as the two aliens conversed. She assumed the ex-Captain was asking some sort of question to clarify… what, she didn't know. Permission? Now that he wasn't the Captain, perhaps he was a war criminal? Difficult to tell what was going on.

The ex-Captain turned and spoke. "As the Captain of this ship, I am under orders to research this space and allow my scientists and those advising me opportunities to acquire military, technological assets and raw materials which the Yollin Monarchy might use for expansion." He looked down at Bethany Anne. "It is our heritage to do such, all great peoples use expansion as the way to move forward."

"No, not all great peoples, just galaxy-sized assholes," Bethany Anne spoke English, but then had TOM translate it into Gaijon.

Bethany Anne turned to the one standing next to the ex-Captain. She noticed his armor, and saw the scrape across the faceplate. "You are?"

"Military Lead Kiel," he replied. It took two tries to acquire the right translation. Bethany Anne bit down a desire to pummel the alien at the moment. This was the one who killed Coach.

"I will deal with you later. You will be brought up on charges for killing one of my people in an unprovoked war."

"War?" Kael-ven interrupted. "Kiel was operating under my orders, and we DID try to limit the loss of life. If that space station were not so ugly and weak, we would have perhaps used other means. In no way did we intend to kill."

Bethany Anne turned back to face Kael-ven. "I will take that into consideration. On the war comment? Yes, your king has declared war on *my* people as have the Kurtherians. My war with the Kurtherians supersedes my war with your leader. I will offer your King one chance when I pass through your gate to leave me alone."

"That will not happen," Kael-ven said. "No one is allowed to pass through Yollin space without obtaining permission first. Simply by using that gate, you will create an incursion and the military will attack."

"Kael-ven, I am personally *counting* on that happening," she said. "Now, tell me, what is standard for accepting the surrender of your people. Our surrender terms might be better, they might be worse. But I will choose the final terms and should you try to bypass my decision, Kael-ven? It will be stopped, and your people may suffer. Is this clear?"

It took her two tries and and then a third, with them repeating her phrase back before understanding was agreed on.

Kael-ven stood taller, the chitinous and angular scales on his body crossing each other as his back straightened and he looked down at the alien. "My name is Kael-ven T'chmon, lately the Captain of the Yollin Deep Space Ship, G'laxix Sphaea. I am offering my life in exchange for the lives of my crew, *all of the lives of my crew*, as the orders I gave them were mine as surely as my orders come from those above me, who represent the King's Decree."

Kael-ven's legs bent in half, and soon his head was level with Bethany Anne's. "Do with my life what you will."

Bethany Anne studied the bent head, the offering of an obviously tender part of their anatomy to deliver a killing blow.

"Kael-ven T'chmon, what happens if I defer taking your life and require seven," here she used a term that the language couldn't translate, "of honorable servitude, never seeking to escape, and never seeking to mislead?"

Kael-ven turned his head up and moved it left and right, "What is this word you used… this 'year?'"

TOM, shit. What is a typical time frame here?

What are you thinking, you wanted seven years?

Yes, it was a standard time of indentured servitude in exchange for something of value used thousands of years ago. I figure we have a little less than five years to get prepared and go through the gate, I want his help and his people's help if possible.

The word, translated is seven solar years, *but Bethany Anne…*

Not now, let me finish this.

"I believe the term is solar years, Kael-ven," she replied.

"On your honor, you will provide for my people and all of them, any under my command, will be spared?"

"Kiel is going to have to face me in combat, Kael-ven. He will survive, but he WILL know pain. I will not allow my person's death to go uncounted."

"Bethany Anne," John said behind her. "You can't set a precedent that you personally will return retribution on every person that happens to kill one of us."

WE HAVE CONTACT

Bethany Anne turned around. "I'm not, John. Kiel is going to be punished, but it won't be in a cell. He will make amends. Their King, however? His ass is mine."

"Oh, well, I'm good with you taking out rulers, they're at your level and all," John agreed. "But I was worried you were going to start taking on all warriors and where the hell would that leave us? Playing with the fuzz in our belly buttons?"

Bethany Anne held in a snort. "I understand, John," she turned back around.

The two aliens had been speaking in decidedly faster tones before the armored one bowed his head and Kael-ven turned to her. "Kiel has agreed and will meet you in battle, but he wants to confirm if he should hurt you that the rest of my people will still be safe from your people?"

Bethany Anne cocked her head and then walked over to the armored alien "How safe do you believe you are from one punch in this armor?"

Kiel looked over at Kael-ven. "Did I understand correctly, she wants to punch my armor?" Kael-ven agreed that was his translation as well. Kiel opened his arms wide, "I wonder if this is going to tickle…." His body, armor and all, slammed back against a wall and toppled over, the alarms ringing in his ears as the suit's HUD confirmed his chest armor had suffered a major reduction.

"KIEL! Are you all right?" Kael-ven called out.

"Yes. No… I'm pretty sure I'm okay, but what did she just hit me with?" Kiel asked as he picked himself up from the floor.

"Her fist," Kael-ven responded.

"That's… not possible." Kiel said but he used the gauntlets to feel a new indentation in his armor. "Or maybe it is," he grumbled and told the suit's command program to shut off the alarms. He wouldn't offer her another free shot like that again.

Lesson learned.

Kiel moved back over to Kael-ven and nodded to the alien. "Accepted."

CLAN TEMPLE NEAR SHENNONGJIA PEAK

"I told you no good solution goes unpunished," Zhu said as Shun shared the news. "We help defeat the enemy and now our asses are stuck on this ancestor-forsaken mountain until we grow old and die."

"I think," Shun said as Bai and Jian looked around, but kept an ear to the whispered conversations, "that our success caused the scientists to request our assistance since they are most familiar with us."

"It isn't so bad," Bai said. "It reminds me of the parks in the city."

"The parks in the city had people cleaning them up, and you didn't worry about bugs and animals that come in the night and take a bite out of you," Zhu bitched.

"They are going after the Sacred Clan," Jian said. His friends watched him as he looked into the trees. He turned to see them all wanting more information. "The Sacred Clan has technology they want. We are merely going to be one group searching for them."

Shun turned and spit into the shrubs. "How the hell are we going to get more silver rounds?"

Zhu pursed his lips. "Let me try, I have an idea." He started walking back towards the group of scientists.

WE HAVE CONTACT

"Great," Bai said. "Send the rube from the country to speak with those from the city," he started out after his friend.

———

THREE WEEKS LATER, QBS ARCHANGEL

The ladies, no men present, sat with Cheryl Lynn at the large table. Each had tablets open and were watching the results of the early sales. Bethany Anne and Gabrielle had something going on up front. They were all going to Japan.

"I can't believe I have this hunk of a man for myself," Jean Dukes murmured as she flipped through the calendar. "Hey, peekaboo Paula is in this shot too!" She turned the calendar around and pointed to the background. "That skank better not be trying to stalk my boyfriend, or I'll put my size sevens up her ass."

"Don't get too wound up, she's in one of Scott's shots as well," Cheryl Lynn told her, turning her own calendar around to show.

Patricia, Barb, and Ecaterina looked carefully. "She looks European, maybe German," Ecaterina commented. Ecaterina flipped through the rest of the pictures, ignoring the guys. She had her own scrumptious man, and she was good with that. He was even taking care of Christina right now, allowing her some time with the ladies.

They had roped Bethany Anne into agreeing to watch Christina again for four hours this coming weekend so they could make a run down to New York and eat at the pizza place Nathan had taken her to when she first went to New York.

"Incredible," Cheryl Lynn whispered loudly. The ladies

all turned to her. "We just sold over two hundred and thirty thousand copies of the calendar, and that's in Australia alone."

Ecaterina was bothered by something, something was eating at her. She picked her tablet up. "Where are the other shots that Mark gave us? You know, the main location to go look?"

Cheryl Lynn told her the internet address and Ecaterina started going through the pictures, looking for clues.

Ignoring the background conversations and the catcalls, she kept looking until she finally figured out what was bothering her.

"We have a problem, sisters," Ecaterina commented. The other ladies turned to her. She set her tablet around and showed a blown-up picture of the woman they were calling Peekaboo Paula.

"She isn't looking to get in the guys' pictures, she's hunting them," Ecaterina said, her accent getting heavier.

"Well, of course! All the bitches are wanting our men," Jean answered, smiling.

"No," Patricia said, understanding dawning. "She isn't talking about grabbing them for a relationship, you mean hunting, hunting, right?"

Ecaterina just nodded her head in agreement. "Yes, I recognize the look in her eyes. It is the same one I use when I'm on the mountain. She is hunting, and she can't be alone. People are chasing our men."

"They aren't hunting just them," Jean said, all humor gone. "They're looking to take out the guys to get to Bethany Anne."

"Well, they just fucked with the wrong people then," Patricia stated, eyes going hard. "Because that shit isn't going to go down too well for me."

WE HAVE CONTACT

NARA, NARA PREFECTURE, JAPAN

There was a sharp knock on his door. Banri Arakawa wasn't expecting anyone at this time of the morning. He and his wife had just finished breakfast.

"Yuko?" she had breathed, but his angry glance quieted her.

He made his way to the door. Perhaps it was his disobedient daughter. While he would be happy enough to see her, she had caused enough grief with her lies and her filthy ways of living on the streets to spite him. She would be expected to be docile and a proper woman for a long time before he would even give a little of his love back to her.

He opened the door, looking to where Yuko's head would be and instead, saw the many medals of a military officer.

"Mr. Arakawa?" The officer asked.

"Yes," he said. "Is something wrong?"

"You and your wife are requested to come with me."

"Did Yuko do something wrong? Why are we in trouble for her disgrace?" He spat out, perhaps he should not have run her off.

"No, your daughter has done nothing wrong. We are to meet with high dignitaries, please dress appropriately. We have only twenty minutes before we must be leaving."

Banri asked the officer to come inside his home as he and his wife changed clothes. The officer could hear the husband and wife speaking in urgent whispers as they changed.

Within twenty minutes, the three of them left in a car. Banri was surprised when they pulled up to a small airport outside of town where a diplomatic helicopter waited for them.

A half hour flight later, the couple was escorted from the helicopter, with many of those attending dipping their heads to the couple in honor.

Banri could not figure out why they were being shown respect.

They were escorted to a large outdoor stadium and through the entrance to one side of the field where there was a large stage set up with many people on it. There were many, many thousands already in attendance and the buzz was deafening as Banri and his wife looked around.

The couple, from a smaller town, and from effectively another time, were overwhelmed. Moved along after a moment to see the crowd, they were in front of the Prime Minister of Japan before they realized who was shaking their hands.

"It is an honor to meet you. I am glad you are not too late!" he told them.

"Why?" Banri asked. "I have asked multiple times, and no one would say what is going on or why. What is it we have done?"

"Oh, no one told you?" he asked, a twinkle in his eye. "I believe the answer is," he looked down at his watch, "going to be evident in just a moment." He was still facing them when the intake of breath from thousands of people in the stadium got their attention.

Banri turned and saw those on the stage looking up. He shaded his eyes to see and saw something coming down through the clouds.

Something large. Really, really large.

A hush descended over the crowd. A spaceship was coming closer. Banri struggled to hear the engines that must be groaning and struggling to keep it in the air, but nothing reached his ears.

Then, many small black ships took off out of the ship and surrounded the area.

Finally, a large Pod, one that looked like a small spaceship slipped out and started to descend into the cleared area in front of the stage, the doors opening. Two men exited first, walking out and looking around. Protection, Banri thought.

"Yuko!" His wife cried out beside him.

Banri turned to those who were now exiting the craft, and there was a Japanese man, dressed in a warrior's outfit and holding a scabbarded sword, who was escorting a beautiful young woman next to him. Her hair was up, and her clothes were exquisite.

It was his daughter.

Yuko Arakawa, the daughter he accused of selling her body on the street, was being honored. She was arriving in a stadium from a spaceship and surrounded by thousands and thousands of his fellow countrymen who were cheering for her.

Banri Arakawa felt a tear start down his face.

He had been wrong. He had allowed his stubborn pride and his old ways to drive his demands and accusations to his daughter. One who had tried, with respect, to get him to believe her.

Banri put his arm around his wife, pulling her in and put his head down by her ear.

"Forgive me, for I am not worthy of being the father of our child, nor the husband of her mother," he paused. "I have been a foolish man."

"You have been, Banri," she replied, barely audible over the crowd chanting. "But this man has always been in you, too. So now, make amends with our daughter and apologize to her."

He nodded agreement and turned towards the two coming up the steps. Banri noticed the patch on the warrior's shoulder. A white fanged skull on a red background, no one sought to shake his hand. He greeted his daughter, eyes filled with tears, adulation coming from the stands.

He tipped his head. "Can you ever forgive me, daughter?" he asked, knowing he could not ever make up for his previous harsh words to her, his shame complete.

She stepped up to him, grabbed him tightly around his waist. He wrapped his arms around her, the tears streaming down his face and dropping to wet her hair.

The crowd's noise, already deafening, went up a notch. Yuko released her father and turned to stand between her parents, putting an arm around her mother and kissing her on the cheek.

She looked down to the craft below, there were four Guards coming out. "Father, Mother, I want to introduce you to my boss, the CEO of TQB Enterprises, her Royal Highness Queen Bethany Anne…"

———

THE END

TO BE CONTINUED IN …

MY RIDE IS A BITCH
THE KURTHERIAN GAMBIT 13

MICHAEL'S NOTES

We Have Contact - The Kurtherian Gambit 12: Written August 29, 2016

Thank you, I cannot express my appreciation enough that not only did you pick up the TWELFTH book, but you read it all the way to the end, and NOW, you're reading this as well.

I'm writing these author notes four weeks and five days after I wrote the Author Notes for SUED FOR PEACE.

Let's get a little Indie Publisher / Author stuff out of the way for those who like to catch up on the series and the 'days and times of a successful (!) indie author.'

———

First, Kindle Unlimited. There is no way at the moment, short of Amazon doing something dramatically screwy to us Indie Authors (which, they have but never when I've been a part of the system) can I even dream of leaving KU anytime soon if I look at income and opportunity.

KU is about a half of my income.

Those that were *preaching* 'go wide' back in Jan-Mar are mostly admitting (not all of them, but a bunch) that the money and rank are just too good to pass up w/ KU… So, now the dark side (being all-in with KU) is a big thing in the Indie community. It's hard to argue with the money, man… it's hard to argue with the money. I wasn't the first to raise this flag, I was merely annoyed that those pushing wide made a religion out of it.

Which has always been my point. I'm not religious (in business), I'm practical. I didn't go wide because I didn't have the time to figure it all out, and staying Amazon seemed like the right choice for me, and it has turned out to be very much so.

Now, new fans look at the quantity of books I have and join KU!

Last month, I was in the top 100 authors on KU for America and England for most KU pages read…SWEEEEET! Mind you, based on the little bonus spiff I was near the bottom (closer to 100 - I might have been #100) but hey, that was a shock and total awesomeness for me.

I don't think I've shared that with anyone but my family at home right now. No author friends, no extended family, no one.

Until you!

Geez, I'm going to have a big 'I love you fans!' moment… Give me a second to get past it … <sniff>

So, the short of it is, I'm in KU as long as Amazon continues loving us Indies as much as they have.

———

Covers!

Have you seen the new covers for books 01-06 and We Have Contact? Books 01-06 (and now 07) are done by Andrew Dobell, and I've talked about him in the past… Phenomenal work.

Jeff Brown of http://www.JeffBrownGraphics.com has done the cover for this book, and will do the covers for Books 08-14. So, maybe by this time (writing the author notes) for My Rides A Bitch (TKG13) we might have new covers for 08, 09, 10, and 11. If not, we will soon after!

Thank you SO much for the compliments on the new

covers, it makes the $$$ that was spent feel like it was well spent!

––––––

Kindles for Military

August is going to be an excellent month. Right now, the affiliate commission is just shy of $800.00. That will pay for the two Kindles to purchase (#3 & #4) and make up for the other expenses for August and the shortage in July.

Now, here is the problem. I've pulled two winners from the nomination page, and I never received info back on WHO they want me to give the Kindles to. So, both times I went ahead and sent it to a Marine Group as a fallback choice. I want to send to specific military personnel who win, yet I don't want to sit on the Kindles, either. So, if you get an email from me (manderle or Mike) talking about Kindles for Forward Deployed Military, it is not spam, folks! :-)

I ordered Kindle #3 but realized I didn't specify it was a gift, so I suspect Amazon in their infinite wisdom preloaded my info on the thing. So, I'll order another and ship this one back… Damn. Plus, #4 will be ordered in a week, so please check your emails if you are signing up to help someone you know to win!

––––––

Book a month

Right now, it is about 34 hours until September 1st. I have to receive and do a final pass on the last ten chapters, compile and send to the JIT authors and get their feedback and publish by tomorrow evening to hit August. It is looking very likely that My Rides A Bitch will be released the first week of October. I WANT to hit September because I want to hit a book a month. However, as I type this, I realize I've released 12 books, two short stories, been a part of 2 Anthologies and two collaborations (The Boris Chronicles) in 10 months. If you include the Omnibuses, then I'm involved in 18 titles in 300 days. For TKG Series Books, that is over 900,000 unique words produced alone.

HEY, I'VE KICKED ASS! LOL…

Wow, that's a relief. It isn't that I want to slow down, it's just pushing against that last day of the month like I'm doing here in August isn't fair to those helping me. So, unless I can speed up my side, I shouldn't be pushing them unfairly at all to make up for my release issues.

———

Christmas Present

See the back of this book.

———

Character requests…from real life ;-)

Anybody know Giorgio A. Tsoukalos (Ancient Aliens)? I have a request from a fan to include him in one of the next two stories, and I think that would be fun (in a good way, not being a bastard, he has enough people harassing him.) So, if you do and could hook an author up, please do!

Also, looking for a retired Navy Admiral that would be willing to join the team as we move into outer space battles and any astronaut fans might know and be able to suggest an introduction.

(I am pretty country agnostic, so I don't care what country they are from… So long as you realize I only speak English so translations, unfortunately, won't work.)

Ok, I think that covers it for who I'd love to talk to and would enjoy being written into a fiction book.

———

Coach's Revenge: Oh yeah, that was me (also known as the *Latest Embarrassing Author Story*)

The other day (last Friday night) I had just finishing chapter 20 and shipped it to Stephen and told him 'no more' for the evening… I was done for the day, and everything else was likely downhill for the rest of the story (5 more chapters), and I looked around to see who I could celebrate with…

But, my family was all gone. Wife in California, one son at a football game, the other at work. So, what should an author do when this happens?

I went to an expensive steak house. (Hell Yeah!) Bob's over in Grapevine, TX to be exact. I had been treated there for Father's day (last year, I think) and decided I was going to treat myself to an excellent steak.

HA!

I get there.

Hostess: Do you have a reservation, sir?

Me: Uh, no.

Hostess: There is presently a long wait, would you care to eat in the bar area?

Another hostess walks me to the bar area, and the only available seats are a comfortable looking leather couch and pair of chairs where the table is a coffee table. The kind of set up where you would enjoy having a drink with friends before your meal, not eating your meal. So, I didn't choose to eat in the bar area. However, I was given one of those 5-inch buzzy things and went right back to the bar area and couch to wait.

So, I sit down and do what any self-respecting indie author does when enjoying himself on this luxurious couch. I pulled out my laptop and started typing another chapter (hell yeah!)

The problem was, it was about forty-five minutes to when my table is done. They buzz me in the middle of an important scene, and I go up to the front, and they take me to a table just around the corner to the right. I sit down, take out my laptop and continue typing (because I'm in the middle of a scene! I can't stop now.)

They come, I get my order taken, and I press on... Right through the scene where Coach is killed, and Penn is thinking about him.

And I can't stop from tearing up. I mean, 200+ pounds of author manliness and I'm freaking tearing up and wiping the tears from my eyes during my expensive steakhouse dinner.

DAMNIT!

How freaking embarrassing...But, I got through the scene and put the laptop away...I'll miss you, Coach, I'll miss you.

UNTIL NEXT BOOK, EVERYONE!

———

THE KURTHERIAN GAMBIT STORE

I've been trying to get this d@mned store open for months. At first, it was 'their' fault (see below) then it was MY fault for …well, busy and didn't want to put out old covers, I wanted the new hotness covers!

Now, we have the new hotness with the first 7 covers and We Have Contact. So, here is the story below. Or, you can just skip all of this and see what I have up so far (only **We Have Contact** right now - more to come).

http://kurtherianbooks.com/We_Have_Contact_Store

THE STORY:

At the end of March this year, I attended the Smarter Artist Summit in Austin, Tx put on by the SPP guys (Sean, Johnnie and Dave). During that event, J A Hess took the stage and presented. One of her favorite merchandising solutions was Society6 (https://society6.com). I was pretty excited to try them, and with such a huge name in the Romance market supporting them, I was happy to move forward with my own plans to offer Kurtherian Gambit products.

Until I hit a snag.

Actually, call it a full-on-catastrophe.

See, I was planning on placing my first product into the store and I had to put my information 'into' the product and, as you may realize, my Series is 'The Kurtherian Gambit'.

And there lies the problem. That name, or more specifically, one word in that name. "Gambit". Not a unique word by a LONG shot. It is a well understood Chess move, a useful phrase for so many books or other I.P. including one from "Marvel". I.E., their character 'Gambit.'

So, my product was rejected for that reason and it pissed

me off. So, I contacted Society6 and asked (in a mostly nice way) 'what the *hell*?'

Here is the response at the time why I couldn't use "Gambit"

Hi Michael,

Thank you for contacting Society6 Support.

We truly do appreciate your comments and questions.

Unfortunately, in an effort to respect the rights of intellectual property owners, we are not able to support the inclusion of certain words, names, phrases, or combination thereof in artist submissions. In this particular case the term "Gambit" was used and we are not able to support the inclusion. Please replace this word to your description accordingly. All words in your listing must be accurate and refer only to the item for sale.

We understand that this particular exclusion may be overbroad as applied to your submission, and we appreciate your patience as we continue to improve our policy and process for the benefit of the overall marketplace.

We apologize for any inconvenience.

Sincerely,
S6 Legal Team

So, I wrote them back…

"Under compliance of the DMCA, we are unable to accept submissions with the term "Gambit" listed in the description or title. "

I know this is inaccurate, I am assuming Society6 knows this is inaccurate (from a legal standpoint) so I'm completely guessing that Society6 was sued at one time or the legal team has decided that from a cost / value standpoint it isn't in the companies best interest to fight it without a 'promoter' to encourage it?

Ok, I get that. So...

Please advise me where and how Society6 is handling their obligation of the DMCA and "Section 512 - which contains provisions allowing users to challenge improper takedowns." So that I may abide by the LAW on this and challenge the UNLAWFUL use of DMCA for a word (not a likeness or unique application).

I look forward to your patience in this annoying and painful effort to support Society6 from the abuse and overarching use of the DMCA and therefore the harmful effects the stifling use of the DMCA is having on at least one (1) of Society6's customers.

Thank you in advance,
Michael Anderle

So, early June, 2016 I received notice that I COULD use Gambit in my storefront on Society6, go Society6! (And me)… But, it has taken me 60 more days to get going…

Finally, my tiny little Kurtherian Gambit store is up now with the beginning of the products…MORE TO COME.

If you have suggestions, drop by on Facebook and fire away on the FB Page here: https://www.facebook.com/TheKurtherianGambitBooks/ or the Amazon Forum pages - I listen ;-)

Ready To Shop? http://kurtherianbooks.com/We_Have_Contact_Store

The world is in ruins…

The cataclysm, brought on by the start of the first Digital World War is complete. Earth has lost billions of people and is now comprised of powerful city-states, not countries. Locations where power, electricity, is possible.

The problem? When the strong survive, not everyone who is strong, is benevolent.

Into this future a man re-emerges from the Etheric where he has struggled to pull himself together, and finally to get himself free.

He made a promise, and Dark Ages or not, he *will* fulfill his promise. For when he was born, you were only as good as your word. For Michael, his word is Honor…
and Honor is *everything*.

The Dark Messiah
Coming Christmas 2016

SERIES TITLES INCLUDE:

KURTHERIAN GAMBIT SERIES TITLES INCLUDE:

First Arc

Death Becomes Her (01) - Queen Bitch (02) -
Love Lost (03) - Bite This (04)
Never Forsaken (05) - Under My Heel (06)
Kneel Or Die (07)

Second Arc

We Will Build (08) - It's Hell To Choose (09) -
Release The Dogs of War (10)
Sued For Peace (11) - We Have Contact (12) -
My Ride is a Bitch (13)
Don't Cross This Line (14)

Third Arc (Due 2017)

Never Submit (15) - Never Surrender (16) -
Forever Defend (17)
Might Makes Right (18) - Ahead Full (19) -
Capture Death (20)
Life Goes On (21)

New Series

THE SECOND DARK AGES

The Dark Messiah (01)
The Darkest Night (02)
Darkest Before The Dawn (03)
with Ell Leigh Clarke

THE BORIS CHRONICLES
* With Paul C. Middleton *

Evacuation
Retaliation
Revelation
Redemption *2017*

RECLAIMING HONOR
* With JUSTIN SLOAN *

Justice Is Calling (01)
Claimed By Honor (02)
Judgement Has Fallen (03)
Angel of Reckoning (04)
Born Into Flames (05)
Defending The Lost (06)
Saved By Valor (07)
Return of Victory (08)

THE ETHERIC ACADEMY
* With TS PAUL *

ALPHA CLASS (01)
ALPHA CLASS - Engineering (02)
ALPHA CLASS (03) *Coming Soon*

TERRY HENRY "TH" WALTON CHRONICLES
* With CRAIG MARTELLE *

Nomad Found (01)
Nomad Redeemed (02)
Nomad Unleashed (03)
Nomad Supreme (04)
Nomad's Fury (05)
Nomad's Justice (06)
Nomad Avenged (07)
Nomad Mortis (08)
Nomad's Force (09)
Nomad's Galaxy (10)

TRIALS AND TRIBULATIONS
* With Natalie Grey *

Risk Be Damned (01)
Damned to Hell (02)
Hell's Worst Nightmare (03) *coming soon*

THE ASCENSION MYTH
* With ELL LEIGH CLARKE *

Awakened (01)
Activated (02)
Called (03)
Sanctioned (04)
Rebirth (05)
Retribution (06)
Cloaked (07)
Bourne (08)

THE AGE OF MAGIC
THE RISE OF MAGIC
* With CM RAYMOND/LE BARBANT *

Restriction (01)
Reawakening (02)
Rebellion (03)
Revolution (04)
Unlawful Passage (05)
Darkness Rises (06)
The Gods Beneath (07)
Reborn (08)

THE HIDDEN MAGIC CHRONICLES
* With JUSTIN SLOAN *

Shades of Light (01)
Shades of Dark (02)
Shades of Glory (03)
Shades of Justice (04)

STORMS OF MAGIC
* With PT HYLTON *

Storms Raiders (01)
Storm Callers (02)
Storm Breakers (03)
Storm Warrior (04)

TALES OF THE FEISTY DRUID
* With CANDY CRUM *

The Arcadian Druid (01)
The Undying Illusionist (02)
The Frozen Wasteland (03)
The Deceiver (04)
The Lost (05)
The Damned (06)

PATH OF HEROES
* With BRANDON BARR *

Rogue Mage (01)

A NEW DAWN
* With AMY HOPKINS *

Dawn of Destiny (01)
Dawn of Darkness (02)
Dawn of Deliverance (03)
Dawn of Days (04)

THE AGE OF EXPANSION
THE UPRISE SAGA
* With AMY DUBOFF *

Covert Talents (01)
Endless Advance (02)
Veiled Designs (03)

BAD COMPANY
* With CRAIG MARTELLE *

The Bad Company (01)
Blockade (02)

THE GHOST SQUADRON
* With SARAH NOFFKE and J.N. CHANEY *

Formation (01)
Exploration (02)
Evolution (03)

CONFESSIONS OF A SPACE ANTHROPOLOGIST
* With ELL LEIGH CLARKE *

Giles Kurns: Rogue Operator (01)

VALERIE'S ELITES
* With JUSTIN SLOAN AND PT HYLTON *

Valerie's Elites (01)
Death Defied (02)

ETHERIC ADVENTURES:
ANNE AND JINX
* With S.R. RUSSELL *

Etheric Recruit
Etheric Researcher

OTHER BOOKS

Gateway to the Universe
* With CRAIG MARTELLE & JUSTIN SLOAN *

THE CHRONICLES OF ORICERAN
THE LEIRA CHRONICLES
* With MARTHA CARR *

Waking Magic (1)
Release of Magic (2)
Protection of Magic (3)
Rule of Magic (4)
Dealing in Magic (5)

SHORT STORIES

Frank Kurns Stories of the Unknownworld 01 (7.5)
You Don't Mess with John's Cousin

Frank Kurns Stories of the Unknownworld 02 (9.5)
Bitch's Night Out

Frank Kurns Stories of the Unknownworld 02 (13.25)
With Natalie Grey
Bellatrix

AUDIOBOOKS
Available at Audible.com and iTunes

WANT MORE?

Join the email list here:

http://kurtherianbooks.com/email-list/

AND NOW

http://kurtherianbooks.com/readers-supporting-military-book-newsletter/

Join the Facebook group here:

https://www.facebook.com/TheKurtherianGambitBooks/

The email list will be sporadic with more 'major' updates, the Facebook group will be for updates and the 'behind the curtains' information on writing the next stories. Basically conversing!

Since I can't confirm that something I put up on Facebook will absolutely be updated for you, I need the email list to update all fans for any major release or updates that you might want to read on the website.

I hope you enjoy the book!

Michael Anderle - August 31, 2016.